MURD
EVERYTH.

MW01145888

Scott Henderson was a partner at a well-known banking firm. He was thirty years old and had never been in love—that is until he met Gail Barrie. Henderson fell hard and fast; but no sooner had he professed his love for the soon-to-be million-dollar heiress (and she for him) than Gail Barrie told him, in no uncertain terms, "I can't marry you, Scott." Within minutes, as if fate was putting an indelible exclamation point on the end of her sentence, Gail Barrie's childhood girlfriend ended up murdered—shot through the heart with a .25 caliber pistol. A .25 caliber was a small gun, just the right size for the hand of a woman. And to make things worse, the evidence seemed to point toward Gail.

But Scott Henderson wasn't the kind of man to give up on the woman he loved—somehow, some way, he would prove her innocence. However, when two more corpses turned up, Henderson came to the grim realization that a mountain of deadly mystery was completely enshrouding the thing he loved best.

FOR A COMPLETE SECOND NOVEL, TURN TO PAGE 177

CAST OF CHARACTERS

SCOTT HENDERSON
His was driven by a passion for the truth and a passion for the woman he loved—even if she turned out to be a ruthless killer.

GAIL BARRIE
She was beautiful beyond words and was about to inherit a million bucks. She was also the prime suspect in a triple murder!

BERNIE WILLIAMS
His seemingly illiterate persona was just a smoke screen for one of the smartest cops on the entire force.

BARBARA MATHEWS
When the going got tough she seemed to be endowed with a calm inner strength.

FERN MEREDITH
Dripping with sexuality, this torch singer and near tramp was pivotal in revealing the identity of a killer.

TONY KINKAID
Not well liked, but the girls found him pretty to look at—handsome and draped in the best of clothes…and always a woman in tow.

CHRIS PETERSON
This hardboiled cop was relentless in tracking down gangsters and thugs, especially when the crime was murder.

PAUL INNES
As the manager of the Cherokee Country Club he was familiar with all the high-class locals—and knew most of their secrets.

.

DANGEROUS LADY

By
OCTAVUS ROY COHEN

ARMCHAIR FICTION
PO Box 4369, Medford, Oregon 97504

*For more information about Armchair Books and products, visit our
website at…*

www.armchairfiction.com

Or email us at…

armchairfiction@yahoo.com

CHAPTER ONE

AFTER THIRTY YEARS of emotional independence, Scott Henderson was in love. He was so much in love that he stayed awake nights thinking about it, which wasn't so good for a healthy young citizen like Scott. Of course, the thoughts were all on the pleasant side, and well worth staying awake for—but that didn't make him any less heavy-eyed the next morning.

There was no reason why Scott shouldn't have experienced romance many years before. He was a personable young man, a potential leading citizen, an ex-army officer who had done a good job for a couple of years, and junior partner in the highly reputable and successful firm of Mathews, Henderson & Company, Bankers & Brokers. He had a compact figure, a nice face, and the esteem of all of his 212,000 fellow citizens in the flourishing industrial city of Cherokee.

He stood now in the midst of the Saturday night crowd at the Cherokee Country Club and stared gloomily at an attractive young lady who was obviously absorbed in a gentleman who was taller, handsomer and definitely more sure of himself than Scott Henderson ever hoped to be.

Beside him stood Paul Innes, 35-year-old manager of the Cherokee Country Club. Paul was tall, slender and inclined to be sardonic. He looked at Scott and followed the direction of that young gentleman's eyes. He said, "You've really gone off the deep end, haven't you, Scott?"

Young Mr. Henderson looked up. He was surprised—and slightly indignant—that his emotions should be so apparent. And then, because the desire to share his happiness and his misery was greater than his reticence, he nodded.

"You said it, Paul. But what chance have I got? Give a look."

The object of his affection was on the broad, stone veranda from which one could look down at the vast emerald expanse of the 36-hole golf course. She had been gazing off into the soft southern moonlight, but now she turned so that her face was visible to those inside the ballroom.

Gail Barrie was young. She lacked only six weeks of attaining her majority, which made Scott feel like an old man.

She was wearing a simple little white dress, which did her figure no injustice. She had dark brown hair that was flecked with red, a clear skin that was almost blond, and gray eyes that could be thoughtful or full of laughter, as the occasion demanded. She was a few inches more than five feet in height and she weighed about 115 pounds, all of which—in the eyes of Scott Henderson—added up to perfection.

Gail was neither alone nor bored. Beside her ranged a young man who was so handsome it hurt. Tony Kinkaid looked like the dream of a Hollywood producer. He had everything plus, and he inspired in Mr. Henderson a ghastly feeling of inadequacy.

Scott said miserably to Paul Innes, "What chance have I got against that?"

Paul was unimpressed. He said, "Kinkaid isn't Gail's type."

"No? I suppose she's allergic to handsome men."

"It isn't that." Paul was trying to be patient with young love. "They simply don't belong together."

"She probably despises him," said Scott, though with very little conviction. "She's just being nice to him because it's socially correct. Actually, she's pining for me." Mr. Henderson made a most inelegant noise, which was intended to put him in his place, and followed with the single word, "Nuts!"

Scott's life had been serene and untroubled until the day Miss Gail Barrie had moved in on him. Unheralded and unsung, she had arrived from Cuba with three suitcases and a personality that he found irresistible. A hometown girl who had lived for sixteen years in Latin America, she moved into the home of his benefactor and business partner, Fletcher Mathews, shook hands with Scott before dinner that night, looked into his eyes and had him hog-tied in one minute flat. That had been two months previously, and nothing had happened since then to relieve the symptoms that kept him moving along the road he fondly hoped would lead to matrimony.

He sought some small measure of comfort from Paul Innes. He said, "You know her better than anybody else in Cherokee. Tell me more."

Paul spoke slowly. He said, "I don't know how well I know her, really."

"Didn't you work for her old man in Cuba for a year?"

"Yes. In a God-forsaken little town in Matanzas Province. I practically lived at their house. But she was just a kid then, and I didn't pay too much attention. All I could see was that she was a neat number who was almost as much Cuban as she was American. That's why I'm surprised at what has happened to you...because I can't think of her as grown up."

"Did she have any heart interest in Cuba?"

"Not that I know of. There wasn't much chance in Miramonte. With me, that town rated zero-minus. Nothing but tired palm trees and stifling heat. There wasn't an eligible single man closer than Havana, and Havana was 175 miles away. She was crazy about her father, and she had a girl named Margaret Allen living with her, an American resident of Cuba whom she had met in school. If there was anything else in her life, I didn't notice it. I also didn't give myself much chance. I hated the place and everything about it. I got out as soon as my year's contract was up. And until Gail came to Cherokee two months ago, I haven't seen her since." He put a cigarette between his thin lips and lighted it. "Of course, she carries glamour," he remarked. "A million dollars usually does."

Scott Henderson looked at him sharply. Then he smiled. "I'd still love her if she was worth twice as much," he said.

"Okay, son. Then why not move in? This Kinkaid is small potatoes."

Scott's private opinion was that Paul Innes had grossly underestimated the gentleman who was hovering over Gail. But Paul's advice gave him some small measure of confidence. He moved across the crowded dance floor, said "Hello" to a dozen young folks whom he had known since babyhood, and stepped hesitantly onto the veranda.

Summer hung heavily over the Country Club grounds. Far off against a clear sky that was studded with stars, he could see the silhouette of The Ridge. In the air there was a faint promise of relief from the sweltering heat. On the eighteenth and thirty-sixth greens, and on the little clock golf green, water sprays were whirling. They made a soothing sound that came to him through the blare of the local orchestra, which was valiantly trying to make like Benny Goodman.

Some of the older people relaxed in easy chairs, most of them sipping cool drinks. Young couples appeared from the ballroom and vanished hand-in-hand toward the automobile parking space, or walked in the direction of the little grove of trees between the tennis courts and the swimming pool. The air was fragrant with the odor of roses and fresh-cut grass. It was all very idyllic for a young man in love—provided he was getting a little cooperation. But cooperation was Scott Henderson's greatest lack at the moment.

A more egotistical person than Scott might have detected a gleam of welcome in Gail's eyes as he horned in. He might also have observed a sign of irritation in Kinkaid's manner, and have taken heart therefrom. All he actually saw was that Gail moved a few inches, making a place for him beside her, and that the very elegant Mr. Kinkaid seemed somewhat annoyed by the intrusion.

The conversation of the next few minutes was slightly less than scintillating. They discussed the younger people and the good time they seemed to be having. Scott did not ask Gail to dance, because he knew what her answer would be. Just a little more than two months previously, her father had been killed in action on Okinawa.

And so they talked idly about the young grown-ups who had been babies in Cherokee when Gail herself was a baby and had lived there, but who were like strangers now despite the warmth of the welcome they had given her. Their conversation appeared to have very little interest to Kinkaid, who had been a resident of Cherokee less than a year, and after a while he walked off to mingle with the crowd in the ballroom. For the first time that evening, Scott was happy. Save for hundreds of people all around them, he and Gail were alone.

He looked after the tall, rangy figure of the retreating Kinkaid and said, "He's the handsomest man I ever saw."

Gail looked at him peculiarly. "Why do you say that?"

8

"I'm only stating a fact. If I were a girl…"

"Don't say it. You probably wouldn't. Tony is too handsome, too sure of himself. Girls don't usually like that. Only sometimes."

"Are you a sometime?"

She said sharply, "Most definitely not. No!"

They turned their backs on the brilliantly lighted windows. They looked out over the golf course toward the pinpoints of light that marked the homes in the swank Brookside section. There was a lot of moon, a lot of inducement to romance, a lot of summer. Scott wished he dared move a little closer…just close enough to touch. He was considering a maneuver when she startled him with a query:

"How would you like to slip off with me for a little while?"

His reaction wasn't very quick. This was better than anything he had hoped for. He wondered what had happened to his repertoire of snappy retorts; he wondered why this girl always left him floundering. If this was love, it wasn't doing him any good. So all he said was, "Would I!" which wasn't brilliant, but was the best he could think of at the moment.

"Have you got your car here?"

"What's left of it."

"Gasoline?"

"Enough. And even if it isn't, and we get stranded somewhere… lady! It's a thought."

She laughed, but beneath the laughter there was an undercurrent of urgency. She asked, "Do you know where the Treadways live?"

"Sure." He gestured toward the dark eminence that was known as The Ridge. "Way over yonder."

"Can you drive me there?"

"Of course… It's a lovely, lonely road. But why?"

"I want to have a little talk with Doris. I understand she arrived this afternoon from Los Angeles."

He nodded. "Her mother's pretty sick," he said casually, "but why the interest? Why tonight?"

Again that unmistakable urgency in her voice. "It's important. I thought she might be here tonight. That's why I came. I've got to see her."

"I thought you didn't know anybody in Cherokee."

"I don't, really. I don't even know Doris. But we lived next door to each other when we were babies. She was three years older than I was. She used to call herself my nurse. I was three and she was six. I haven't seen her since I left here when I was four."

He said, "Why should I argue against something that gives me a break? I'll show you the view from the top of The Ridge. I'll take a long time showing it to you."

She said, "Let's go casually. I'd rather nobody saw me leaving."

They sauntered the length of the veranda and walked down the five stone steps leading to the walkway. The parking lot was filled with cars, and most of the cars seemed to be filled with young couples more or less pleasantly engaged. "Love," said Scott. "The world is full of it. It must be wonderful."

He found his car, and thanked his luck that it hadn't been hedged in. "The crate," he said. "Climb in, honey—and we'll git goin'."

They rolled along the tree-lined, curving driveway and turned south toward The Ridge. They moved slowly through Brookside, past homes that were dark and homes that were bright. The houses were all expensive, and some of them were beautiful. They had lawns with trees on them, and beds of well-tended flowers, so that the air was rich with summer perfume.

They climbed The Ridge. Scott said, "Even though I don't understand it—this is great."

She said, "It's great for me, too."

"You say the smartest things."

"I'm not feeling very bright, Scott." She put her head back against the cushion and stretched out her legs. The faint glow from the dashboard enabled him to see what he already knew: That they were very nice legs. Her eyes were half closed. He didn't try to talk.

He swung suddenly from the main road and braked to a halt in a little glade that looked down into the broad valley. He snapped the ignition and light switches. "This," he said, with not too much confidence, "is the view I said I was going to show you."

She sat up. There was no protest about his stopping. The night closed in on them. She looked down at the twinkling lights. She said, "Dad always told me it was beautiful. I think he was homesick for it—much as he loved Cuba."

They were silent for a while. Scott reached out his hand and let his fingers close over hers. She didn't draw away. Her hand was soft and warm, and he dared to let himself believe that it was responsive.

Somewhere he found a spark of courage. His voice wasn't quite steady as he said, "I'm going to do something, and then I'm going to ask a question. Ready?"

Her gray eyes looked into his. She didn't say anything or do anything. She just sat there. Waiting.

His arm went around her. He drew her to him and bent his face over hers. Her lips parted under his, and for a few seconds she was rigid.

Then something happened that, to Scott, had all the power of an earthquake. She was quiescent no longer; no longer passive. Both arms went around his neck. Her body pressed against his. Her lips were eager. A skyrocket exploded inside of him. This was wonderful. Unbelievable. Fantastic.

They clung to each other interminably. Time dropped away. There was no world beyond the windows of their car.

Her arms released. With obvious reluctance, she drew away. He said, "Good Lord…" Then he went on without looking at her.

"That's the thing I was going to do, Gail. Now for what I intended to ask. Will you marry me?"

She turned so that she faced him. She said steadily, "I love you, Scott," and he knew that she meant it.

He said, "When—that's what I want to know. When will you marry me?"

She didn't answer. She didn't move. He regarded her intently.

She was crying. And he knew instinctively that she wasn't crying because she was happy. It was the sort of crying that hurt. It hurt all the way through.

She caught him to her again and kissed him passionately. Then she drew away.

"I love you, Scott," she repeated. "Isn't that enough?"

He said, "No, it isn't enough. What I want…"

She said, "I won't marry you, Scott."

He asked dazedly, "Why?"

"Because I can't. Because it's impossible. Because..."

And that was as far as she went. She broke down then and cried in his arms. As though from a distance he heard her voice. She said, "I can't marry you, Scott. And you mustn't ask me why."

CHAPTER TWO

SCOTT TRIED TO FIGURE IT OUT. He said, half to himself and half to Gail, "So I'm the guy you love and yet you won't marry me. It doesn't come out even."

She said, "Isn't this enough for now?"

"Couldn't be better. But it's the distant future I'm thinking of, when silver threads are amongst the gold and your grandchildren are clambering over your knee."

She smiled and pressed his hand. "If I ever have grandchildren, sweetheart, I'll count on you to be their ancestor. But, believe me, Scott, that's as much as I can promise. I can't even explain now. But someday..."

He said, "I'd love to debate the point, but I'm too happy. The wise man takes what he can get, or words to that effect. So..." He wrapped her up again most efficiently. The response was all he could have asked for, and more than he expected. When he came up for air, he said, "If that's a sample, the process of becoming a grandfather should be fun." He regarded her critically. "You know, you're quite a gal."

"Thank you..." She glanced at her wrist watch and sat up straight. "Scott! It's horribly late. Let's get going."

"Aw, no. I'm happy here. This is a lot better than talking to Doris."

"I think so, too. But I've got to see her. Right away."

"She can't wait until tomorrow?"

"No."

"Okay, honey. If that's what you want..." He started the motor, backed into the main highway and started moving forward slowly toward the Treadway home. "I'm grateful to Doris in any event. If she hadn't come home, you wouldn't have invited me to take you riding; and if I hadn't taken you riding, I wouldn't be practically a grandfather."

He recognized a brick wall when he encountered one. She had her reasons and he credited them with being good ones. And after what had just happened, nothing seemed to have any importance. He was way up in the stratosphere and loving it.

And so, as he drove as slowly as the car would move in high gear along the fringes of the fashionable Brookside residential area, he tried to explain to her how happy he was. He confessed that he'd been pretty jealous when he had observed Tony Kinkaid hanging around her at the Country Club all evening. "He's got it," stated Mr. Henderson. "I figured that if he was moving in, I'd have to move out before I ever got started."

She said, without looking at him, "How much do you know about Tony?"

"Nothing. He flashed into town about a year ago. I believe he represents some big electrical supply firm. Somebody put him up at the Club, and he was elected. He's a queer bird. He looks like Country Club and acts like Country Club and yet…"

"Yet what?"

"I don't know. This doesn't seem to be the proper time to take a rap at an unfortunate rival."

"He's not a rival, sweetheart."

"Say that again. The sweetheart part."

She smiled. "Sweetheart," she repeated. "Anyway, I don't like him. Not even a little bit."

He said, "Congratulations, Scott. Now your own homely puss need never annoy you. Anyway, what I was driving at is this: I've never figured out whether Tony belonged with our crowd or with the gang that runs Valley View."

"Valley View? What's that?"

He smiled. "I keep thinking of you as a native of this hamlet. I forget you've never even visited here since you were a baby. Valley View, my sweet, is an intriguing excrescence just beyond the city limits where a melancholy gentleman named Sax Bailey operates what he calls a cabaret. He serves dinners and puts on a show featuring an exceedingly hot torch singer named Fern Meredith. Downstairs he has a complete gambling layout: roulette, dice, blackjack and what-have-you. I more than suspect that his apparatus is rigged, and that the suckers haven't got a chance. But the society crowd of this teeming metropolis rushes out there in droves to be taken. Tony goes there quite often. He…" Scott fumbled for a cigarette and stopped talking. "Naughty, naughty!" he said. "Mustn't kick a guy in the teeth when he's down."

"Go ahead," she insisted. "This could be important."

He couldn't grab that one. How in the world could the private life of Tony Kinkaid be of any importance to Gail? He said, "You know how Cherokee is—or do you? People gossip. Tony is handsome. Fern Meredith gives the impression of needing asbestos clothes. She's supposed to be the boss's gal friend. So there you have what might, or might not, be a cute, illicit triangle. And I feel like a bit of a heel for mentioning it."

She listened without comment. That surprised him, because he had fancied that she was going to press the subject. But apparently she had heard all she needed to know. Just another thing he couldn't understand, another topic he felt had been carried as far as she wanted it carried.

He dipped over The Ridge. The countryside was still beautiful, still bathed in rich, mellow moonlight. But the houses were more widely separated. Some of them achieved the dignity of estates. He stopped under a pair of magnificent oak trees between which was the commencement of a driveway.

"Heah y'are, Missy. The residence of Massa Treadway an' fam'ly. What gives now?"

The house was set far back from the road, screened by trees and heavy shrubbery. There was a walkway between neatly trimmed hedges. There was a lawn smooth as velvet. There were flowers in profusion. There was a background of rolling countryside, cut through by a tiny silver stream known simply as The Brook.

The house looked very large and very white. It was of Colonial architecture. A veranda spanned its entire width, marked by a half dozen Doric columns, each two stories in height.

There was a dim light in the entrance hall downstairs, just beyond the screen door. Upstairs two yellow squares marked the windows of Mrs. Treadway's room. Gail opened the car door and got out. Scott Henderson started to do the same, but she stopped him. She said, "Wait here, please. I'll only be a few minutes."

He was puzzled, but there didn't seem to be anything to argue about. So he said, "Okay, Gorgeous," and climbed back into the car.

She moved into the shadowed walkway leading to the veranda. He looked after the trim, slender figure with approval and proprietary pride.

Happiness triumphed over his puzzlement. He had just discovered that he'd had a lot of capacity for love bottled up in him for thirty years. He was still shaken from the intensity of her response. That was a nice memory. He reviewed it briefly and ecstatically. He dismissed her refusal to consider an immediate marriage. Maybe she figured she was too young.

And she was young, of course. She still had almost six weeks to go before reaching her twenty-first birthday. He wondered whether he'd be criticized for robbing the cradle, and in response to that he told himself, "Oh hell! What of it?" Certainly they'd acted the same age back there when the car was parked. Nine years' difference: that sounded like a lot. But a man of thirty wasn't old by any standards.

He was a trifle sorry that she was so wealthy. He knew all about that since his firm, Mathews, Henderson & Company, was the trustee of her father's property and the executor under his will. Fletcher Mathews and Major David Ellsworth Barrie—Gail's father—had been lifelong friends. Barrie's final act before shoving off for active duty had been to turn over all his property to the firm—which meant to Mr. Mathews.

He'd made his fortune in Cuba—most of it, anyway. Something to do with the finding of naphtha deposits. Scott had heard that they could take it out of the ground and put it right into the fuel tanks of automobiles. The coming of the war had given the property terrific value. Major Barrie had sold out, lock, stock and barrel. And now the money derived from that transaction belonged to Gail...or would the day she became 21. He knew it would amount to approximately a million dollars after payment of inheritance taxes to the State and Federal governments. Yes, he wished it might be different, but he was too sensible a person to let that worry him.

He turned away from practical thoughts to the contemplation of a rosy future. He felt beautifully callow and sentimental. The world was painted in gay colors.

The soft stillness of the night was broken by a sound. It was a sharp, severe, sudden noise and it seemed to come from inside the Treadway home. Scott Henderson thought:

That sounded like a shot.

Ridiculous. But the idea persisted. There was no logic to it, but there it was. He felt nervous and jumpy. There was no reason for that, either. He started to get out of the car, thought better of it, and settled back behind the wheel, leaving the door open.

For what seemed an interminable time there was silence. And then, clear and shrill, there came the sound of a woman's scream.

Scott was out of the car, running toward the house. He was afraid without having the faintest idea of what he feared. His feet made sharp, scraping sounds on the gravel walkway. He leaped up on the veranda, crossed it, and flung open the unlocked screen door leading into the entrance hall.

The first thing he saw was the figure of a woman. Not Gail. He didn't see Gail anywhere. This woman was bigger and heavier and older than Gail, and she was dressed all in white. Mrs. Treadway's nurse: that's who it was.

The screen door slammed behind him, and the nurse turned. Her cheeks were pallid, her eyes big and round and terrified. Mary Potter knew Scott, though he didn't recognize her. She said, "Oh…" and pointed to something on the floor.

Scott Henderson ran forward. The body of a woman was lying there. A young woman. His first feeling was one of relief. It wasn't Gail.

This girl wore a thin housecoat. It was of a pretty, flowered material. And just below the left breast, there was a dark, ugly stain that was no part of the pattern. He looked down at the oddly grotesque figure, at the plain, sweet face; at the dark hair that pressed against the floor. He said, "Doris!" and looked at the nurse.

Miss Potter said, "Oh, God… Oh, God…"over and over again. She said, "Miss Doris is dead…"

Scott looked around. He opened his lips to ask about Gail, then changed his mind. He didn't know why.

There was no sign of Gail. She wasn't in the hallway. She wasn't in the living room or in the room beyond.

Doris was dead.

And Gail Barrie had disappeared.

CHAPTER THREE

SCOTT HAD NEVER BEFORE seen the body of a person who had been murdered, and he wasn't enjoying the experience. Doris was sprawled on the floor. She looked uncomfortable. He told himself that he was a damned fool. A dead person couldn't be uncomfortable. And that snapped his thoughts back to Gail Barrie, who had walked into that house a few moments before the shooting and now had vanished.

He said to the nurse, "What happened?"

Miss Potter said, "I don't know. I heard a noise. It sounded like a shot, but that seemed ridiculous. Then I thought I'd better look anyway. I found her…"

"What was she doing downstairs?"

"I sent her. She was all tuckered out; the long train ride and all. I thought it'd be good to get her out of the sickroom."

"How long ago was that?"

"Fifteen minutes. Maybe twenty."

"Who else was here?"

Miss Potter looked surprised. She said, "Nobody else. Just us."

"The servants?"

"They've been gone since right after dinner."

"And you're sure that only you and Doris and Mrs. Treadway were here?"

"Of course I'm sure. Just the three of us." She looked at Doris and then at Scott. "Of course, somebody else *must* have been here…"

That's what Scott Henderson was thinking. Somebody else had been there, and he knew who that somebody was. He had seen

Gail walk into the house. And that's all he had seen. She and Doris were downstairs. Now Doris was dead and Gail had disappeared.

His thoughts were racing, making great circles around the idea of Gail and coming back always to the same point. He said, "Do you know whether Doris had been expecting anyone?"

"I don't think so."

One idea hit him between the eyes. He had to find Gail, had to speak to her before anyone else did. He wanted to ask more questions, but that seemed to be the wrong play. Obviously, the nurse hadn't heard her; didn't know anything about her. He wanted Miss Potter out of the way.

He said, "Look, you go back upstairs to Mrs. Treadway. This will be tough on her…"

"She's too ill to understand what it's all about."

"I'd advise calling the doctor, anyway. Is there a phone upstairs?"

"Yes."

"Call from there. But before you do, give the police a ring."

She looked frightened. "What do I say?"

"Just answer any questions they ask. Tell them they'd better send out right away." He tried to make his voice sound authoritative. "Run along now."

She started up the stairway—a solid, compact young woman; quietly efficient and badly frightened. Scott found the courage to give her what he fancied was a reassuring smile. He said, "Don't forget: call the police first."

He heard her moving about in the upstairs hall, heard the sound of the telephone dial. Time was closing in on him. The name Treadway carried a lot of weight in Cherokee. The cops would be there in a hurry.

He was not familiar with the Treadway home, but its arrangement was simple enough. He walked through the downstairs rooms, snapping on the lights in each, peering into closets and behind draperies. He was badly shaken, and more frightened than he cared to admit.

He finished his search of the downstairs rooms. He went through the kitchen and the butler's pantry. He returned to the hall that bisected the house. He opened the screen door and stepped outside.

His eyes had become accustomed to lights, and so the night seemed blacker and more forbidding. Everything seemed to be in order. Nobody in sight. Back beyond the edge of the property there was woodland: tall, stately pines and venerable oak trees. He wanted to search the edge of the woods, but realized that hc didn't have time, and that it wouldn't be so good if he happened to be outside when the police arrived.

He went back inside the house, nursing the thought that perhaps Gail had gone upstairs. There must be a back stairway. She could have used that.

Young Mr. Henderson had been through a fair share of experiences in his thirty years, but this was a new one. He knew he had to do something, but couldn't figure what. There was the fear that something had happened to Gail, something dreadful. But even more than he feared that, he feared something else. It stemmed back to her insistence on seeing Doris immediately, of regarding her visit to this house as more important than being alone with the man she had just said that she loved. There had been some compelling motive for the visit to the Treadway house, some reason why she couldn't wait until the morrow to see Doris.

Odd about that, too. Gail was almost 21. According to her, she hadn't seen Doris since they had lived next door to each other and played together as little children. When Gail left Cherokee, she was four years old; Doris, seven. Gail hadn't been back since. The more he turned it over in his mind, the less sense it made.

A siren wailed through the summer night. Scott hadn't had time to decide what he was going to tell the police. He was on the spot, and he didn't like it. He was terribly in love, and the girl he'd been making love to a few minutes since should have been with him—but wasn't. It was confusing and frightening.

The siren stopped abruptly. Scott heard heavy feet crossing the veranda. The screen door opened and two men came in.

They didn't look like policemen. They were in civilian clothes. One of the men was tall and broad, the other short and wiry. Scott felt a sense of relief at sight of the big man. He moved forward with his hand out. He said, "Bernie!"

Bernie Williams grabbed Scott's hand, and crushed it. He said, "What gives, Scott?"

Henderson felt better now. This was a breather. He wasn't afraid of being pushed around.

Bernie Williams was a cop, but Bernie was his friend. They had gone to the same grammar school and had attended high school together. They had played on the high school football team. That was when their acquaintanceship had ripened into a friendship that—on Bernie Williams' part—amounted almost to idolatry.

Bernie had been a good football player, but definitely weak on the scholastic side. The academic standards of their school were high, the eligibility rules rigid. So Scott Henderson had not only played football, but he had labored diligently through two fall semesters to stuff enough knowledge into Bernie's head to keep him eligible for the team. Bernie was grateful. He thought Scott was a genius. He never understood how any kid could know so much and be so nice.

Bernie had played his quota of football, and then abandoned all thought of graduating. He possessed an innate shrewdness and unusual powers of observation. But Latin and mathematics floored him. He left school, and the next thing Scott heard, he was a rookie patrolman on the Cherokee force. Their contacts since then had been cordial but infrequent. Bernie had become a detective, and—from all reports—a good one.

The smaller man came forward. Bernie said, "Meet Sergeant Peterson, Scott. Chris Peterson. He's in charge."

Peterson looked alarmingly efficient. His bright eyes ferreted through the hallway, and came to rest on the body of Doris Treadway Colby. He knelt beside her and made a couple of simple tests. He got up and said, "Deader 'n hell. How'd it happen?"

Scott said, "I don't know."

"You was here, wasn't you?"

"No. I was in my car. It's parked by the gate."

"Who is she?"

"Doris Treadway. She's Mrs. Colby now."

"Hmm!" You could almost hear Chris Peterson's brain clicking. He knew everything there was to know about everybody in Cherokee. "I thought she was livin' in L. A."

"She does live there. Her mother is ill. Doris got home this afternoon."

"Cute reception she got." He looked up at Scott. "Let's have it the way you know it. Where do you fit in?"

The young man hesitated. He looked toward his friend Bernie Williams for help, and saw Bernie's keen, level glance fixed on him. No use trying to dissemble with Bernie…the big guy knew him too well.

"Well?" Peterson's voice was crisp. "What's all the thinking for?"

There was a sound from the back of the house. All three of them turned toward it. The rear door opened and Gail Barrie came in. Her face was pallid. She moved toward them swiftly and looked down at Doris. She said, "Is she…?" and left the question hanging.

Bernie said, "Yes, ma'am, she's dead all right."

Sergeant Peterson broke in. His voice had softened, but it still was freighted with the unmistakable tone of authority. He asked, "Who are you?"

She shook her head, as though rousing herself from a nightmare. There was something in her eyes that was more than grief or shock. Scott could see that she was fighting for self-control.

She moistened her lips and said, "I'm Gail Barrie."

"Oh…" The name registered with Chris Peterson. Every man, woman and child in Cherokee knew about the young lady who had been born in Cherokee and had come back to await her twenty-first birthday when she would come into possession of a fortune estimated at more than a million dollars. "Gail Barrie, huh?"

"Yes."

"She a friend of yours?" By "she," he meant Doris.

"Yes."

"You here when it happened?"

Scott tensed. Gail hesitated, then said, "Yes, I was here."

"All right, Miss Barrie. S'pose you give out. What did you see?"

Again that hesitation, as though she weren't quite sure of herself. "I came to see Doris. The front door was unlatched. I walked in. I saw two people standing back yonder, sort of under the stairway. Then there was a shot. Doris fell. A man ran out the back door."

"You get a good look at him?"

She shook her head. "No."

"If you was that close…"

"I was looking at Doris. I knew that something terrible had happened, but I didn't know what. She started to fall and I tried to catch her."

"And the man ran out the back way?"

"Yes. I tried to do something for Doris. I saw she was dead…"

Bernie Williams said, "Take it easy, Miss Barrie."

Chris said, "After you decided she was dead, what did you do?"

"I ran out the back door. I thought maybe I could see the man…or where he went."

"Did you?"

"No."

"But you seen him when he was running toward the back door, didn't you?"

"I saw it was a man…that's all."

"Tall, short, thick, thin? What kind of a lookin' man?"

"I—I don't remember."

"Think hard. We gotta have something to go on."

She said, "I'd only be guessing. But if you want a guess, I'd say he was about average size."

Chris Peterson shrugged disgustedly. "Ain't that my luck. Somebody sees a murder and ain't got no idea what the guy looked like." He looked at Bernie, who had been moving about the reception hall. "Find the gun?" he asked.

"No."

"Take a look outside. Careful where you walk. There may be footprints."

"Okay, Sarge."

Bernie moved slowly and heavily toward the back door. Scott hated to see him go. He felt safe with Bernie around. Chris was something different. The little sergeant was keen and alert, and forbiddingly impersonal. He spoke to Gail. "You say you just got here when the thing happened?"

"Yes."

"Kinda late, ain't it?"

She didn't answer. He went on, "How come you wanted to see her so sudden?"

Again Scott Henderson got the idea that Gail was choosing her words with too great care. She said, "I haven't been in Cherokee since I was four years old. The only person I really remembered was Doris. I heard that she had gotten back to town today and thought it would be nice to drop in on her. Scott drove me over."

"And then…?"

"He waited in the car. I came inside."

"Just in time to see her get it, huh? But you don't know whether the man was short or tall or what? How you know it wasn't Henderson?"

Her hand went to her lips. "It wasn't!" she cried.

"How come you're so sure?"

"I know it wasn't. He was in the car…"

"That's the way you peg it. He could of maybe got out."

Scott said quietly, "I could have, Peterson. But I didn't."

"Okay," Chris's glance clashed with Scott's. "Keep your shirt on. I wasn't saying you did. I'm just a poor dumb dick trying to learn things." He turned again to Gail. "You didn't see nothing of the guy after you followed him out the back door?"

"No."

"And you wasn't scared?"

"Yes, I was frightened."

"You run out a minute or so after it happened. You just come back. That's quite a little while, Miss Barrie. It was long enough for us to get the call at headquarters and for me and Bernie to drive out. What was happening all that time?"

She said carefully, "I walked toward the woods."

"That takes a lotta guts."

"I wasn't thinking about myself. I walked as far as the brook. I didn't see anything. I stayed there a while, looking around. Then I came back."

Peterson said softly, "When did you get that bruise?"

Scott was startled by the question. He followed the direction of the detective's glance. He didn't like what he saw.

On Gail's left arm there was an ugly red mark; the sort of bruise that appears on sensitive flesh, and turns black and blue the next day. As a bruise, it wasn't much. But this Scott Henderson was sure of: It hadn't been there earlier in the evening.

Gail looked at her own arm. She seemed surprised and frightened. She said, "I don't know…"

"You had it long?"

She shook her head. She looked appealingly at Scott, as though she had reached the end of her resources and was begging him to take over.

He was thinking desperately. Too many things were too vague. He said, "I know when she got the bruise, Peterson."

"Oh, you do, huh? How come you do, and she don't?"

Scott said, "It's just a trifle embarrassing."

"I don't embarrass easy."

"On the way over here from the Country Club, I parked for a little while on The Ridge. I asked Miss Barrie to marry me."

"I'm listening."

"She said Yes. Naturally…in a situation like that…"

Chris Peterson's eyes glittered. "I get it. You clinched. Young love on the loose. You grabbed her so tight she bruised."

The two men stared at each other. Scott didn't like the sergeant. He didn't like anything that had happened, was happening, or gave promise of happening.

Peterson said, "You must be a hell of a lover, Henderson; that's all I gotta say."

Gail looked gratefully at Henderson. For a moment, he felt fine. Then a new thought hit him.

He started wondering what it was she was grateful for. And where she really had gotten the bruise.

CHAPTER FOUR

BROOKSIDE WAS A SPRAWLING, sparsely settled area on the outskirts of Cherokee. All who could afford it had built homes in Brookside that they could not afford. Around each house there was plenty of room for lawns and trees and flowers.

Normally, Brookside was quiet and tranquil at night. Particularly on the far side of The Ridge where the Treadway house was located. But now—quite suddenly—it stopped being tranquil.

Automobiles came from all directions, converging on the Treadway home. First there was a prowl car in which there were two uniformed policemen; then the Treadway family doctor, an elderly, kindly man with gray hair and stooped shoulders; then the coroner and his assistant, then a ramshackle car, which disgorged two fingerprint men. The Treadways rated a lot of attention, and they were getting it.

There was a brief lull, then more cars arrived. In the first was a tall, rangy chap named Bill Daggett. He was forty-one years of age, perpetually on the edge of being drunk, and worked for Cherokee's morning newspaper, the *News-Herald.* He barged inside and started firing questions at Sergeant Peterson. Peterson countered with a question of his own. He said, "How'd you get here so quick, Daggett?"

The reporter grinned. "Our headquarters man was there when the call came in from here. He phoned the night city editor, who phoned me at the Country Club."

"Too bad," commented Peterson caustically. "They got you before you finished getting nice and plastered. I suppose you told everybody."

Daggett said, "Listen, copper," and waved his hand toward the great outdoors.

A procession of automobiles was turning into the driveway. "A lovely social evening," stated the reporter, enjoying Peterson's discomfiture. "Thought you'd enjoy meeting a few of Cherokee's nice people, Chris."

The first person inside the house was Barbara Mathews, nineteen-year-old daughter of Scott Henderson's partner. Ordinarily, she was gay and bright and vivacious. Not beautiful by any standards—not even pretty, perhaps—but she was the sort of girl about whom young men buzzed eagerly. She saw Gail, and ran across the hall to her.

For the two months Gail had been in Cherokee, she had been a guest at the Mathews home, and she and Barbara had become fond of each other. There was only a trifle more than a year of difference in their ages. They started talking, and Scott could see Barbara glancing occasionally at the body on the floor.

Other people streamed in. Apparently Bill Daggett had flung a bombshell into the Saturday night crowd at the Country Club. Behind Barbara trailed a very young Air Force lieutenant. He wore silver wings, ribbons of the European theater, three battle stars, three overseas stripes, and four decorations. He looked like a kid home on vacation from military school. Barbara introduced him briefly as Lieutenant Homer, and Scott remembered him as a gawky youngster who only three years ago had been a pleasant, awkward nuisance around the club tennis courts.

Another car produced the tall and handsome Tony Kinkaid and a young couple named Pearsall. Two more cars added ten of Cherokee's nicer and more curious people. Then another car bearing a couple whom Scott knew only casually, plus Paul Innes, the manager of the Country Club. Sergeant Chris Peterson made no effort to conceal his disgust. He said to Innes, "You forgot the band."

Paul said, "Don't blame it on me. Daggett made sure everybody at the Club knew about it."

"Good old Bill," Peterson's eyes dwelt unhappily on the *News-Herald* man, "Someday he's gonna get his ears pinned back, and I wanna be there."

Innes said, "He's a damned nuisance. But he's a good reporter."

"Too good. And being a louse doesn't help any, either."

Peterson assigned the two patrolmen to the job of herding the crowd into the living room and keeping them there. There was an incessant chatter in which women's voices were pitched higher than usual, while the men talked softly.

Bits of truth filtered through the haze of conjecture. Not for twenty years had Cherokee experienced the thrill of a society murder, and that one had not been a mystery: Just a married couple who happened not to be married to each other, plus the wife of the erring gentleman. Exciting but not puzzling, and long since forgotten.

Scott Henderson stood on the fringe of the group that centered about Gail. Tony Kinkaid towered above them all, his too-handsome face showing interest and solicitude. Chris Peterson stood it as long as he could and then shouldered through. He said, "Break it up, folks; break it up. Miss Barrie, s'pose we go upstairs where we can hear ourselves think. You, too, Henderson."

Kinkaid started with them toward the steps. He said. "I'll go along, too."

"Who are you?"

"A friend of Miss Barrie's."

"Lawyer?"

"No."

"Then you stay here."

Kinkaid's face flushed. He said, "Tough cop, huh?"

"I'm gentle like a lamb." It was apparent that Sergeant Peterson and Tony Kinkaid were not destined to become good friends. "But I don't need no zoot suits today, so you go peddle your merchandise somewhere else."

Tony's eyes got hard. Then he smiled. He said, "Okay, Sherlock. I hope you break your neck."

Henderson moved to the vicinity of Paul Innes. He said, "How did that hunk of manly beauty get in on this?"

Innes shook his head. "That I wouldn't be knowing, Scott. He just seems to get around. The minute he heard that Gail Barrie was here, he sort of took over."

Scott said, "He's not my favorite gent."

"Nor mine. But what can we do about it?"

They went upstairs: Peterson, Scott Henderson and Gail Barrie. Peterson called the doctor into the hall and asked whether the nurse could be spared for a few minutes. They went into the guest room at the back of the house, a spacious, lovely room done in gay, flowered chintz, and not at all the sort of place for a murder investigation.

Miss Potter came in, looking badly scared. Much to Scott's surprise, Peterson was gentle with her. His questions were quiet and adroit. She repeated what she had told Scott. Just that and no more. Peterson let her go, and looked at the others. He said, "You might as well relax. We still got a lot of talkin' to do."

Scott took out a pack of cigarettes. He offered one to Gail and then said, "Sorry, I forgot you don't smoke." He extended the pack to Peterson who said, "No, thanks," and then pulled a cigarette out of his own pocket and lighted it. He pulled a small straight chair from its place against the wall, reversed it and sat staring at them, his arms across the back of the chair. "Quite a mess," he commented.

There was a knock on the door. Bernie Williams came in. His broad, heavy face showed worry and concentration. He walked across to Peterson and handed him something.

Bernie said, "I fished this out of the brook, Sarge."

"This" was a neat little pearl-handled .25 caliber automatic. Peterson, his wizened face impassive, removed the clip, inspected the gun, sniffed it, and smiled. "Nice work," he proffered. "One bullet fired—probably a little while ago. In the brook, huh?"

"Yes. I was using my flashlight and saw it on the bottom. The brook is pretty shallow, you know."

"How far from the house, Bernie?"

"Two, three hundred yards. Right beyond the edge of the woods."

"Our ballistics man might find something here." Peterson exhibited the gun to Scott and Gail. "Either of you ever see this before?"

They both said "No."

"Neat little weapon." Peterson seemed talking to himself. "Just goes to prove what I always said: It ain't the size of the gun that counts, it's where the bullet hits. This thing don't look like hardly more than a toy. Sort of thing a lady might carry around, thinkin' it was cute."

He looked hard at Gail. Scott looked at her, too, and saw her flinch. Peterson said, "You never toted no gun, did you, Miss Barrie?"

"No."

"Ain't you been livin' in Cuba—some little God-forsaken town?"

"Yes."

"Never carried a gun there?"

"No. Cuba is quite civilized, you know."

"I don't know nothing. I ain't right bright." He studied the gun then addressed Gail again. "Ever shoot a gun, Miss Barrie?"

"Yes."

"An automatic?"

"I've used both automatic and revolver."

"Why?"

"The same reason most people do. Target practice. For fun."

"Pretty good shot?"

Scott got up from his chair. He said, "What goes on here? Miss Barrie told you she never saw that gun before. Now you're trying to tie her up with something just because she knows how to use one. Well, I can use an automatic, too. I'm a damned good shot. So, I'll bet, are twenty-five percent of the people downstairs."

"Well, whaddaya know. Excitable as hell, ain't you, Henderson?"

"Not ordinarily. But you're getting way out of line."

"Ain't I the bad boy. You better report me to the Chief. You explain to him how you think a cop ain't got no right to question the only people who were right on the spot when a dame was murdered. But before that, you might explain to me why you're so quick to get sore when I start doin' my job."

Scott opened his lips for an angry retort, but Bernie Williams horned in. His placid, steady voice said, "Take it easy, Scott. Ain't a lick of sense getting Chris mad. He's got to play it his way."

"Thank you, Mister Williams." The sergeant's voice was heavy with sarcasm. "It's real nice having somebody along to smooth the way for me. Meanwhile, much as I appreciate your help, you can keep your yap shut from now on."

Bernie's eyes narrowed and he smiled. He said to Scott, quietly, "Don't mind him. He can't help being a louse."

Peterson took it. He said to Gail, "You say you walked in the house, heard a shot from under the steps, saw a man run away and then Mrs. Colby staggered into view and fell down. Is that the way it was?"

"Yes."

"You went to her, figured she was dead, and then ran out after the man?"

"Yes."

"You went as far as the brook. You stayed there quite a while. What were you doing all that time?"

"Looking."

"You didn't see or hear anything?"

"No."

"You still can't remember what the man looked like?"

"No."

"Okay. So you stood there, smelling the flowers. You didn't see no man, you didn't have no gun, and after a long time you come back in the house. Have I got that straight?"

"Yes."

Scott said, "Don't you believe her?"

Peterson said, "Hell, no. Her story stinks."

Scott said, "Are you accusing Miss Barrie—"

"I ain't accusing nobody. I ain't even expressing opinions unless somebody tries to shove me." Peterson ground out his cigarette in a tiny jade ash tray and stood up. He said, "That'll be all for now. I'll be seein' you."

He walked out. Puzzled, Scott waited until he heard him moving downstairs, then turned to Bernie Williams. He asked, "What does that mean?"

"It means," said Bernie carefully, "that he isn't making any arrests right now. I figure you can go whenever you want."

"Funny..." Scott smiled thinly, "...brother Peterson doesn't like me much."

"He doesn't like anybody. But he's a good cop."

Scott turned to Gail. He said, "I'd like to take you home. Alone."

She hesitated, but only for a moment. Then she nodded. They went downstairs, and Bernie talked briefly with Peterson. He rejoined them and said, "Yeh. You-all can go. You'll be seeing a lot of Peterson, I think. Try playing it gentle."

Paul Innes came over to join them. He said, "This is rotten. Is there anything I can do?"

Scott shook his head. "Nothing. You see how it is. I suppose they're bound to put the heat on anybody who happens to be around when something like this occurs."

"Sure..." Innes said, "I'd like to help. You can call me on my private number at the Club."

"Private number?"

"Yes. Doesn't come through the switchboard. Better make a note of it, Scott. It's 41732. I might be useful if they want someone to confirm what was going on at the Club. The normalcy of it, you know. Probably doesn't mean a thing, but it might help."

Henderson thanked him and took Gail's arm. Tony Kinkaid and Barbara Mathews joined them. Barbara looked worried. She stated that she intended to drive Gail home, but Scott cut in. He said, "I'm driving her home, Barbara. See you at the house."

He started out of the house with Gail. Bill Daggett interposed himself. He said, "Hey, I want a few words with you…"

"Nothing doing, Daggett. Get your dope from Peterson."

"That horse's neck? What I think of that guy…"

He followed them out to the car, and they got rid of him only by clambering in and riding off.

Scott drove slowly, retracing the road that had brought them to the Treadway home.

He wanted to say something, but didn't know where to begin. Gail sat rigidly beside him, staring into the night. The pinewoods closed in on them. Scott spoke softly. He said, "Only one thing is important, Gail. I love you terribly. I want to marry you. But I've got to ask questions." He put his right hand caressingly on her shoulder. "Look, honey," he asked, "what happened?"

She didn't say anything, and after a while he went on:

"That bruise," he said, "it wasn't on your arm when we left the Country Club. I held you tight when I kissed you, but I didn't hold your arm. You didn't get the bruise from me. Where did you get it?"

She said, "I—I don't know…"

"That's not true, Gail."

"It is…"

"If it's all you're going to say, that's all right with me. Anything you do is all right with me. I want you to understand that. But the fact that I love you doesn't make me stupid."

She was silent for a long time. They dipped down from The Ridge and rolled slowly across the valley, past the Country Club, toward the Mathews home, where Gail was staying. Not until then did she speak.

"Listen carefully, Scott," she said. "What I'm going to say won't make sense—but it's all I can say. There are some things I can't tell you. It isn't that I don't want to. I can't. You must believe that."

"If you believe I love you, you can trust me."

She said, "You mustn't go on loving me. Or, if you can't help it, you mustn't do anything about it."

"That doesn't make sense."

"I'm serious. Stop thinking about me. Stop trying to fit together the pieces of a puzzle you don't understand. Stay out of this."

"Stay out of what? I don't understand what you're driving at."

She reached over and switched off the ignition. He braked the car to a halt, and put his arms around her.

For an instant, she was rigid. Then her whole body crumpled. Her arms went around his neck and she clung to him.

He said, "Look, you're worried, and I think you're frightened. I'm the man you're going to marry, remember? How about letting me share this with you?"

She said, "I can't!"

He kissed her, and then let her go. He started the car and drove on silently. He pulled up in front of the Mathews home.

Scott said, "I'm playing it your way, sweetheart. I have a hunch you're going to need me. When you do, I'll be here."

CHAPTER FIVE

IN THE DAYS that followed, Scott Henderson learned that the aftermath of murder is neither private nor pleasant.

The expensive but unpretentious home of Fletcher Mathews in the older section of Brookside became the focal point for the officious and idly curious, as well as for friends who were genuinely eager to help. And the center of everyone's interest was Gail Barrie.

To the public in general, Gail was a fascinating figure. That she was young and pretty was incidental; that she was native to Cherokee and yet a stranger to the city was interesting; that she had been an eyewitness to the murder of Doris Colby was tremendous.

On all counts, the attractive Miss Barrie shaped up as what newspaper men call "good copy." Within a month or so—on the occasion of her twenty-first birthday—she was to come into sole possession of the fortune left by her father, a war hero. Scott knew that the net amount of her inheritance would be around a million dollars. Gossip put that amount up to several times the true figure.

Newspaper reporters haunted her. Bill Daggett was in the vicinity of the Mathews home so often as to become a nuisance. He had arrived at the scene of the murder early enough, and had seen enough, to know that there was more to the case than appeared on the surface. He had a social entrée, which merely meant that he could be more obnoxious than the average newshound. His daily stories carried a sting.

In addition to the unpleasant publicity, there was the usual routine of legal formality: the coroner's inquest, which decided that Doris Treadway Colby had met her death by means of a gunshot wound at the hands of a person or persons unknown; questioning by a genial but competent District Attorney who knew and liked Scott Henderson and had been a close friend of Major Barrie's in the old days. The three local papers carried photographs; all sorts of photographs. Of Doris, of Gail, of Scott, of the Mathews and Treadway homes, which were referred to as "palatial estates." There was even a picture of the little .25 with which Doris had been killed.

That fact had been established. The ballistics expert at the modern police laboratory, of which Cherokee was so proud, stated positively that the gun that Bernie Williams had fished out of the brook had been the murder weapon. It checked with the bullet that had been extracted from Doris's body. The great unanswered questions were: Who had owned the gun; who had fired the shot?

Doris's funeral was not a private affair, despite the best efforts of the family to make it so. The only ray of consolation in the situation was that the mother of the victim was too ill to grasp the tragedy.

Under the shrewd direction of Sergeant Chris Peterson, Cherokee's detective force worked indefatigably. Chris got in everyone's hair. He turned up in unexpected places with unexpected questions. Only the fact that his partner in the investigation was the slow-moving, slow-thinking Bernie Williams kept the police probe from being unbearable to Gail and Scott.

To complicate things still further, Gail Barrie was in a mental and emotional slump. Scott tried to rally her. She remained in the house constantly, and in her room most of the time. She avoided being alone with Scott. Except for a brief, innocuous interview with the press—on the advice of Fletcher Mathews' attorney—she refused to see reporters.

Unfortunately, Mathews himself was away. Two days before Doris' death, he had left for Washington. During his absence, Scott was in complete charge of the prosperous banking firm of Mathews, Henderson & Company. But what was more important was that he was in charge of the more personal side of the affair.

He was made no more cheerful when, three days after Doris' death, he received a call from Bernie Williams. Bernie wanted to have a private chat with him, and they selected Scott's office in the Cherokee National Bank Building. Bernie drifted in about six o'clock, a huge hunk of young man, who was abysmally worried. He produced a rank pipe and a tobacco pouch, and at Scott's suggestion waited patiently until the last office employee had left.

Academically, Bernie had been a lost ball in the high weeds. His separation from the rigors of formal education had brought him great relief. He entered upon police work gleefully, and had become a first-class cop. He was honest, unswerving, tireless and shrewd. He possessed that native instinct without which no man becomes a topflight police officer.

He spread a newspaper on the top of Scott's black walnut desk, and used it as a resting place for his tremendous feet. The hum of traffic drifted up from the street eight stories below.

The day had been sweltering. The pavements of the downtown area radiated heat, which rose in shimmering waves and sent the solid citizens home gasping. Private and municipal swimming pools were jammed. There seemed scarcely a breath of air to relieve the oppressive sultriness.

Bernie gazed steadily at his friend. The two young men liked and trusted each other. Scott fired up a cigarette and waited for Bernie to speak. He didn't have to wait long.

Bernie said, "Scott, you and your gal friend are needing a friend at headquarters. I'd like to be elected."

Henderson smiled. "You're it."

"What I'm saying right now is off the record." Bernie was deadly serious. "I got a proposition to make."

"I'm listening."

"This Doris Colby thing looks like it has cooled off. But it hasn't. Chris Peterson is on the ball. He never quits until he knows the score…and he doesn't know it yet. Neither do I. Somebody's going to discover a lot of truth, or else they'll uncover some facts that will add up worse than the truth. Me, I'm only interested in finding out what really happened. You can help."

"How?"

"By telling me things you haven't told Peterson. By laying all your cards on the table. You're in love with Miss Barrie, ain't you?"

"Yes." Scott said it simply, without adornment.

"She's in more of a spot than you think. Lacking any other good suspect, she's ready-made for having herself a bad time."

"You mean Peterson would frame her?"

"Nope. I hate the guy's guts, but he's honest. Miss Barrie holds a bad hand. Chris is positive she knows more than she's telling. He thinks maybe she killed Doris."

"That's absurd."

"Is it?" Bernie lowered his feet from the desk and leaned forward. He didn't look like a big, lumbering ox now—he looked like a highly efficient policeman. "Can you swear she didn't?"

"Of course, I can't swear it. But I know…"

"Don't you see? You ain't got a chance, Scott—unless you come clean. This is between you and me. You either trust me a hundred percent or you don't trust me at all. There are angles I don't get. Neither does Peterson. My idea is that your best bet is to play on my team. I'll try to see it your way. What I believe, I'll keep to myself. It ain't according to Hoyle, but I say to hell with regulations. What we want to know is who killed Mrs. Colby. If we work together, we can maybe dope out something that's right before Peterson succeeds in proving something that's wrong."

Scott did some fast thinking. He trusted Bernie. He knew he needed what Bernie was offering. But, oddly, he was frightened. He said, "You mean that anything I tell you will stay between us?"

Williams shook his head. "That ain't exactly the way I mean it, Scott. If we try to handle this together and it leads to Miss Barrie…well, she'd be out of luck. That's my job. It's the way I see things, and the way I do 'em. I'd figure, too, that you'd have to want it that way, even if you *are* overboard about the girl."

"And if I say 'No'?"

"I'll be damned sorry. Because I still got my job to do, and I'll have to do it the best way I can. Think it over, kid. I ain't shoving you."

Scott got up and walked to the window. On the way he touched Bernie's shoulder lightly, an unconsidered, spontaneous gesture of friendship. He stood looking down at traffic: at buses pulling out from the business district for the residential sections, buses jammed with irritable, perspiring workers, eager for a night's respite from the smothering heat.

He felt that he had been pushed into a corner. He'd been presented with an alternative. Yet he was frightened. Suppose he talked freely to Bernie. Suppose what he said had the effect of tightening a noose around Gail Barrie? Instinct told him that the thought was outlandish. Common sense made it plain that it wasn't.

He wondered what he'd be thinking—wondered what his course of action would be—if he knew that Gail was guilty. He gave that one a going over, and didn't get anywhere. The thought was incredible, but there it was. Hell of a thing to fall in love, and then have something like this rise up and smite him. He could try to shield her, right or wrong. He could... He made his decision suddenly. He said, "Okay, Bernie. I'm taking you up."

The young man seemed neither surprised nor elated. He waited until Scott sat down again. Then he said, "I'm gonna start slamming questions at you. You're too close to this. Maybe there's an angle you missed."

"Shoot."

"First: How well do you know Miss Barrie?"

"Well enough to want to marry her."

"That doesn't mean a thing. That's how you feel, not what you know. Hell, I was cut in the head once about a dame. I didn't know from nothing, but she was keeping me awake nights, just the same. I'm asking what do you know—really."

Scott said, "Practically nothing. She was born here. She was four years old when she left. I never saw her until the second of June, this summer, when she got to town and went to stay at Mr. Mathews' home."

"She never visited Cherokee in all that time?"

"No."

"So all you know about her is what she told you?"

"I wouldn't say that. In August, 1943, her father was here for quite a while. He was a captain then, and he'd just been ordered overseas. He'd sold out everything he owned in Cuba except his home in Miramonte. He turned his holdings over to Mr. Mathews to handle for him."

"Mathews personally?"

"Actually, yes. Legally, no."

"Spread that out a little."

"Few men nowadays leave their affairs in charge of an individual. The individual might die. So the papers were drawn in the name of the firm: Mathews, Henderson & Company. We're a corporation." Scott smiled slightly. "Legally, we can't die."

"Pity Doris Colby wasn't a corporation."

"Barrie's property was in fairly liquid form. Good securities, plus a lot of war bonds. Our firm was made trustee, with Gail as the sole beneficiary. Then there was a will that made us the executors. Under either the trust deed or the will, Gail would come into the property, in the event of her father's death, when she reached 21."

"When will that be?"

"September seventh."

"No strings attached?"

"None."

"Ain't she kinda young to have that much money?"

"She will probably leave it with us. I can't say for sure, because Mr. Mathews hasn't discussed it with me, but that's the way I would peg it."

"Keep going."

"Barrie—who had been promoted to Major—was killed on Okinawa, May 22nd. We heard it first from Gail. She was notified by the War Department, and immediately cabled us. She got here a couple of weeks later."

"So much for that." Bernie poured tobacco from his pouch into the bowl of his pipe, tamped it down, lighted it deliberately and blew a cloud of smoke at the ceiling. He said, "When were you and Gail planning to get married?"

Scott started to say something, and then changed his mind. Williams' eyes missed no detail of his change of expression. "You said you'd come clean," he reminded.

"We hadn't discussed any date. It just happened the other night, you know. When we were on the way to Doris's."

"And since then?"

"She's been up in the air like a kite. So we haven't got around to discussing it again."

"Mmmm! Now a question that I know has been bothering Chris a lot. Gail left here when she was four. She's nearly twenty-one now. Almost seventeen years she hadn't seen Doris, and even then Doris was only seven. How come she had to rush over there the minute she heard Doris was home?"

Scott shook his head. "I don't know. She asked me if I'd drive her over and I said 'Yes.' "

"Did it strike you as funny?"

"I wasn't thinking about that. A fellow named Kinkaid had been hanging around her all evening. All I could think of was the opportunity of getting her away from him. Do you know Kinkaid?"

Bernie laughed. "And how I know him."

"What does that mean?"

"I tangled with him about three months ago. Out at Valley View Lodge."

"No kidding."

"I'll say I'm not kidding." Mr. Williams seemed vastly amused. "I don't peg this Kinkaid exactly. He looks like something out of a magazine advertising section—sort of picture you look at and figure that if you wore hoozis clothes you'd look that good yourself, except you never do. Somehow, you never think of a real handsome guy being tough. That's the mistake I made."

Bernie was smiling. Whatever it was he had to tell, it didn't seem to have made him angry.

"Well, one night I drift into Valley View. That's county—not city—which is why Sax Bailey gets away with it. He's a tough egg, that Sax, but nice. Anyway, there's a setup out yonder. Blonde babe named Fern Meredith sings with the band. Class...oh, boy!"

Bernie lifted both hands and brought them down in symmetrical curves. "Like that."

"I've seen her."

"Then you know. Anyway, she's supposed to be Sax Bailey's particular gal friend. Only not too particular. And according to rumor, she's been giving him the runaround with this Tony Kinkaid.

"The night I'm there, Kinkaid, Bailey and the gal seem to be having it out. Kinkaid offers to bounce Bailey around on the floor. It's none of my business, but Sax has been nice to me and I don't want to see him get messed up. So I walk over and advise Kinkaid to pipe down. He asks if I'm a cop, and I say 'Yes,' only I'm off limits and ain't got any legal rights.

"Well, Kinkaid asks me why don't I step outside and finish the argument. That's okay by me. We find a nice quiet spot, and I give him a final warning. I could have saved myself the trouble."

Scott looked at the brawny figure of his friend. "You mean he whipped you?" he asked incredulously.

"Whipped me? Brother, he mowed me down. Then he helped me up and said, 'Let's forget it.' I said that was fine with me. We went inside and had a drink together. I don't like the lad, but I'm telling you, kid—don't ever mix with him."

Memory of the affair seemed to afford Bernie a lot of amusement. And it gave Scott food for thought. He hadn't pegged Kinkaid that way. It was a new slant on a man about whom Cherokee knew nothing.

Bernie Williams came back to important things. He said, "This I gotta ask you, Scott. That bruise Gail had on her arm the night Doris was killed. Did you put it there?"

Scott said carefully, "I told Peterson..."

"I ain't Chris. I'm Bernie Williams, remember. And I'll tell you I don't believe you bruised her."

Their eyes met and held. "All right," said Scott reluctantly. "I don't think I did, either. It's possible, of course."

"So if you didn't, she got it between the time she chased out after the murderer and the time she came back."

"It could have been that way."

Bernie said, "Thanks, kid. It might be important. I've been thinking about that bruise. It wasn't made by running into something in the dark. It was made by a person. Chris thinks so, too. He thinks it all the time. I have an idea maybe she caught up with the guy who killed Doris."

"Then why wouldn't she say so?"

"Because maybe he scared her. Maybe he said she'd get a dose of the same. People will hold out a lot of information if they're scared enough." He lighted a match, watched it burn, and then dropped it into an ashtray. "You got any idea if that gun was hers?"

"I don't think so."

"She could have used it, dropped it in the brook…"

"Now you've gone screwy, Bernie. If that happened, where did the bruise come from?"

The big man shrugged. "I was just thinkin' out loud. Sometimes you get a new slant that way."

He framed the next question carefully. "Could Gail be in love with this Kinkaid number?"

"She could—yes. But she didn't act that way."

"I wonder if he knew where she was going when she left the Country Club?"

"I don't know that, either. But he's a stranger in Cherokee. Doris has been living in Los Angeles for two years. Kinkaid came here about a year ago."

"From where?"

"I'm not sure, but I think it was Cleveland."

"I'll check on the lad… You know, one thing struck me as funny. Right after the word got around that Doris had been killed, a lot of people showed up at her house. That was natural, in a town like this. But why Kinkaid? Why did he get over there so fast?"

Scott said slowly, "He could be in love with Gail. And when he heard that she was there…"

"Or he could be interested in the million she's on the edge of getting. It just struck me as funny…"

Scott said, "But you haven't got any motive. He didn't know Doris."

Bernie said, "Look, kid—what do you reckon is holding Chris Peterson up? He ain't looking for evidence. He's looking for motive. Until he finds that, he can't move. Neither can I. Apparently nobody had any motive for killing Doris, but she was killed just the same. And the person who did it meant business— they weren't just having a little target practice. Find a motive, and you've got the case pegged."

Scott said, "Kinkaid was still at the Country Club when Gail and I left. He was still there when they heard the news."

"Check. But you tell me you stopped on The Ridge long enough to do a hunk of proposing. From a guy like you, that wouldn't come easy. So that took a lot of time. Kinkaid could have beat you to the Treadway house. He could easily have returned to the Club before the crowd there heard the news. He might then have gone back to Doris's house—just to make it look right."

"You mean you think it might have been Kinkaid?"

Bernie shook his head. "I don't think anything, Scott. Not yet. But I can tell you this much: I ain't checking Mr. Tony Kinkaid out of the picture."

CHAPTER SIX

SCOTT HENDERSON was about to have dinner with Gail Barrie and Barbara Mathews. He parked in front of the Mathews home, which was a gray-stone-and-red-brick affair and one of the older residences in Brookside.

For a couple of days Scott had been regretting the absence of Fletcher Mathews. Mathews was a stocky, gray-haired gentleman of fifty-six, who had been like a father to Scott. He had taken him into the office immediately following his graduation from college, taught him the intricacies of the banking business, schooled him in practical finance, held a place for him while he was in the army, and then had reorganized the corporation, changed its name and taken Scott into the firm. Despite the difference in their ages, the men were friends. There was a mutual admiration and mutual trust. And right now, Scott found himself plagued by the idea that perhaps he wasn't handling things the way Fletcher Mathews might have done.

He sighed as he got out of the car and walked across the tiled veranda. This was a fine, sturdy home, belonging to a fine, sturdy citizen who had served his community well. Mathews had been successful in his business, but had never lacked time for civic affairs. He had twice been mayor of Cherokee when Cherokee was sadly in need of brains and incorruptibility. He had been offered a United States Senatorship, and had turned it down. He lived in the big house with his daughter, Barbara, and in all the years Scott had known him he had never discovered any quality in the man that was less than admirable.

Scott shoved open the screen door and stepped inside. He saw nobody. A tantalizing fragrance came to him, and he walked back to the kitchen. The two colored servants—Leander and Oleander—were preparing dinner. Scott sniffed and said, "Baked ham! It isn't possible!"

Oleander looked up, delighted. "Sho' Lawd is, Mistuh Scott. Us been savin' our points jes' fo' this."

Scott said, "That's too much. Don't you think so, Leander?"

The combination butler-chauffeur-gardener grinned broadly, "Nossuh, Mistuh Scott," he said. "They ain't no sech a thing as too much eatments."

Scott said, "Where's Miss Barbara?"

"She ain't come in yet."

"Miss Gail?"

"She's up in her room." Oleander's eyes betrayed concern. "She sho' ain't been herse'f sence Miss Doris was killed. Don't do nothin' but sit at the window. Ain't no sparrer don't eat more 'n her."

"Hasn't she had any visitors?"

Leander and Oleander shook their heads. Leander said, "Plenty visitors, all right, Mistuh Scott, but she don't see none of them. 'Ceptin' that Mistuh Kinkaid," Leander's tone indicated that he didn't entirely approve of Tony.

A gay voice called from the front of the house. The door slammed. Barbara said, "Hi there! Where's everybody?"

Scott made a gesture to the servants, bowed solemnly before the fragrant ham, and pushed through the swinging door. Barbara was in the front hall, bubbling over with vitality and good spirits. He put one hand under her chin and brushed her forehead with his lips. He said, "The late Miss Mathews."

She laughed. "Couldn't help it, Scott. And I'm not very late. Where's Gail?"

"Oleander says she's upstairs."

They looked at each other, their faces suddenly grave. Scott nodded toward the living room and they walked in there and sat on the big overstuffed couch.

Between these two there existed a delightful and unusual relationship. They knew—and had discussed frankly—that Fletcher Mathews entertained the hope that they would someday fall in love and marry. Six months before, Scott had said, "So what do we do, Half Pint?"

She said, "Nothing."

"You know how your father feels?"

"Sure. But that still doesn't mean…"

"I'm too old, eh?"

"Be yourself, Scott. You're a child. A swell child, and even a trifle precocious. But we're not in love with each other, or are you?"

"I admire you," he said, half-seriously, half-jokingly. "You're an admirable screwball. But I'm not in love with you, either."

And that was that. It was a nice relationship, and it was the way they both wanted it.

Scott said, "What's happening isn't so good, Barbara. We've got to snap Gail out of it."

"How? She's sweet and lovely and stubborn as hell."

He said, "I understand she's seen Tony Kinkaid a couple of times."

"That gorgeous heel!"

Scott smiled. "If we could just get her started…take her out somewhere…maybe she'd let herself get back in circulation again. Unless she gets a grip on herself, she's liable to get morbid."

Barbara glanced at the toes of her sensible shoes. "We'll work on her at dinner. Perhaps we can sell her on a movie. If that misses fire, we'll take her riding later tonight."

He agreed, but he wasn't optimistic. Nor did he get more hopeful as they ate the luscious dinner that Oleander had cooked and Leander served.

Gail toyed with her food. She smiled brightly, and laughed when either of them said anything that was supposed to be funny, and steadfastly maintained that she wasn't going to any movie that night. She said she was tired. She said she had things to do. She made a score of excuses, any one of which might have been valid except that it wasn't.

There was nothing in Gail's manner to betray morbidity. She looked lovely unless you happened to catch her off guard. Then there was something in her eyes... There were little lines about the corners of her lips...

After dinner they went on the veranda together. They talked inconsequentially: about reconversion, about Barbara's manifold activities, about the beautiful weather they'd been having...about everything except the things that all were thinking.

After an hour Barbara—none too adroitly—said that she had a letter to write. She said she'd be back in a half hour. She went upstairs, and the minute they were alone Scott walked over to Gail's chair and seated himself on the arm of it. He dropped one arm across her shoulders, tilted her chin back and bent his face to hers.

Again—as always—the fierceness of her response astounded him. It was magnificent, it was everything it should be, it left him thrilled and shaken...except that in her passion there was an intensity that transcended the physical. It was as though she was clinging to something that was in danger of slipping away from her.

Barbara rejoined them and discoursed lyrically on the beauties of the night, and the advantages of driving in the moonlight. Gail Barrie shook her head. She said, "You're a wonderful salesman, Barbara, but just for tonight include me out."

"Aw, Gail..."

"I'm tired. I want to turn in. I'll look at the moonlight through my window. I'll even let some of it into the room. You and Scott run along and have your drive."

They argued. They pleaded. They didn't get to first base. Finally Scott rose and said, "The gal is stubborn as an army mule." He held out his hand. "Let's go, Barbara."

She caught something in his glance. Obviously, he wanted to talk to her. Well, she wanted to talk to him, too. They told Gail good night. Scott kissed her. They watched her start upstairs, after closing the front door. Then they piled into his car and started across the valley toward the wide rolling countryside beyond The Ridge.

Scott said abruptly, "It's bad medicine: all of it."

Barbara nodded. "She's changed, Scott. When she first got here she was a different person. She had been shocked by her father's death—they must have been awfully close—but she knew how to take it. She went places. She did a tough time readjusting her life but still wasn't going to let herself be whipped down by something she couldn't change. She acted like a sane, normal girl who was having help. That thing the other night...Doris's death...changed her completely."

Scott said, "Have you tried to find out why?"

"I tried. No soap."

"She rallied from the news about her father. But she hasn't bounced back from this."

"Not an inch."

"She needs help," said Scott, "but she won't accept any."

"What kind of help?"

"If I knew the answer to that one, I wouldn't be so worried."

Barbara said, "You don't believe she told the truth about what she saw at Doris's house, do you, Scott?"

"No."

"And the police don't believe her either, do they?"

"No."

"You think she recognized the murderer?"

"Yes."

"Then why... Good God! Scott, it doesn't make sense. Here's a sweet, normal girl. And believe me, she is... I saw enough of her in the past two months to know that…a sweet, normal girl who all of a sudden starts acting like a crazy woman. Why don't you force it out of her? She's in love with you like crazy."

He said, "I've tried every way I know. I've been gentle. I've been tough. I've teased her, begged her, bullied her. I'm licked."

They drove a long time without talking. The hands of the dashboard clock approached midnight. Scott said, "I could do with a drink."

Barbara nodded. "I could do with three drinks."

"Valley View Lodge?"

"Sold."

He stopped the car, backed into a side road, completed his turn and started back toward the western end of The Ridge where the Lodge was located. He said, "I'll buy you a stack of chips. Maybe this is your lucky night."

There were thirty-five or forty cars in the parking space next to the Lodge. From inside came the sound of an energetic local orchestra beating it out. Scott and Barbara went inside, crossed the miniature dance floor and walked through a door marked "Recreation Room." On the way they passed Sax Bailey, the quiet, expressionless, middle-aged man who operated the place and was supposed to own it. With him was a gorgeous blonde, resplendent with curves that her gown made no effort to conceal. As soon as they got beyond earshot, Barbara said, "What it takes, that Fern Meredith has got it!"

Scott laughed. "I never did go much for the voluptuous type."

"I bet you say that to all the skinny girls."

Valley View Lodge was on the low side of The Ridge. Its dining room was on a level with the road. In the rear it overhung a cliff, and the gambling room was downstairs.

The room was thick with cigarette smoke. The roulette wheel was clicking merrily. There was a crowd clustered about the dice game. In front of a tiny table, four people sat on high stools playing blackjack against an impassive houseman.

They recognized a dozen people in the room. They waved at each other and called greetings. Barbara found a place at the roulette table, and Scott bought her ten dollars' worth of 25-cent chips. Yellow ones. She put one quickly on the line between 17 and 20 and the ball dropped into the pocket marked 20. Barbara squealed and the dealer, who had seen her before, gave her a cold professional smile as he shoved 17 yellow chips at her and left the one she had just bet.

She looked like a kid, and she was playing with a kid's enthusiasm. Luck was with her, but she wasn't a natural gambler and refused to bet too many chips at a time. Scott loved her freshness, her delight over her modest winnings. Once he leaned over and said, "It's a pity Gail didn't come. She'd have enjoyed this."

A waiter brought drinks. Barbara drained hers, put five chips on the second dozen and won ten when number 13 hit. Everybody seemed to be having a good time except a few who were losing more than they could afford. Valley View was Cherokee's outstanding hot spot. Its popularity was based on good food, good service and an atmosphere that made its patrons believe that they were raising hell.

Sax Bailey was a good manager. He kept the riffraff away, he was courteous, he employed a bouncer who could sense trouble a mile off and had the ability to nip it before it ever got really started.

Barbara's forty chips built up to more than a hundred. She was having the time of her life. Her laughter rang across the room with each trivial winning. It was infectious. People came to watch her.

At 12:30 there was a surge toward the stairway. Somebody said, "The show's going on," and Scott shoved all of Barbara's chips at the dealer. He said, "She's cashing in."

The wealthy daughter of a wealthy man, Barbara was as delighted with her $28 profit as though she had made a million. She insisted on returning Scott's original ten. She said, "All right, we'll see the show."

The orchestra was still selling the latest swing. Scott knew that the show wouldn't go on for another fifteen minutes at least. But he also knew that if Barbara kept on playing, she'd lose her modest winnings and with it much of the kick.

He walked up the stairway with her, and into the dining room. He looked around.

At the far end of the room was the bandstand. In front of it was the dance floor, jammed now with older people who were dancing conservatively, and younger ones who were jitterbugging. There was a liberal sprinkling of uniforms, including at least a dozen young men who had just returned from the fighting fronts and who had ribbons on their chests and little parallel gold bars on their left sleeves.

Around the edge of the room were tiny booths, large enough to afford a degree of privacy, yet small enough to permit an unobstructed view of the dance floor. It was all very hectic and gay, and Scott had succeeded in throwing off the depression that had gripped him earlier in the evening.

He circled the room with Barbara, looking for an empty booth. Far down near the bandstand, he thought he saw one. He grabbed Barbara's hand and quickened his pace.

But the booth was not empty. Neither of them knew that until they got there.

Two people were in the booth. A man and a girl. They were sitting very close to each other, talking earnestly, unmindful of the crowd, the music, the dancing.

The man in the booth was Tony Kinkaid. Kinkaid, the magnificent.

The girl was Gail Barrie.

CHAPTER SEVEN

SCOTT COULDN'T SEE Barbara's expression, but he had a fair idea. And he knew that he himself wasn't giving any notable demonstration of nonchalance.

Gail was staring up at him, her cheeks pale, her eyes too bright. Of the four, only Tony Kinkaid seemed at ease. He rose elegantly, smiled, and said, "Well, here we are. Just one big, happy family."

Scott didn't say anything, for the simple reason that he couldn't think of anything to say. Tony gestured largely toward the table. "How's about having a little drink with us?"

"No, thank you."

Scott kept his eyes on Gail. She seemed to be frightened, though of what, he hadn't the faintest idea. He tried to make himself believe that she was merely embarrassed, but knew that wasn't the whole answer. She was appealing to him to understand something he couldn't understand. He said, "We're on our way out."

Gail still hadn't spoken. Barbara said, "Have a good time, folks," and moved off with Scott. On the way around the room they passed Fern Meredith. She was watching them oddly, with wise, sultry eyes. Briefly, her glance went to the booth in which Tony Kinkaid and Gail Barrie were sitting, and then back again to Henderson and Barbara.

Scott and the girl got outside and went to the parking space. They climbed into his car and started in the general direction of home. Barbara said, "Was I surprised! You could have knocked me down with a crowbar."

Scott managed a sickly grin. He said, "Light up a couple of cigarettes, will you?"

She carried out his instructions and poked one of the cigarettes between his lips. Barbara said, "I know. You don't get it."

"I'm afraid I don't."

"That makes us unanimous. I'm only sure of one thing. It isn't love."

Scott said, "Gail wasn't so tired, after all. That was a stall. She wanted to get us out of the house."

"Keep talking."

"She must have had a date with Kinkaid. Simply didn't figure we'd be at Valley View."

Barbara touched his hand. "Snap out of it, Scott. And quit being jealous because he's beautiful and you look like a bum."

Scott laughed. There wasn't much mirth in it, but it was a laugh. "You know," he said, "you're a good kid. It's a pity we couldn't fall in love with each other." He was staring into the night. "How do you peg it, Barbara?"

"I don't. I haven't got a thing to go on but my instinct. There's some tie-up between Gail and God's-gift-to-women. My guess is that she went out with him because she figured she wouldn't run into us, whereas if they'd stayed at the house, they couldn't have missed."

"He's been making a terrific play for her," stated Scott miserably.

"Check. She's not hard to look at, and she's wealthy."

He was thoughtful and silent. Barbara said, "You may as well get it off your chest."

"Okay." He chose his words carefully. "I know Kinkaid has been chasing Gail. Until the night Doris was killed, I couldn't see where she was having any. That night she was different, somehow."

"Isn't that the night you and she did your first hitting in the clinches?"

"Yes…"

"Did you believe her, or was she putting on an act?"

"I believed her."

"I believe her, too. Ever since then, when your name has been mentioned, Gail's been starry-eyed."

"Kinkaid may have known that she was headed for the Treadway house that night. Because she and I parked for a while, he—or anybody else—could have had time to get there ahead of us. I still believe Gail knows who shot Doris."

Barbara said soberly, "Or perhaps Kinkaid does."

He looked at her, startled. "You don't mean…?"

"I don't mean anything, Scott. I'm playing copper. I'm trying to think like Chris Peterson would think if he knew everything we know. I'm doing it because I think you and Gail are the two swellest people I ever met, and I don't like the fog you're walking around in. So I'm going to crash through with a piece of unasked advice: Don't question her. Don't mention tonight. She'll either tell you, or she won't. Questioning won't help."

He said awkwardly, "And if you learn anything…"

"I'll let you know. Now let's forget it…or anyway, let's pretend we do."

He stopped in front of the Mathews home and took Barbara inside. He said, "I wish your father was here."

"Ditto."

"When do you expect him?"

"Next week: that's all I know. You haven't heard anything at the office?"

"Nothing definite." He kissed her lightly and opened the front door. He said, "Thanks, Barbara. You're a good guy to have around."

He drove home slowly. He couldn't peg this one. He had the uncomfortable feeling that the answer was right there, but it kept eluding him. And the more he thought the more elusive it got.

He put his car in the garage and rode the elevator up to his eleventh floor apartment in Cherokee's newest and tallest residential building. Living room, bedroom, bath, and kitchenette. He was proud of it. But tonight he didn't give it a thought. He pitched his coat on the couch and sprawled out in an overstuffed club chair. After a while he got up and started to undress. He snapped out the lights and lay down, trying to fit the pieces of the puzzle into their proper places. He got exactly nowhere.

He spent a sleepless, miserable night. The following morning, even after he had showered and shaved and absorbed two cups of steaming coffee, his mirrored reflection looked haggard. He wanted to call Barbara, but thought better of it. If there was anything to report, the kid would call him.

He went to the office and tried to work. At noon he ate lunch at a cafeteria, which was about the best Cherokee had to offer in the way of a restaurant. He was joined by two young men who worked in the Cherokee National Bank. They were very jovial young men, and they knew a lot of new jokes. The jokes were good and Scott tried to laugh, but his efforts were not too successful. He went back to the office, tried to lose himself in the intricacies of a new bond issue that the firm was considering, and was just about to give it up when the telephone rang. He picked up the receiver, said "Hello" and heard Barbara's gay voice.

"Western front," she said. "Nothing to report."

He questioned guardedly. "What time did she get home?"

"Around one-ish. Went straight to her room."

"This morning?"

"More of the same. Much casual conversation. No mention of anything we're interested in. A little while ago she received a beautiful box of flowers…"

"I sent 'em."

"On the beam, Scott. Cute idea. She grabbed 'em and ran upstairs. She was crying."

"Lovely," he said. "Old Scott Henderson! Never makes the wrong play."

"This was right. She's probably hugging them to her bosom right now. Lovely bosom, if you ask me...though of course you're too much of a gent to notice such things."

He grinned in spite of himself. They talked a little more and then she rang off. He turned back to his work, and this time had a little more luck. But he wasn't so absorbed that the telephone failed to be at his ear with the very first ring it gave. He said, "Hello..."

A woman's voice came to him. Not Barbara's voice, nor Gail's. A voice he didn't know. "Mr. Henderson?" it asked.

"Yes. This is Scott Henderson."

"This is Fern Meredith."

At first he didn't get it. Then he remembered. The torch singer at Valley View Lodge. The come-hither blonde who was reputed to belong to Sax Bailey and to be playing around with Tony Kinkaid. Scott said, "Yes, Miss Meredith...?"

"You know who I am?"

"Of course."

"I'd like to talk to you. Right away. It's important."

He felt an odd sense of excitement. He asked, "How important?"

"That's what I'm trying to find out. It's about something that happened last night."

He said, "Where can we meet?"

"Suppose you came to my apartment...would your reputation be ruined? I know this isn't New York, but I'd rather see you privately."

"Where do you live?"

She gave him the name and address of one of the older apartment buildings. He said, "I'll be delighted to come over. When?"

"Now."

"I'll be there in five minutes."

"Nine-C," she said. "Come right up. They don't stop you in this joint."

The lobby of the apartment building was old and dingy. An elderly man on duty in the lobby paid no attention to Scott, nor did the elevator boy ask questions when he stepped into the cage and said, "Nine, please."

He pressed the buzzer at the door marked 9-C, and got no answer. Then he rapped. The door opened. A pleasantly husky voice said, "Come right in…"

The apartment consisted of a single room with a recess that obviously did duty as a kitchenette. There were two doors, one of which was partly open—that led to the bathroom. The other door, he concluded, opened into a bed closet.

The place was shabbily furnished. The furniture looked old and tired. The dun-colored rug had holes in it. The window drapes were languid and neglected.

Fern held out her hand. She was dressed simply, as though for the street. He had wondered about that. Maybe he had been thinking in terms of seductive negligee. Whatever he had expected, this was different.

He studied the girl. No possibility that anyone would ever mistake her for a boy. Here, in the bright light of early afternoon, she looked a trifle older than when she was working at Valley View. Thirty, perhaps. A couple of years one way or the other. Her skin was lovely, her eyes a rich deep violet, her hair golden blond. He didn't know much about such things, but he got the impression that it was natural.

She waved him to a chair, shoved a pack of cigarettes in his direction, and seated herself. She crossed a pair of exceedingly well-shaped legs and he caught a brief vista of flesh above the rolled stocking. She saw him looking. She smiled. He felt himself flushing. He wanted to say, "So what! I'm human." But he didn't say it. He sat there smoking, waiting for her to speak.

She said, "You seem to be taking this in stride, Mr. Henderson. Weren't you surprised by my call?"

He nodded.

"I took a chance," she went on." I know something about you." She smiled, and a dimple appeared. "I've been here several months, you know. I've got good ears, and you hear a lot in a spot like Valley View…if you're willing to listen. Drunk or sober, people talk. You'd be surprised how much dirt I could dish up about the good folks of Cherokee."

He still didn't say anything.

"I want to ask you just one question," she said, and he caught the urgency in her voice. "It's none of my business, but I'm asking it anyway. It's this: Aren't you pretty fond of Miss Barrie?"

His eyes narrowed. He studied her. She was leaning forward, as though a great deal depended on his answer. He said, "Yes, I'm fond of her."

"Fond enough to try to keep her out of trouble?"

"Yes."

She sighed and settled back. She said, "Thanks. That'll make things easier. I got a lot on my chest, and if I can't spill it to you, I'm out of luck." She reached for a cigarette, and he held a match for her. "What do you know about me?" she asked suddenly.

He shook his head. "Very little, except what everybody knows."

"Have you heard that I'm supposed to belong to Sax Bailey?"

Her directness was startling. He blinked and said, "Yes."

"Of course you've heard it. You've probably also heard that I've been cheating—with Tony Kinkaid."

His embarrassment amused her.

"You needn't say anything, Mr. Henderson. I just want you to know that I'm playing my cards face up. That's so you'll believe me when I tell you that I think there's trouble brewing. Serious trouble. Involving Tony and Miss Barrie."

CHAPTER EIGHT

IF SCOTT HENDERSON had not been so worried, the situation would have amused him. Here he was, an earnest and successful young businessman, conversing intimately with a very blond and seductive young lady who confessed that she wasn't too heavily endowed with morals. What made it more incredible was the fact that Gail Barrie was the topic of discussion. He told himself that this simply wasn't being done in the best society. And anyway, nothing could possibly be as important as information. He wanted facts—even a few theories—to tie in with all the things he couldn't understand.

Fern said, "We better start off with me. The best I can hand myself is that I'm a high-class tramp."

Her eyes were steady. Scott felt embarrassed. This didn't seem to be the spot for a conventional contradiction. Anything he might say would sound silly, anyway. So he let it ride.

"It's true what they say about Dixie," she went on easily. "I'm more or less the personal property of Sax Bailey. Singing with his band is just gravy."

Henderson waited.

"Until recently," stated Fern, "I've played things his way. Then I met Tony Kinkaid. Tony's a prime louse, but I'm in love with him."

"What do you mean, he's a louse?"

"He's conceited. He's strictly on the prowl and doesn't give a damn for anybody but himself."

"You know that—and you're still in love with him?"

"Uh-huh. It makes me out a dope, but that's how it is."

"I see..." Scott was disappointed. "So what it adds up to is that you're jealous of Miss Barrie."

She said, "No." She said it matter-of-factly, without emphasis.

He shook his head. "I don't get it."

"You wouldn't. My slant is new to you. That's why I started off by admitting that I'm a tramp.

"Tony is playing around with Miss Barrie," she continued. "I saw them at Valley View the other night. That wasn't the first time. I think he's trying to muscle in."

"What does that mean?"

"He wants to marry her."

"And you still say you're not jealous?"

"I still say it. From what I've heard, Miss Barrie is just about to come into a hunk of money. If Tony could marry that, he'd be sitting pretty. That's something I can understand. I'm not jealous. But if she didn't have a dime, I'd feel different. Follow me?"

"Frankly, no."

"I'll diagram it. In a million years Tony wouldn't marry me. He's not as high class as he looks, but he still rates a long way above me. He could marry Gail, and I'd still be available behind the scenes. That's as far as my ambition goes. Maybe it hits you as funny, but I've been around too long to start kidding myself now. If Tony can horn in on a million bucks, I'm for him. It would prove he was a smart cookie. It wouldn't prove anything else."

Fern's realistic philosophy was a trifle bewildering, but Scott appreciated her honesty. He said, "Let's concede that you're not jealous. Then what am I doing here?"

"I'm afraid."

"Of what?"

"I don't know. There's something between those two that I don't like. It's a lot more than a smart guy trying to marry money..."

Scott said, "Supposing you've got him figured correctly, it doesn't follow that you also understand Miss Barrie. Who's to say she hasn't fallen in love with him...the same as you have?"

"I worried about that. But I don't anymore."

"Why not?"

"Something happened last night..." She looked past him at a picture that hung, rather crookedly, on the wall. She said, "You were surprised to see her at the Lodge, weren't you?"

"Perhaps."

"You and Miss Mathews got out fast. I watched Tony and Miss Barrie. They were doing a lot of talking. They didn't seem to be very happy. As soon as the show ended, they left."

She leaned forward in her chair. "So far," she said, "Nothing. Being in love with the louse, I was upset. I've got a cubbyhole overlooking the parking lot. Sax calls it a dressing room. I think different. Anyway, it's got a window. You can see things through a window if you know where to look."

"What did you see?"

"I saw Tony and Miss Barrie walk out to his car. They seemed to be having lots of no fun. They stood by the car facing each other. I couldn't hear what was being said, but they were having it hot and heavy. And this you got to believe. All of a sudden he slapped her. Smacko! Right in the face. Twice. And hard. She took it. Then she walked around the car and climbed in. He slipped under the wheel and they drove off. Mind you, he didn't shove her into the car. She got in herself, meek as a lamb. So I'm asking you... Would you peg Miss Barrie to act like that?"

"Definitely not." Then he said, "Of course, you could be lying."

"I could be. But I'm not. That's why I wanted to see you. Right now, we seem to be on the same team. Those two are in something up to their necks. You wouldn't like anything to happen to her, and I'm riding herd on him. If I'd seen him kissing her, or making passes, I'd have been sore. This way, I'm worried."

Scott said, "I'm probably wrong, Miss Meredith...but it seems to me you're building something out of nothing. You think he's not in love with her. But you think he wants to marry her. Okay so far. Except that it doesn't check with this slapping episode."

"Some girls..." she said, "...like it."

"Gail wouldn't."

"Then why did she take it?"

Scott couldn't think of an answer. Oddly enough, he believed Fern. Her story made even less sense than anything else he'd encountered, so it fitted perfectly. Fern Meredith said, "Tony is pulling a fast one. I'd bet my lace panties on that. What it is, I haven't any idea. All I'm interested in is keeping him out of a jam."

Scott got up and held out his hand. He said, "Thanks for talking so frankly. Maybe I might get a new slant."

"You'll tell me if you do?"

"Yes. But I'm not optimistic."

He left Fern's apartment and rode the elevator down to the street level. Nobody paid any attention to him.

Odd character, this Meredith girl. She was stumbling around in the same fog that enveloped him. Their interests were identical. He wondered how she would have reacted had he told her all he knew: about Gail's actions on the night of Doris's murder; of Kinkaid's arrival at the Treadway house with the first carload of friends and morbidly curious people from the Country Club; of Gail's refusal to go out with him the previous night.

He knew it was up to him to do something, but what that something was he couldn't figure. After all, Gail was a stranger in Cherokee. Sure, she'd been born there. Older residents had known her father and mother. They'd even known her when she was a baby. But she hadn't even visited Cherokee since she was four years old. Sixteen and a half years. That was quite a stretch. A lot of things could have happened in sixteen years.

There was only one person in Cherokee who really knew anything about Gail. Paul Innes, manager of the Country Club. Paul had worked for Gail's father in Cuba. He had lived in the little town of Miramonte for a year. He'd been like one of the family. Scott decided to have a talk with Paul. Not to tell him anything, but to ask questions. He went into the coin booth of the nearest drugstore and dropped a nickel in the slot. The operator answered and he said, "Four one seven three two." That was the private line at the Club, the one that didn't go through the switchboard.

Innes answered promptly. He said he wasn't busy. He told Scott to come right out, or, as an alternative, offered to meet him downtown. Scott told him to wait where he was. He got his car and drove across The Heights and into the valley beyond.

The golf course looked beautiful in the brilliant sunshine. Here and there he could see men and women playing. Some kids were slamming balls around on the tennis courts. A half dozen people were splashing in the pool. He walked through the huge main hall of the Club and into the office marked MANAGER—PRIVATE. Paul Innes unwound his long figure and stood up to shake hands. He was five years older than Scott, and looked more than that.

He said, "What's on your mind, Scott?"

Henderson tried to keep it light. "I'm in the mood to make a nuisance of myself. Got some time to throw away?"

"All you want."

They faced each other across Innes' desk. Scott said, "I'd like this to be between us. It's quite personal..."

"Quit apologizing. Let's have it."

It wasn't easy. Scott fumbled for a few moments and then said, "Aw, hell, Paul—it's about Gail Barrie."

"Yeah? What's she up to now?"

"Nothing... That is...well, you may as well know it. I'm in love with her. I've asked her to marry me."

Innes grinned. "Is that bad?"

"No. But I've been doing a lot of thinking. I suddenly realized that I don't know her at all. You do. Maybe you can tell me some things."

Paul Innes stretched back in his chair and laughed. "That's quite an order. What I know about Gail you could write on a postage stamp."

"Didn't you live in Miramonte for a year when you worked for the old man?"

"Yes. And what a year! I hated it."

"Why?"

"Have you ever lived in a little Cuban town miles from anywhere? Heat that would knock you on your ear, people you didn't know or understand? Except that Barrie had been swell to me, I'd have walked out before the year was up. I stuck it out because he needed me. I was an expert accountant, and he couldn't replace me easily. But, brother—I didn't like it. If it hadn't been for my weekends in Havana, I'd have gone nuts."

"Weren't you almost a part of the family?"

"Sure. I had to be. There wasn't anything else. Bridge games at night. I'll never play bridge again as long as I live. Barrie, myself, Gail and her girlfriend. They didn't like it, either. The bridge, I mean. They liked Cuba because they'd lived there all their lives."

Scott said, "Tell me more."

"There isn't anything to tell. Gail went to school with this other girl—her name was Margaret Allen—in Havana. Margaret was a little older than Gail, but they were intimate friends. Margaret's old man had represented some news service down there. Barrie probably figured she'd be a perfect companion for Gail. When he died, she went to live with the Barnes in Miramonte. The two girls were more like Cubans than Americans. Barrie's company maintained a school. Gail and Margaret taught in it. They ran the house for the old man. They stayed in Miramonte when Barrie was commissioned. When I was there, they were both kids. I didn't have a lot to do with either of them."

Scott said, "Was Gail interested in men?"

"I wouldn't be knowing. She certainly wasn't interested in me. I was her father's friend. I suppose I looked old to her. And there were damn few young men around Miramonte."

"But those few...what about them?"

Paul shook his head. "I was never sufficiently interested to find out. I suppose Gail had the same interest in them that any other normal youngster would have. She had a certain amount of freedom. What I mean is that they didn't fence her in the way they do Cuban girls."

"That was her life: keeping house, teaching school, playing bridge at night?"

"Just about."

"And you never caught any hint of there being...well, anything important under the surface?"

Innes frowned. "I don't know what you're driving at."

"Neither do I. It's only...well, there are times when I can't understand Gail. I thought perhaps you had the answer."

"I have." Paul concentrated on his explanation. "It's being raised in another country. The American who grows up in Cuba isn't either American or Cuban. Gail's instinct runs one way, but her background pulls against it."

Scott drew a deep breath. He wanted to go on, but didn't know how. Paul Innes said, "If you want to know whether Gail always seemed to be a nice, normal girl—the answer is 'Yes.' She and her father were crazy about each other. She even seemed to love that crummy, steaming little town. Does that answer everything?"

"I suppose so."

"Look..." Innes spoke earnestly. "I don't know you very well, Scott. I'm five years older than you are. But I can see that something's eating on you. You've fallen for a girl you can't understand. If you want my advice, I'll hand it to you this way: Quit worrying. Her blood is American. Before she's been in this country a year, she'll forget all the Cuban customs she's been brought up with. And that's all I can figure that could be wrong. Or am I merely making it more complicated?"

"No...you've helped a lot." Scott shoved a pack of cigarettes across the desk. After they had both lighted up, he spoke again, trying to make his voice casual:

"How well do you know Tony Kinkaid?"

"Not at all. He moved here about a year ago. I don't like him."

Scott said, "You remember last Saturday night here at the Club...?"

"Kinkaid and Gail?" Paul Innes laughed. "You're really overboard, aren't you? Get this. Kinkaid is nothing more or less than a wolf in wolf's clothing. A kid like Gail might be interested in him for a few days...but no longer. They simply aren't each other's type."

Scott said goodbye and went back to his car. He'd had his talk with Paul Innes. And he hadn't advanced an inch.

He had a premonition of impending danger. He felt that important things were about to happen.

But he had no faintest idea how soon they would happen, or how tragic they were to be.

CHAPTER NINE

ON FRIDAY NIGHT Scott Henderson dined at the Mathews home. Steve Homer, the young lieutenant with the baby face and service ribbons, who at the moment rated number one in Barbara's affections, was there.

After dinner the couples separated. Barbara and her lieutenant found two chairs around the corner of the veranda where the shadows were deep. Henderson and Gail found two other chairs where they could look across the valley and hold hands and pretend that everything was just dandy.

Their evening was not an outstanding success. When it came to simple conversation, they were stymied. Scott didn't mention Valley View or Tony Kinkaid or Fern Meredith. He didn't ask Gail why she had permitted Kinkaid to slap her around.

He talked about love and moonlight and honeysuckle. He felt rather sappy, and knew that he sounded that way. Yet—oddly enough—the thought that she was really in love with him persisted. He wasn't an expert on that sort of thing, but he had a hunch.

He left shortly before midnight feeling happy and futile and bewildered. He went to his apartment and turned in. Being young and healthy, he went to sleep promptly and didn't know anything more until the morning sun streamed in through the window. He rode to the office and put in an unusually heavy Saturday morning.

He was proud of being a member of the firm of Mathews, Henderson & Company. He missed his senior partner and wanted to have things shipshape when Mr. Mathews returned. He telephoned Gail and chatted for perhaps ten minutes. Lots of words, but they didn't mean a thing. He called a friend and suggested golf for the afternoon. Golf was good for him. He shot usually in the low eighties, and that required concentration.

The game was pleasant enough, but it didn't seem important. The result was that he turned in a snappy 78. It was the first time he'd ever broken eighty, and he knew he should have been excited. Joe Harrigan, his partner, was the enthusiastic one. He told everybody in the locker room about it. He dragged Scott to his house, and plied him with highballs. He gloated over Scott's achievement. He kept on gloating all through dinner.

Scott checked out shortly after ten. He put his car in the basement garage and went into the lobby. A huge, muscular figure uncoiled itself from a brown leather chair and came to meet him. Bernie Williams looked like a mountain…a very worried mountain. He said, "Where the hell have you been?"

Scott told him. He said he'd been playing golf with Joe Harrigan and that he had dined at Joe's house. He didn't mention his 78. He was sick of it. Bernie said, "How long ago did you leave there?"

"Five minutes. Ten, maybe."

"Can you prove it?"

"Of course…" Henderson caught a tenseness in the other's manner. He said, "What gives, Bernie? Why the Old Sleuth stuff?"

Bernie moistened his lips. He said, "Me and you gotta get goin', Scott. There's hell to pay."

They left the building, walked toward Bernie's car, which was parked at the curb. Scott said, "Let's have it."

Bernie let Scott have it, all right. Between the eyes.

He said, "Fletcher Mathews has been killed."

At first it didn't register. Things like that never do. They are too incredible. Scott said, "What the hell are you talking about?"

"Just what I said. I know it's tough, but I hadda give it to you quick. We're on our way there now."

"On our way where?"

"To his house."

"But he's in Washington…"

"Guess again. He got in early this evening. He went from the airport to the Country Club. He was asking for you. Then he went home. Just a little while ago we got a call from one of the servants. Mathews was dead. Shot. They found the body near a hedge between the house and the garage. It could have been anything. To me it says murder."

Scott's initial reaction was a terrible sense of loss. No time yet for grief to assert itself. Fletcher Mathews had been a second father. He was the finest, kindliest man Scott had ever known or ever expected to know. This was something too tragic to grasp at once. It had to sink in. It had to find its way through his brain to his heart.

Bernie started talking. He talked swiftly and roughly. He said, "I'm pouring it into you, Scott. It's lousy. It's worse than lousy. I gave it to you the short way because we ain't got a lot of time. You can think about Mr. Mathews later. Right now I want you to have other things on your mind."

"What other things?"

"What you're stepping into. Chris Peterson is at the house. When I got the news, I was off duty. That's how come I could go after you. I didn't want you to hear it from somebody else, especially from Chris. He'd jab it into you and turn it around. He's an okay cop, but that's how he works. This way you can be prepared."

"For what?" An idea hit Scott, and he said sharply, "Gail Barrie?"

"She was there. Nobody around the house, only just her and Mr. Mathews."

"Where were the others?"

"I ain't got all the details yet. Barbara Mathews was out. The servants were in their house back of the garage. It ain't so good. Peterson hasn't been able to get Miss Barrie out of his mind since the night Doris Colby was killed."

They whirled over The Heights and through curving, tree-lined streets to the Mathews home. The scene struck a chord of recollection in Scott's mind. He'd seen it all somewhere before: The house lighted up, interested neighbors and curious passers-by herded into a group by a burly policeman. A prowl car standing at the curb. A squad car nearby, just like another night. Just like the night at the Treadway house.

He and Bernie shoved past the patrolman on duty at the front door. They walked into the living room. The first person Scott saw was Gail. Her face was ashen, her eyes too big and too bright. The servants, Leander and Oleander, were there, too. Oleander was crying. Leander was saying, "Ain't no use weepin', honey…ain't no use weepin'…" over and over again.

Sergeant Chris Peterson was there, too—small, wiry and hard-boiled. He stared unblinkingly at Scott.

Scott walked across to Gail and put his arms around her. Her body was rigid. She looked at him, saying nothing. Her eyes said it all. Peterson asked Bernie Williams, "Where did you pick him up?"

"At his apartment house. He golfed all afternoon and took dinner with the Harrigans. Left there about ten minutes before getting home."

"Neat." Chris's voice was clipped. "Real neat."

He turned back to Gail. He'd evidently been in the process of grilling her when Scott arrived. He said, "So you was in your room, all by yourself. You didn't even know Mr. Mathews was home."

She nodded.

"What did he say to you?"

She said, "I told you I didn't see him. I was in my room."

"You heard the shot?"

"I don't remember."

"Hmm! Somebody shoots a gun right in back of the house. There ain't nothing around here except a lot of quiet. But you didn't hear it."

"I didn't say that. I said I don't remember. If I heard it, I probably thought it was a backfire."

"I've heard that one before, too. Funny how nobody can tell the difference."

Scott said, "When you hear a noise like that, you naturally think backfire…"

Peterson snapped, "Keep out of this. When I want your opinion, I'll ask for it."

Bernie whispered, "Better play it his way, Scott."

Chris went on with the girl. "So after you didn't hear no shot, but thought what you didn't hear was a backfire—what did you do?"

"Nothing."

"What's the first you knew about something being wrong?"

"I heard Oleander scream."

"And you didn't think that was a backfire, too?"

Scott flushed and started to say something, but Bernie grabbed his wrist.

Gail was terrified, but Peterson's hostility made her angry. She stared at him, waiting for his next question. It came soon enough:

"What did you do after you heard Oleander scream?"

"I ran downstairs."

"How did you know which way to run?"

"She was still screaming."

"Okay. Keep talkin'."

"I ran around toward the garage. She and Leander were this side of the hedge. Mr. Mathews' body was lying on the path."

"And was you surprised!"

A plainclothesman walked into the room. He said, "Can't find no gun, Sarge. We looked everywhere."

Peterson nodded. His bright little eyes never left Gail's face. He said, "Where would you guess the gun was hid. Miss Barrie?"

She looked straight back at him. She didn't answer his question.

"Ain't no brook nowhere around," Peterson went on. "But I got a hunch the gun ain't far away."

Another car roared up to the front of the house. Same old stuff. Technical boys. Coroner. A bright-faced lad from the D.A.'s office who said, "Hi, Scott. 'Lo, Bernie." Fingerprint men. Peterson talked to them quietly, and they went about their duties. The youthful assistant district attorney stayed where he was, listening. Peterson picked up where he left off with Gail.

"So you come downstairs and seen Mr. Mathews' body. What happened then?"

"I felt for his pulse. I felt his heart. I realized he was dead. I sent Leander to telephone for the police."

"How much time did all that take?"

"I don't know."

Peterson swung on Scott. "You're Mathews' partner, ain't you?"

"Yes."

"You knew he was flying home this evening?"

"No. I didn't expect him until next week. He probably came shipside."

"We can check that. You didn't know he was comin'. Miss Barrie didn't know he was here. Leander and Oleander was in their house. Maybe he just killed himself." Chris looked disgusted. "I don't think I'm getting a lot of cooperation around here. I don't like it that way."

Gail said, "I've told you all I know."

"Which is another way of saying you've told me all you're *gonna* tell. Okay, Lady. You always seem to be around when murders happen. You ain't on trial now. Nobody can make you talk if you don't want. But just for the books, I ain't satisfied."

The young assistant district attorney said, "Why aren't you satisfied?"

"First, we ain't got the gun."

"That's logical. If the murder was committed by someone from outside, he'd have taken the gun with him."

"That's the easy way of figurin'. Me, I like it the other way. But my second reason is neat." Peterson looked at the others in the room. "This ain't official. It ain't an accusation. It's just the way things strike me."

He drew a deep breath. "Think this one over. Miss Barrie could be telling the truth. I ain't got a lick of proof that she ain't. But…" and his voice became hard. "But *if* she killed Fletcher Mathews, she couldn't possibly cook up a better story than the one she has just told us."

CHAPTER TEN

SCOTT HENDERSON said, "That's rotten, Peterson."

"So it's rotten. It's still the way I think. If Miss Barrie killed Fletcher Mathews—I ain't saying she *did*, mind you—she couldn't make a smarter move than to have cooked up that story." He bowed to Gail with mock politeness. "That's all for now, Miss Barrie."

She said, "May I go?"

"Sure. Just tell me where."

"Upstairs with Barbara."

"When did she come in?"

"Just before you got here."

"Alone?"

"She was with Lieutenant Homer. They had planned to ask me to go riding with them. When she found out what had happened…"

"I'm sorry for her," said Peterson simply.

Scott took Gail's hand. He said, "Want me to go up with you, honey?"

"No. Join us later. Right now, I'd like to be alone with Barbara."

"I understand…" He tried to bolster her morals. "Don't worry, Gail. Things will work out all right."

She squeezed his hand and walked out of the room. He admired her courage, but that didn't dispel his bewilderment.

The door opened and several people entered. There were two policemen and three other men. One was a portly real estate operator named Cummings. The second was Paul Innes, manager of the Country Club.

The third was Tony Kinkaid.

One of the policemen remained in the hall with the civilian trio. The other one walked into the living room to report to Peterson. He said, "Here they are, Sarge. What'll I do with 'em?"

Peterson said, "Dining room. And keep the door closed until I call you."

He turned around and spoke to the colored man-of-all-work. His voice was unexpectedly gentle. He said, "Leander…?"

"Yassuh, Cap'n…?"

"Tell me in your own words what happened?"

Leander's ebony face was lined with grief. There were traces of tears on his cheeks. He said, "I dunno nothin', Cap'n 'ceptin' only what Miss Gail done tol' you. Nor neither Oleander, she don't know nothin' likewise."

"Where were you at the time?"

"We was in our house, Cap'n. That's back of the garage. We went there soon as we washed up the supper dishes an' straightened aroun'."

"What were you doing?"

"Just settin' an' talkin'."

"About what?"

"I dunno fo' sure, Cap'n. If I recollect rightly, we was discussin' 'bout a baptizin' a week ago come Thursday. Oleander was sayin'..."

"Never mind that. What was the first thing you knew about anything being wrong?"

"We heard a noise. Oleander, she jumped. She said, 'Leander! That sounded like a gun.' "

"What did you say?"

"I said, 'Hush yo' big mouth. That wasn't no gun.' "

"And then...?"

"Well, me an' her did a lot of arguing.' She kep' on sayin' it was a gun, an' I kep' on sayin' it wasn't. I said they wasn't nobody 'roun' heah had a gun, an' if they did have, they wouldn't be shootin' it that time of night."

"What time was it?"

"I don't remember exactly, Boss...but maybe a little befo' ten o'clock. Anyway, Oleander ain't no gal to leave drop an idea once she gits her teeth into it. She said she knowed she was right...an' fo' once I got to admit she was. She said she was goin' downstairs an' have herself a look aroun'. I tol' her to go right ahead. So she did. Next thing I know, I heard her yellin'. An', Cap'n, I mean yellin'. She split the night wide open. I went runnin'. An' there they was."

"They?"

"Oleander an' Mistuh Mathews. He was layin' in the path an' she was kneelin' down 'longside of him screamin' an' cryin' an' talkin' to him."

"Did you know he had come back home?"

"Nossuh. Us wasn't expectin' him until next week. Tuesday, I think Miss Barbara said. Anyway, Oleander kep' tellin' me he was dead. She kep' on sayin' somebody kilt him. She showed me her hand. It was all over blood."

"What did you do then?"

Leander's face was solemn. He said, "Cap'n, I kneeled down there on the path 'longside of Oleander, an' we prayed fo' the soul of the finest man that ever lived. We was still prayin' when Miss Gail come out of the house an' ast us what was the matter."

"Did she look surprised?"

"Wuss than that, Cap'n. She looked like even if it was true, she couldn't b'lieve it. She looked so terrible that Oleander got up an' put her arm aroun' her. Seemed like as if she was goin' to faint or somethin'."

"After you told Miss Barrie that Mr. Mathews was dead, what did she say?"

"Nothin' special, Cap'n. She just looked down at where he was layin', an' she sort of said, 'Oh, God! Another!' That was all, Cap'n. She didn't say nothin' else."

A hard calculating light came into Peterson's eyes. "That's all she said, eh? She just said, 'Oh, God! Another!' You're quite sure about that?"

"Yassuh. I remember distinctly."

"Did you hear her say that, Oleander?"

The sobbing colored woman nodded and said. "Yassuh. Tha's all she said."

Scott didn't like Peterson's expression of achievement. Nor did he relish the cause of it. "Another!" Another what? Another murder, obviously. That referred back to Doris."

Peterson said, "Thanks to both of you. I ain't goin' to keep you any longer. Maybe you better go upstairs and see if you can do anything for Miss Mathews."

The servants left. Henderson was regarding Chris Peterson with new respect. He had handled Leander and Oleander expertly. He had been gentle and kindly and patient. The man was clever. He could play more than one tune. He wasn't always the tough, explosive cop. He was persistent—and dangerous.

Peterson turned to Bernie Williams. He said, "Bring Cummings and Innes in. Leave Kinkaid where he is."

The two men came in together: Cummings, short and pudgy; Paul Innes, tall and solemn. Both appeared to be badly shaken. Peterson said, "What do either of you gents know about this thing?"

They looked at each other. Cummings said, "You tell him, Paul."

"There isn't much to tell," said Innes. "The Club was pretty crowded. I was busy. It was after dark when Fletcher Mathews arrived. He asked whether Scott Henderson was anywhere around. He said he wanted to see him immediately. He said it was important."

"Go ahead." Peterson obviously had no intention of hurrying Innes. Things were going well.

"I told Mr. Mathews I didn't know. I knew Scott had been playing golf, but I wasn't sure whether he'd gone home. I sent one of the boys to look for him."

"Were you surprised to see Mathews?"

"No. I had heard he was out of town, but that didn't mean anything. He told me that he'd come back sooner than he expected. He'd been able to grab a shipside seat on a plane out of Washington and hadn't had time to wire anybody. He repeated that he wanted to see Henderson right away. He said he had come straight to the Club because he knew Scott was usually there Saturday evening. Just about that time the boy came back and said that he couldn't find Henderson. Mr. Mathews told me he was going home—to his house, that is. He asked me to have Scott call him in case he dropped in at the Club later."

Peterson said, "Let me interrupt, Mr. Innes. How did Mathews look? How did he act?"

Innes looked puzzled. He said, "I'm afraid I don't understand what you're driving at?"

"Did he seem excited or worried? Was there anything unusual in his manner...as though he might have anticipated trouble?"

Paul Innes shook his head. "Definitely not. He seemed tired from his trip, but that was all. Aside from being anxious to talk to Henderson, I'd say that there wasn't anything on his mind."

"Okay. What happened next?"

"He said he was going into the bar to bum a ride home. He had come from the airport in a taxi. I offered to drive him home, but he said 'No.' He knew that Saturday is my busiest time. He reminded me again to tell Henderson to call him, and then went into the bar. That's all I know."

Peterson turned his attention to the paunchy, florid gentleman. "How about you, Mr. Cummings?"

"I don't know anything, really. Mr. Mathews came into the bar. Most of us had been playing golf all afternoon and were shooting dice for the drinks. We had shot a lot of dice and had a lot of drinks. We invited Mathews to join us, but he refused. He asked whether any of us had seen Scott Henderson. We said we'd seen him on the links, but not since then. Then he asked one of us to drive him home."

"What time was that?"

"Around ten o'clock. Maybe earlier. Tell you the truth, we were all a little high. You know how it is on Saturday night."

"Yeh, I know. So who offered to drive him home?"

Hell, everybody offered. But Tony Kinkaid offered first, and that's who he went with."

"What was Kinkaid doing there?"

"Same thing we were, only not as much of it. He was drinking by himself."

"Was he drunk?"

"No. That boy never gets drunk. He could drain a distillery and walk out sober. You can ask Lew. He's the bartender."

Peterson said, "Lemme get something straight in my own mind, Mr. Cummings: You say Kinkaid was by himself. Any reason for that?"

Cummings looked embarrassed. He said, without conviction, "Of course not."

"Let's try that one over," suggested Peterson. "Mathews has been murdered. This ain't no time to hold back."

Cummings appeared to be quite unhappy. He said, "Wee-ell, we're not very fond of Kinkaid. No reason, you understand—that is, nothing specific. Maybe it's because we don't know him very well…"

"I get it. So he was practically alone, and when Mathews asked someone to drive him home, everybody offered—but he went with Kinkaid. How do you figure that one?"

"I was surprised. Except that Kinkaid insisted. He said he was going anyway. He said it would be a shame to break up our drunken brawl. Those are the words he used, our 'drunken brawl.' Of course he was kidding, but he's peculiar that way: you never really know whether he's kidding or not."

"In other words," persisted Peterson, "your idea is that Mathews would have preferred going home with one of you, but that Kinkaid forced himself on him. Is that it?"

Cummings said, "I didn't say that, you know. Of course, we're old friends of Fletcher Mathews, and maybe he would have preferred one of us…"

"Thanks, Mr. Cummings. And thanks to you, Mr. Innes. Now would you mind leaving the room? I don't care where you go— but I'd rather not have you here while I'm talking to Kinkaid."

The two men vanished. At a signal from Peterson, Bernie Williams went to the dining room and returned with Kinkaid.

Tony looked like the picture of what the well-dressed sportsman should wear. He had on a checkered sports coat over a light flannel shirt that was open at the neck. He wore slacks that hung perfectly from his slender hips. He looked very tall, very blond and very arrogant. He even seemed faintly amused.

He looked around the room. He looked at Chris Peterson and Bernie Williams and Scott Henderson. He was calm and self-possessed. He said, "Just like old times…"

Then he looked at Chris Peterson.

"All right," he said, "let's hear you accuse me of having murdered Fletcher Mathews."

CHAPTER ELEVEN

PETERSON DID NOT SPEAK immediately. His hard eyes bored into the handsome young man who faced him jauntily. After a while he said, "Wise guy, huh?"

"I believe so."

"All right, sonny. Go ahead and show us how wise you are."

Tony Kinkaid seemed to be enjoying himself. Every move he made was straight out of Hollywood. He dipped into his coat pocket and produced a tobacco pouch and a pipe. He filled and lighted the pipe.

"First of all," he stated blandly, "I haven't the faintest shred of an alibi. When Mathews asked for a lift, several of his friends offered. I was apart from the group, but I insisted on driving him. Reason? I was bored. I dislike stuffed shirts, especially when they've been drinking. Mathews wasn't too happy about accepting a favor from me, but apparently I forced his hand.

"I drove him home. Except for a downstairs light and two lighted windows upstairs, the house was dark. I didn't see anybody. I had plenty of opportunity to do anything I might have wanted to do. What actually happened was that Mathews thanked me, got out of the car, and started toward his front door. I drove off."

"Where to?"

Kinkaid smiled. "This is another part of my story that should make you happy, Sergeant. I figured I didn't want any part of the dance at the Club. So I started for Valley View Lodge. I feel more at home there."

"So I've heard."

"But just before getting there, I changed my mind. I decided to go back to the Club, anyway. So I did. I can't prove any of this. If I had killed Mathews, I'd have had plenty of time to get rid of the gun."

"How did you know he had been shot?"

"Well, spreading unpleasant news seems to be a Cherokee habit. Besides, the dumb cop you sent to bring me here told me the whole story. He also told Cummings and Innes. He was quite talkative, in fact. I could see that things might look bad for me, except that I can't figure why I would have killed him. Maybe you know."

"Maybe I do." Peterson was annoyed by Kinkaid's insolence. The play had been taken away from him. The suspect was dominating the scene, not the detective. It gave Peterson a feeling of inferiority. He said, "How come, if you was in the bar with all them other fellows, you wasn't with them?"

"They don't like me very much," stated Kinkaid promptly. "In fact, I'm not too popular in this town."

"I could guess why."

Tony remained unruffled. "Any more damaging evidence you'd like me to give against myself?" he inquired.

Peterson said, "You're playing it cute, ain't you? Smart slicker making a monkey out of a small-town cop. I bet you feel good. I bet you ain't gonna keep on feeling that way indefinitely."

"Why, Sergeant! That sounds like a threat. Don't tell me you're thinking of taking me downtown and giving me a working over."

"I've heard worse ideas."

"I wouldn't advise it. Not unless you're sure you could make your charge against me stick. Because when I got out I'd make the department sweat. And if that didn't pan out, I'd get hold of the boys who worked on me—one by one of course—and take them to pieces."

"Tough, ain't you?"

"I'm tough enough for that." He grinned cheerfully at Bernie Williams. "Ask him," he suggested.

Peterson said, "You say you was headed for Valley View after you left Mathews at his house. You been hanging around that joint a lot, haven't you?"

"I like it there."

"You like it with your little playmate, huh?"

"I do."

"Don't you know Sax Bailey is bad medicine?"

"You scare me to death."

"You been playing it two ways, Kinkaid: Fern Meredith out at the Lodge, and Miss Barrie at the Country Club. I got a hunch there's something between you and Miss Barrie."

"She's a charming girl. And I understand that she's worth about a million dollars."

The sheer effrontery of the man had Peterson stumped. He said, "You trying to marry her?"

"I don't discuss my love affairs, Sergeant. Though you probably wouldn't understand that."

Scott Henderson had been watching interestedly. He was thoroughly angry. He hated Kinkaid's arrogance, his soft-voiced coarseness. He, too, had been wondering about Kinkaid and Gail Barrie. He didn't say anything, because this was his turn to keep quiet. But there seemed to be something unsaid. Kinkaid's tactics had saved him from a grilling. Kinkaid was smart. Scott wondered whether Peterson was keen enough to estimate him correctly.

Peterson said, "I'm not making any charge against you, feller. But I'm busting out with ideas. You got over to the Treadway home mighty quick the night Mrs. Colby was killed. You had a neat chance tonight, provided you wanted to do anything. I got a feeling the two killings are tied up. I figure you in 'em some way. I'd watch my step if I was you."

"Thank you, Sergeant." Kinkaid was scathingly polite. "Your solicitude overwhelms me. Anything else I can do for you?"

"Yeh. You can get the hell out of here."

Kinkaid left. His exit was superb. If he was holding anything back—if he had any worries—he gave no sign. Bernie whispered, "The guy's good," and Scott nodded. That was the trouble: Kinkaid was too good. Bernie seemed to be thinking the same thing. He said, "Someday that lad will outsmart himself."

Eventually the house was cleared of officialdom. Peterson seemed to be more than moderately unhappy. Two of his men reported that they still hadn't found the gun, and that they hadn't located any shell. It didn't mean a thing, except that if there wasn't a shell, Mathews had probably been killed with a revolver, not an automatic. Nothing much to go on there. Bernie left with his chief. Scott Henderson went upstairs.

He knocked on the door of Barbara's room. He went in and found Barbara sitting on the bed, and Gail standing near her. He could see traces of tears on their faces. But Barbara wasn't crying now. She was looking straight ahead as though trying to adjust herself. He knew that full realization hadn't hit her yet.

He seated himself on the bed. He took Barbara's hand. He couldn't think of anything to say. They sat there for a while, and then suddenly she turned and flung her arms around him. She started crying.

He didn't try to stop her. He figured it would do her good. He felt like crying, too. It was as though he had lost a father for the second time.

Leander and Oleander were in the hall, clinging to each other. After a while, Barbara stopped crying. She said, "I'm all right now, Scott."

He held her tight and said, "Good going, kid."

She asked, "Is Dad downstairs?"

That was a tough one. He shook his head. "They had to take him. Autopsy..." It seemed so damned coldblooded. "I'll go downtown later," he went on. "I'll attend to the arrangements."

They talked a little more. He urged her to take an anodyne, and she agreed. He said, "Mind if I talk to Gail for a few minutes?"

She said, "Don't worry her too much, Scott."

Scott went to the door and called Oleander. He left her in charge of Barbara. He looked at Gail for the first time. Her face was white. He said, "Let's go down on the veranda, Gail."

She didn't protest. They walked through the downstairs hall, ghostly with silence. They went onto the veranda and leaned against the stone railing.

The night was clear and hot. There were a million stars. The huge oak which shaded the front of the house in the daytime, whispered in the gentle breeze that drifted in from across The Ridge. Scott said, "I'm going to say something, sweetheart. Before I say it, I want you to remember that I love you. No matter what has happened—no matter what happens in the future—I love you. I can't help it."

He fell silent. Then he spoke again:

"Nobody will ever quite understand what Fletcher Mathews meant to me. I won't even try to diagram it. But he meant this much: that I'm going to find out who killed him. I'm going to see that his murderer is punished. I don't know who is going to get hurt...but no matter who it is...no matter *who*, Gail... I'm going to follow through. Do you understand?"

She said, "You're talking about me, aren't you, Scott?"

"I hope not. But I don't know."

"And what you're trying to say..."

He stared off into the night. "I'm not just trying, Gail. I'm saying it. Even if it were you..."

Her body was rigid. Her right hand was clenched and pressed hard against her lips. She looked small and lonely and helpless.

She looked like a very young girl who was very much alone, a girl who desperately needed help. There was a stricken light in her eyes, as though she had fought beyond the limit of her strength. Scott said miserably, "Don't hold it back, honey. It'd do you good to cry."

Still she said nothing. There was something terrible and frightening in her grief, as though she could hold on just so long and would then break completely. He felt oddly out of the picture. There was so much about her he didn't know and didn't understand.

He stood watching her. There wasn't anything he could do. Nothing she would let him do.

And then she lowered her hand from her lips. She spoke, and he knew that she was trying valiantly to keep herself from cracking up. She said, simply, "I didn't kill Doris or Mr. Mathews."

She didn't spread it out. That was because she couldn't, because it was too difficult to put things into words. She had to say them the easy way. He took her left hand in his. He knew she'd go on if he gave her time.

"A little while ago," she said, "you told me that no matter what happened, you loved me. I'm saying the same thing. I love you. I'll always love you. Try to remember that."

He nodded. "I've never been up against anything like this, Gail. I've never been hit so hard. That's why I've got to be honest."

He hesitated briefly before going on. "You're right in the middle of this, darling. I haven't any idea how or why. If you'd only trust me..."

As though impelled by a common impulse, they turned and faced each other. And then his arms were around her and he was holding her tight. All the fear and grief that she had been fighting to hold back boiled over. He spoke to her in whispers, saying nothing...hoping that the mere sound of his voice would soothe her.

And then the storm was over. She spoke from the shelter of his arms, without looking at him. She said, "I want to tell you, but I can't."

"Yes, you can, dear. I'm sure you know who killed Doris. I know where you must have gotten that bruise on your arm. There couldn't be any reason strong enough for you not to tell someone. Anyone. It doesn't matter who. Surely you don't deny having seen someone that night at Doris's, do you?"

"I don't deny it, Scott. I don't admit it, either."

He was overwhelmed by a feeling of utter futility. He said, "I love you so much, and understand you so little. I know you're not thinking straight. There isn't anything bigger or stronger than murder. There isn't anything that could justify your keeping to yourself whatever it is that you know. If you're afraid..."

She said, with quiet dignity, "I'm not afraid of being hurt, Scott."

Henderson looked down at her tear-stained face. He said roughly, "This louse Kinkaid is mixed up in this. He's got some sort of a hold over you. That night at Valley View Lodge..."

She said gently, "You mustn't push me anymore, Scott. If I could tell anybody, I'd tell you. But I can't. All you can do is to make us both more miserable than we are. If I told you any more, you'd try to help. And you couldn't help. All you could do would be to make things worse."

He was incredulous. "Worse than what has happened already?"

"Yes." She said it with a sincerity that almost convinced him, despite its apparent absurdity. "Worse than anything that has happened already. Things that have happened can't be undone. Nothing can bring back Mr. Mathews or Doris."

He knew that he was beaten. He released her hand and turned away.

She touched his sleeve. Her voice was tiny and pitiful. She said, "Will you kiss me good-night, Scott...please...? It may be the last time."

CHAPTER TWELVE

THE NEXT MORNING was gloomy and miserable and wet. It was as though a master stage director had played a melancholy mood straight across the board, denying even the slightest hope of natural youthful resilience having a chance to assert itself.

The hilly, curving streets of Brookside were washed with rivulets of dirty gray water. The lawns and gardens were soaked.

Water hazards on the Country Club golf course became lakes and small rivers. The crest of The Ridge was capped with thunderclouds. The downtown section of Cherokee was depressing; the streets shiny and black.

It was then that they brought Fletcher Mathews back to his home.

In a city such as Cherokee there aren't many people who grieve sincerely when a man dies, but Mathews' death caused more genuine grief than that of any other citizen might have done. All his life he had been kind to people, had helped those who needed help, had contributed generously to charities, had played an upright and leading part in civic affairs, even to serving two terms as mayor when actually he loathed politics and public life.

There wasn't much to it in an official way. Bernie Williams talked to Scott briefly on the telephone. He said that Mathews had been killed by a .25 caliber revolver. The technicians at the police laboratory stated that the bullet had been fired from a revolver. Scott didn't ask how they reached that conclusion. He didn't care. The thought struck him that Doris Colby had been killed with a .25 caliber gun. Not the same gun, of course, because the police were holding that. But it seemed that the killer had a penchant for lethal weapons of smaller size. Anybody could use a .25 caliber gun.

But it seemed definitely to be the sort that a woman would select.

Time dragged heavily on Sunday. People were, for the most part, considerate, and eager to be of help. Businessmen speculated among themselves as to the terms of Mathews' will. Mathews, Henderson & Company was the State's most important private banking firm. If things developed as anticipated, Henderson would automatically become a powerful figure in the financial life of the city.

But Scott wasn't concerned about that. His thoughts were primarily of Barbara, and secondarily of Gail Barrie.

Of the two, Barbara rallied more quickly. She had been hit hard, but she was taking it beautifully. It was Gail who seemed stunned; Gail who required the greater degree of looking after. So Scott talked privately with Barbara and asked her to take care of Gail. He talked privately with Gail and suggested that she must take care of Barbara. By mid-afternoon he saw that both girls were doing what he suggested, and that this necessity for helping someone else was helping both.

The funeral was Monday morning. The skies were still gray and forbidding, but there was no rain. The house was smothered in flowers. It seemed as though everybody in Cherokee attended the simple ceremony. And then it was all over, and Scott and the two girls came back to a house that would always be empty. Oleander had made some fresh, strong coffee and fixed a light lunch. She and Leander fussed around the three young people, scolding them into eating. She railed at them for not doing the things they would normally do, and all the time she was crying into her apron.

They sat around all afternoon and all evening and talked. They tried to snap themselves out of it because they realized that this was the beginning of something. They didn't talk about the man who had left them. They didn't talk about anything much, really.

Scott went home about eleven o'clock. He felt completely sunk. He undressed, put on a robe, turned out the lights and pulled a chair to the window. He sat staring across the stanch industrial city, the city that Fletcher Mathews had helped to build. He felt more alone than he had ever felt in his life. More so than when his father died, more lonely than he would ever feel again.

And the next thing he knew, it was Tuesday morning. A new day had started. A new era was under way.

He went to his office in the Cherokee National Bank Building. This was another step he had dreaded. The office help was all there: clerks, accountants, salesmen, financial experts, secretaries, bookkeepers, office boys. Their faces showed what they felt. Grief—and curiosity. David Gardel of Gardel & Landsberg, the firm's lawyers, dropped in shortly before noon.

He told Scott about the will. He said that Scott now owned forty percent of the stock of Mathews, Henderson & Company, and that he had been placed in complete control. The firm— which now meant Scott Henderson—had been named as executor. Sixty percent of the profits were to be given to Barbara. Scott, as an individual, was designated her guardian until she should reach the age of twenty-five. Gardel said that Mathews had left a lot of money; that the estate would be huge, even after deduction of taxes. He said Barbara was perhaps the wealthiest young woman in Cherokee, perhaps in the State. He said he'd be standing by if and when his help or advice should be needed. He got up and put his hand affectionately on Scott's shoulder. He said, "I know how you're feeling. We all feel that way. But you've got a job to do. Start doing it as soon as you can."

It wasn't easy. Routine business seemed absurdly unimportant. But there were things that had to be done, and that helped. It wasn't until late afternoon that an odd thought came to Scott Henderson. It was then that he remembered the terms of the trust agreement and will left by Major Barrie. Mathews, Henderson & Company were the trustees and executors. Today that meant Scott. It meant that, at least until Gail Barrie's twenty-first birthday on the seventh of September, he had complete charge of her affairs.

Tuesday night was slightly less difficult than the previous night had been. The girls were trying, and meeting with some small measure of success. Wednesday was still better, and from then on the trend was in the right direction. The impact of the original shock was wearing off. Their grief was no less deep, but time was already helping to make the blow bearable.

Barbara's courage was magnificent. Within a week she was back at her Red Cross chores. Occasionally she dragged Gail with her. Both had sense enough to know that anything was better than staying in the house, brooding. And Scott's work at the office became heavier. He was probing into matters that theretofore had been in the hands of Fletcher Mathews.

More and more, as the days dragged by, Scott's thoughts dwelt on the subject of murder. Apparently the police had accomplished nothing. No gun had been found, no arrest had been made. As far as Scott knew, nobody thought of Gail in connection with Mathew's death, and no public mention had been made of Tony Kinkaid. Kinkaid's story advertised the fact that he had had the opportunity, but no one could figure a motive. Particularly Chris Peterson couldn't figure one. He couldn't find a shred of evidence against Kinkaid, and he was too shrewd a policeman to make an arrest unless he had a reasonable assurance that he could make it stick.

Ten days after Mathews' death, Bernie Williams dropped into the office in the late afternoon. Scott was still using the smaller of the two private offices. He had converted Mathews' big corner office into a conference room.

Bernie closed the door behind him, dropped his huge muscular bulk into a chair, lighted a cigarette and looked at his friend. He said, "I figured it was about time you'd be wanting to talk to me, Scott."

Henderson nodded gratefully. He said, "You're right, Bernie. I've been wondering whether they've got hold of anything that I don't know."

Bernie shook his head. He said, "Not a toothpick. But Peterson isn't letting up."

"You still working with him?"

"Yeh." Bernie came to the point. "He still thinks Kinkaid and Gail Barrie know a lot. So far he hasn't been able to find anything that looks like proof."

"What do you know about Kinkaid?"

"Not much more than you do. We checked on him, of course. He seems to be a wrong gee, but you can't prove it. He holds a new job every couple of years. He has a trick knee, which is what kept him out of the army. The gals go for him hot and heavy, but that's no news to you. He has belonged to good clubs wherever he's lived...which is a lot of places...and also seems always to have had friends in what you nice, respectable muggs call 'the underworld.' "

"What does that add up to?"

"Nothing. Lots of guys get a kick out of that. They like to take friends into dives and introduce 'em around... You know: 'Meet my friend, Bloodygut Louie' or words to that effect. Makes 'em feel tough. All I know about Kinkaid is that I think he's smoother than fresh butter. The way he shoved it into Chris Peterson the night Mr. Mathews was killed was smarter than you know. He got Chris sore—but he also made it look as though he wasn't worried."

"If that's true," said Scott carefully, "what is Chris really thinking?"

"You want it straight?"

"Yes."

"Gail Barrie."

"That's ridiculous. What possible motive..."

"Chris is trying to figure that one. So far there ain't any answer. A good-looking gal with a million bucks! Brother, why would she ever want to do anything except go shopping? It's got him stumped. But I'm afraid he'll work something out sooner or later."

"What do you mean: 'Afraid'?"

Bernie didn't evade. He said, "Look, kid. In high school I wasn't too bright. But on this job, I'm a long way from a dope. I think what Chris thinks: That there's some sort of a tie-up between Kinkaid and Miss Barrie. And whatever it is, it's still on."

Henderson frowned. "Mind explaining that?"

"She's seen him three or four times recently. Twice when she was downtown, they just happened to meet. Once, and maybe twice, he's been at the house."

"How do you know all this?"

"Hell, Scott—be your age. Cherokee ain't the sticks. We got a good police force. Ever since Mathews was killed, we've kept an eye on Kinkaid and Gail Barrie. Not a regular tailing job, but enough so we wouldn't be out of touch. Chris has checked back. He knows about that night at Valley View, for instance: the night when you and Barbara were so surprised to see Kinkaid out there with Gail."

"Where did he get that?"

"Lots of people saw you. They gossiped. And Sax Bailey supplied the finishing touches. He keeps a close eye on Kinkaid, because the lovely brute has been muscling in on Fern Meredith."

Scott said slowly, "You're positive about Gail having been with Kinkaid several times recently."

"It's right out of the feed box. How do *you* peg it?"

"I don't. That's on the level, Bernie. I'm taking your word for what has happened since Mr. Mathews was killed. I know something of what went on before that. I can't figure any of it. They aren't in the same league—and what's more, I'd bet anything in the world that she dislikes him intensely."

"I got that hunch, too, Scott. Which ain't so good. If Gail had fallen for him, it'd be simple. This idea makes a guy try to figure another angle. Except when I finish thinking, I'm always back where I started. It's like that damned geometry you tried to hammer into my thick skull when we were in high school: Take a handsome louse and a rich girl to start with. The way the problem sets up is that you're trying to prove he's making a play for her because he'd like to grab himself a husband's slice of that dough. Only this comes out different. Somebody is awful dumb, and it ain't Tony Kinkaid."

Scott picked up an envelope from his desk and stared at it. It didn't mean a thing, but then nothing seemed to mean anything these days. He said, "You're being pretty swell about this, Bernie. And just for your information, we're on the same side of the fence. I'm in love with Gail Barrie. But if I turned up anything that connected her with Fletcher Mathews' death, I'd forget that."

"I believe you. That's why I'm trailing along. One of these days, an idea will pop out... Until then..."

He started to get up. He stretched out his big hand toward Scott just as the door opened.

Gail Barrie was in the doorway. She seemed surprised to find Bernie Williams there. She said, "I'll wait out here, Scott, until you're through."

Scott said, "Come on in. Bernie's an old school friend."

She shook her head. "I'd rather wait until I can see you alone, Scott. It's very important."

CHAPTER THIRTEEN

BERNIE MOVED TOWARD THE DOOR. He said, "I gotta be goin'—honest. Bye, Scott. Evenin', Miss Barrie."

She looked after his huge figure. Her eyes were thoughtful. Then she seated herself across the desk from Scott.

He said, "When I see you looking so pretty, I want to do something about it."

She smiled. "We'll leave that until later. This is a business call."

"Meaning you'd rather talk here than somewhere else?"

"That's it. I'm afraid I'm going to startle you."

He shrugged. "So what? When you're with me, I can stand anything."

Twice she started to speak. Twice she changed her mind. He leaned across the desk and said, "Look, honey—don't try to pick the right words. Let's have it—whatever it is—in your own way."

"Thanks… But it still isn't easy." She looked past his shoulder and through the window. "Did Mr. Mathews ever discuss Dad's estate with you?"

"No-o…except in the most general way."

"Did he ever tell you about something I am planning to do, and which he thought was ridiculous?"

"No."

She seemed to be disappointed. "Then I'll have to start at the beginning."

"Sounds like a good idea."

"I'll be twenty-one on the seventh of September, Scott. Until then you…of course, I know it's the firm, but that's really you…will be acting as executor and trustee. But the day I'm twenty-one, everything belongs to me outright, doesn't it?"

"Yes."

"I'm asking you what I asked Mr. Mathews a long time ago. On my birthday, or as soon after as possible, I want the entire estate converted into cash and turned over to me."

Henderson blinked. He said, "Let's have that again, honey."

She repeated it. He said, "Are you crazy? Do you know how much you're worth, Gail?"

"Mr. Mathews said it would be approximately a million dollars."

"And you want one million dollars in cash?"

"Yes…"

He said, "I never heard of anything so absurd. What in the world could anybody want with that much currency?"

"That's how I want it, Scott. I know you can't convert it all into cash immediately. But Mr. Mathews said that Dad's holdings were what he called liquid; that they could be converted into cash quite simply. He promised some time ago to start doing it."

Henderson backed against the window. He was staring at Gail as though unable to credit the evidence of his senses. He said, "That's the most cock-eyed thing…"

She didn't say anything, and he went on slowly: "I've been looking things over these last few days. Mr. Mathews evidently had started converting your securities into cash. I couldn't figure why. I still can't. What's it all about?"

"Don't make it too difficult for me, Scott. I've been over the legal side of it with your lawyers. Mr. Mathews had them here one day to talk to me. Legally, I can do whatever I choose to with my money. I can make a bonfire of it if I want."

"But one million dollars in cold cash..."

"I know. I couldn't use it to buy things with." She smiled timidly and shook her head. "I don't mean you're to hand it to me in a package, Scott. But I want it deposited in my name. I want the bank notified that within a very short time I'll make large withdrawals against it. I suppose that even a strong bank like the Cherokee National has to make special arrangements for that sort of thing."

Scott said, "The estate isn't settled yet, Gail. There's a lot of red tape..."

"Mr. Gardel explained that. But I'm sure, from what he and Mr. Mathews said, that most of my money can be made available within a month or two."

Scott lighted a cigarette and puffed furiously. Then he asked, "Didn't Mr. Mathews try to argue you out of this?"

"Yes."

"And when you wouldn't give in?"

"He said he'd do what I wanted, that he had no choice. You haven't any choice, either, Scott."

He let that ride. Thoughts—and not particularly pleasant ones—were chasing each other through his mind. He said, "What do you want with all that cash?"

"I can't tell you. But please believe me—I'm not as crazy as I sound. It all ties in..." She choked off the words, but he snapped at them.

"What all ties in?"

"Everything." She wasn't as sure of her ground now. "It's all part of things I can't explain to you. But that isn't the point. What I'm driving at is that as soon as I'm twenty-one, that money is mine. I can do anything I want with it. Nobody has a right to insist on knowing why."

"That's true... Except maybe I have more right than anyone else would have."

She said, "Let's don't play that way, Scott. I came to your office because I wanted to keep this one thing businesslike; impersonal. I wanted to tell you…and then to ask you not to mention it again."

He said sharply: "Is it Tony Kinkaid?"

"I can't answer that."

"You know if he ever got his hands on your money… Damn it! Gail—what's that man got on you? What's the answer to all this? Why can't you trust me? Don't you know I want to help? Can't you understand what's going on in my mind?"

"Yes… That's why I'm sorry I came to Cherokee." She made a little gesture of helplessness. "All my talking didn't do any good, did it?"

"I don't know what you mean by 'good.' As trustee and executor I have responsibilities. I have the right to do everything in my power to keep you from making a terrible mistake."

"It's a little late for that now."

"Why? That's all I'm asking: *Why?* If you'd give me the slightest hint—even the most implausible explanation…"

She rose from her chair. She came over to the window and stood close to him. But she didn't touch him. She said pleadingly, "Do what I'm asking, Scott…please. Don't keep asking questions that I'm not going to answer. There are a lot of things you don't understand. Keep away from them. Let me alone." She was talking swiftly, desperately. "Stay out of it. It's no good for either of us. If anything ever happened to you…"

He said, "Nothing's going to happen to me. And what might happen to other people has already happened. I don't know why you want to do this thing, but I can guess. So I'll ask you once again. Are you in love with Tony Kinkaid?"

Her eyes met his levelly. "You want to believe I am, don't you, Scott? You want to believe it because once you do, it will make other things plausible. All right…go ahead and believe it. Maybe thinking a few rotten things about me will help you."

He said, "That's the first time I've ever heard you go corny."

He took her by the arm, walked her back across the office and shoved her into a chair. He said, "Suppose—in order to protect you—I went to the Probate Court and stated that I thought you were temporarily deranged?"

"You couldn't prove it."

"I might. God knows there isn't a man, woman or child in Cherokee who would believe that what you are suggesting is sane. I might make it stick long enough to snap you out of this way of thinking…"

"You wouldn't do that."

"Like hell I wouldn't. I'd do anything I had to do."

"It wouldn't work, Scott. It would only stir things up, make them more difficult."

"And dangerous?"

"And dangerous."

Scott said, "I suppose you know that the police are still interested in you."

"I guessed as much."

"There's *that* angle…"

Gail nodded. "Yes…you could do that. You could tell them about this talk. That would make them sure of a lot of things that still wouldn't be true. It could cause a lot more misery—"

"To whom?"

"To me, for one. To you." She sighed. "I can't stop you, Scott, if that's the way you want to play it. You can't make me tell you anything, no matter what you do. I've been over all of this with Mr. Mathews. You couldn't think up any argument that he didn't offer. We could talk all night, and I'd still feel the same way. I suppose you would, too."

He sat tensely, waiting for her to go on.

"Because you don't understand everything, Scott…you won't concede a single point. I'm young…but I'm not that young. I know what I want to do…and I'm going to do it."

Suddenly she started to cry. She said, "Why does it have to be this way? We're making a mess of everything."

He was badly shaken. "Knowing only what I know," he said steadily, "I've got to play it my way."

"What does that mean?"

"I'm going to make it as difficult as I possibly can. I'm going to help you whether you want me to or not."

His words seemed to frighten her. She exclaimed, "Scott! You can't! You mustn't!"

"That's how it's going to be, Gail."

She turned wearily toward the door. She said, "I was afraid of this. I was more afraid of it than almost anything else that could have happened."

She looked at him for a long time. Then she said, "Let's leave all this in the office—if we can. But before we drop it, I've got this to say: I still want my inheritance converted into cash as soon as possible."

He didn't answer. He closed the windows of his office, shoved some papers into the top drawer of his desk. He was completely and utterly miserable.

He said, "I'll drive you home."

She shook her head. "I've got Barbara's car downstairs." There was a pleading note in her voice. "Will I see you tonight?"

"Perhaps. I don't know."

She turned abruptly. She walked through the outer office, past the rows of empty desks, and through the door into the hallway.

Scott Henderson stood rigidly, looking at the ground glass panel that bore the legend: "MATHEWS, HENDERSON & COMPANY—BANKERS."

"Damn! This is a thousand times worse than I thought it was."

CHAPTER FOURTEEN

FOR SCOTT HENDERSON the next forty-eight hours were maddening. He was up against something bigger than he was: dead end, brick wall, immovable body...no matter what he tagged it, it came up trouble.

He was grateful for the pressure of work made necessary by the firm's reorganization. He promoted a bright lad named Magruder to handle much of the routine stuff he had looked after while Fletcher Mathews had still been around. He delved into transactions that theretofore had been the exclusive concern of Mathews. He consulted with big business men and local industrialists on financing projects that were still in the formative stage. He held endless consultations with Gardel & Landsberg, the lawyers. He worried about everything, but most of all, he worried about Gail Barrie.

Worrying about her was easy. Easy as stepping into a readymade suit if you've got a stock-size figure. She was the perfect contradiction: the sweet, unsophisticated girl just out of high school; the intelligent, mature woman who knew all the answers; the obstinate person who wouldn't listen to reason; the trembling, frightened girl who was very much in love and didn't bother to conceal it when she was alone with him.

She was a girl who told many things, but not the things that were important. She held the key to the problem, and she wouldn't let him in on it. He loved her—and was furious with her.

She had demanded that he help her to do something fantastic. One million dollars in cash! Not all in one lump, perhaps, but as soon as possible. That could mean but one thing: She was planning to transfer her fortune to someone.

His threat of having her subjected to a sanity test had been sheer bluff. She was sane enough. Certainly, he couldn't prove she wasn't. No one could. There was a modern slang word for it. Screwball. But being a screwball wasn't being insane.

He held a lengthy conference with David Gardel, with whom Gail and Fletcher Mathews had discussed the matter. The net result was zero. It was her money. She could convert it into silver dollars if she wanted to and pitch them one by one off the roof of the Cherokee National Bank Building. Except that if she tried doing that, one might take it for granted that she was slightly deranged. This thing—whatever it meant—she was doing calmly and deliberately. She had returned to Cherokee with the idea of doing it. She had discussed it with Fletcher Mathews and with Mathews' lawyers.

The police hadn't gotten anywhere. Scott was just a trifle sorry for Chris Peterson. He didn't like the man, but he agreed with Bernie Williams that Chris was a good cop trying to do a good job. He wished him luck, too. His desire to see the murderer of Fletcher Mathews caught and punished was far greater than any other emotion. Greater even than his love for Gail.

Peterson was not clairvoyant. All he could do was to investigate patiently and indefatigably. When he had enough facts, when they fitted neatly into a pattern, he'd make an arrest. Scott believed that if he told Peterson everything he knew, Gail would be the victim.

He was willing to risk that. But only provided he could be convinced that she was the guilty person. So far he didn't have any such belief. She knew things about Doris's death that she wasn't telling; she'd had all the opportunity in the world to kill Fletcher Mathews. Mathews might even have had a talk with Gail when he returned suddenly from Washington. But that was guesswork. It couldn't be proved, except by Gail. Leander and Oleander had gone to the servants' house. Barbara had been out with her lieutenant. And the vital element of motive was still lacking.

Or was it? Suppose Mathews had refused pointblank to become party to Gail's absurd insistence upon converting her fortune into cash? Scott shook his head. That didn't come out right, either. Inspection of the Barrie estate file showed that Mathews already had started the ball rolling. More than one hundred thousand dollars worth of liquid securities already had been sold and the proceeds deposited to the credit of the trustee's account in the Cherokee National.

So Scott didn't have any motive there, either. He didn't have anything.

There seemed to be only one other possible answer: that Gail actually was in love with, and under the influence of, Tony Kinkaid. Kinkaid might have dished up a yarn of imaginary trouble, which had aroused her sympathy...provided she was in love with Kinkaid.

Henderson studied that possibility. It could be that Gail had been stalling him; that the affection she had bestowed so generously was phony.

Proceeding from that basis, the conclusion was easy enough. Perhaps Kinkaid had killed Doris Colby. There seemed to be no motive, but for a moment he forced himself to accept it as truth. Gail might have known what Kinkaid had in mind. Her trip to Doris's house could have been to forestall the killing. Arriving too late to prevent the murder, but not too late to identify Kinkaid, her infatuation might have impelled her to protect him.

Kinkaid had driven Fletcher Mathews from the Country Club to his home just a few minutes before Mathews' death. That didn't look so good, either. Gail might have witnessed the shooting, or have drawn inescapable conclusions. Having protected Kinkaid once, she could have protected him a second time.

Logical. Sound reasoning. A lovely case against Tony Kinkaid, with Gail cast in the role of accessory. Everything fitted. It fitted so perfectly that Chris Peterson might swing into action if he knew it. But there were two flaws. Not logical flaws, but flaws just the same.

Scott could not make himself believe that Gail would play any active part in any murder, either before or after its commission.

And his instinct protested that she was not in love with Kinkaid.

If either of those beliefs were true, the theory washed out.

And he was right back where he started.

He didn't go to the house Tuesday or Wednesday nights. He telephoned and asked Oleander to tell the girls that he was too busy. That didn't sound like such a hot excuse, even to him. But Barbara might believe it, and Gail would understand.

All day Thursday he was unusually busy. A million little details crowded in on him, and shoved important things out of the way. The office force was working hard. At six-fifteen he shooed them out, despite their willingness to remain.

He walked into his private office. He didn't close the door between that and the main office. He dropped wearily into the club chair in which important clients usually sat, lay back and closed his eyes. Business facts, financial figures, personal problems, were all mixed up. They paraded through his mind without order or sequence.

The sharp ring of the telephone snapped him out of it. The switchboard operator had plugged in the line to his desk before leaving. He picked up the phone and said, "Mathews, Henderson & Company."

The voice of Barbara Mathews came to him, "Scott?"

"Hi, Barbara."

"Are you busy?"

"No…"

"Can you come out here, right away?"

Something caught at him, frightened him. He said, "Anything wrong?"

"I don't know. But I want to talk to you."

"I'm on my way."

He locked the entrance door to the office, fidgeted impatiently while waiting for an elevator, moved swiftly through the lobby to the parking space a half block away, fumed at the lackadaisical efforts of the attendant to get two other cars out of the way so that he could get free.

He drove fast. Premonition rode with him. He tried to be sensible about it. Why conjecture, when he'd know in a few minutes? That's why he hadn't asked any more questions on the phone. Step on it, Scott! Fast, but not too fast! Attaboy! Scott Henderson, always under control. Nuts! He was thinking that way. It was better than trying to pin something down.

Barbara was waiting for him on the veranda. Her eyes were worried. She smiled when she greeted him, but there wasn't much mirth in it. She didn't waste time with social trivia. No "Will you have a drink?" No "Where have you been keeping yourself?" Just sit down and start talking. Don't waste time. It's important.

She said, "I might as well come straight out with it, Scott. Gail has gone."

He locked the fingers of his hands together. That made him sit steady, made him look calm. Inside, he was doing nip-ups.

"Gone where?"

"I don't know."

He made an effort to smile. It was feeble, but it was something. Trying to help Barbara. She was up in the air like a kite.

"Tell me more," he suggested.

"She left here about an hour ago. I wasn't at home. Oleander saw her go out with a suitcase. She drove away in a car."

"Whose car?"

"Oleander doesn't know. She didn't pay any attention. She says it may have been a private car, or it may have been one of those old jalopies they're using for taxis."

"Did Gail say anything?"

"No. Oleander says she was dressed as though for a trip. Suit. Hat. Nobody wears hats around here in summer unless they're going away."

"Have you looked upstairs?"

"For a letter of some sort? I've looked, Scott. In her room, my room, everywhere. Not a word. I thought maybe I'd get a phone call from her. That's why I didn't call you immediately."

He said, "What do you think?"

"I don't."

"How has she been acting for the last couple of days?"

Barbara answered carefully. "Peculiarly. Night before last, when she came back from your office, she turned in early. Said she had a headache. Steve was here with me. After he left, I went upstairs. I heard Gail crying. I went in and inquired. She said she hadn't been crying, but that wasn't the truth. All day yesterday, all day today, she's walked around like someone in a daze. I tried to find out why, but she wouldn't tell me a thing. Did you and she quarrel?"

He said slowly, "Not exactly. You couldn't call it a quarrel." He talked swiftly, telling Barbara everything that had happened in his office two days previously. He tried to give it to her straight, without embellishment. When he finished, she was staring at him.

"It gets crazier and crazier," she said. "I'm worried."

"I'll double that in spades."

"She could be walking out, figuring that you're fed up with her. Or maybe…"

They didn't hear the telephone. Leander shoved through the screen door, beamed at Scott, and said, "Gentlemun on the phone asked was you heah, Mistuh Scott. I tol' him I'd find out. He says was you heah, he craved to talk with you."

Barbara followed him into the hall. Scott said, "Hello," and Bernie Williams' voice came to him through the receiver. Bernie said, "Stick around a few minutes, will you, kid? I want to come out and talk something over."

The waiting was interminable. Gail walking off. Bernie asking no questions…simply announcing that he was on the way. Not so good. No sense speculating about it, except that the two things were bound to be connected.

Bernie's car made a lot of noise. It coughed and spluttered and creaked. It stopped at the curb with a gasp of relief. Bernie joined them on the veranda, said "Howdy" to Barbara and looked around to make sure they were alone.

He said, "There's hell to pay."

Scott said, "Let's have it."

"It's liable to be a wallop."

"I can take it."

"Okay, kid." Bernie seemed to have difficulty getting started. Then he let fly.

"Gail Barrie and Tony Kinkaid are at the Cherokee Hotel," he said. "They got married about an hour ago."

CHAPTER FIFTEEN

FOR AN AWKWARD minute they stood where they were, not looking at each other, not doing anything. Scott and Barbara heard the words, but the full significance did not immediately sink in.

Bernie pulled up a chair and dropped into it. He said, "Why shouldn't we sit down?" There didn't seem to be any reason why they shouldn't, so they sat down.

Scott was trying to take it in stride. He was trying to conceal the things that were seething inside: the incredulity, the sudden sharp pain, the fear. He was trying to convince himself that even if what Bernie said was true, it wasn't as bad as it sounded. He didn't speak, because at the moment he couldn't trust himself. It was Barbara who broke the silence. She said, "You're sure, Bernie?"

"Yeah. Couldn't be surer. Got the tip from Marty West, assistant manager at the Cherokee." He turned to Scott. "You remember Marty, don't you? Played a darn good tackle on Eastern." Scott nodded, and Bernie continued. "He gave it to me off the record. Said they checked in with one suitcase each. Registered as Mr. and Mrs. Anthony Kinkaid. He gave 'em a three-room suite on the tenth floor. Corner. I beat it down to the license bureau. It was there, all right."

Barbara said, "I wonder why...?"

"He's a good-looking so-and-so," stated Bernie. "Knocks 'em over right and left. Why shouldn't Miss Barrie fall, too?" He looked uncomfortably at Scott. "I know how you feel about her, kid. But I gotta call 'em as I see 'em. No matter how things were between you, it's just a lot of damns over the water now. This Kinkaid is a smart cookie."

Barbara said, "That's not the whole story, Bernie. I can understand Kinkaid's end of it, of course. But why Gail?"

"Women are all a little nutsy. Even the best of 'em."

He pulled out a pack of cigarettes and shoved them in Scott's direction. He said, "Here I am shooting off my mouth with a lot of words that don't mean anything. I ain't trying to butt in, Scott. You know that. It struck me that Chris Peterson was gonna find out about this thing pretty quick. Chris is on the ball all the time. He's likely to show up here any minute, and start shoving you around. It seemed like a good idea to get here first." He looked appealingly at Barbara.

She answered his unspoken plea. She said, "It's a mean set-up, Scott. But Bernie is right. This way you've got a chance to adjust yourself. If you heard it first from Peterson, you'd probably blow your top…"

He reached out and pressed her hand. He said, "Of course you're right, Barbara—you and Bernie both." He gave a short, bitter laugh. "Scott Henderson! The great lover. The irresistible. The colossal idiot!"

"Layoff that stuff," growled Bernie. "It ain't getting you anywhere."

Barbara said to Bernie, "They registered. You checked the license. Are you sure there was a ceremony?"

He grinned. "You're a keen babe. Been that way ever since you were in high school. Yeah, I checked that angle. Married by Municipal Judge Aleck Mooney." He looked away from Henderson's misery and said gently, "You rather I scrammed, Scott? Come back after dinner, maybe?"

"No." Scott had a grip on himself now. He said, "If that's how it is, that's how it is. For the record, I'll say I'm still in love with her. I'd still do anything to keep her from getting in deeper than she is already."

"Nice goin'. How much does Barbara know?"

"Everything."

"Good." The change in Bernie's manner was almost indiscernible, but it was there. He became suddenly the professional policeman: kindly, considerate, but competent. He said, "I don't like any part of it. It ties Kinkaid and Miss Barrie up too tight, and they were tight enough before. Kinkaid showing up at the Treadway house right after Mrs. Colby was killed. Him bringing Mr. Mathews home the night…" He saw Barbara's face and tried to choose his words more carefully. "Anyway, Miss Barrie was home that night. Kinkaid was here. Maybe other things have been happening. Things I don't know about."

Scott spoke steadily. He said, "There have been."

"Scott!" Barbara's voice was sharp with warning. She knew what he was about to tell, and she was afraid. "You'd better think it over first."

"That's all I've been doing. Bernie's on our side, and that's why it's important for him to understand what our side is." He was calm enough; outwardly at least. "Gail is mixed up in something that none of us can understand. If she had any part in your father's death, Barbara…that's her lookout. I don't mean to sound heartless or tough. I told her what I'm telling you now. What I mean is, I'd do anything for Gail. A lot more than you realize. But I wouldn't protect any person who was mixed up in Mr. Mathews' death."

Bernie Williams wasn't talking. He slouched back in his porch chair, waiting. Listening.

Scott told him briefly and graphically about Gail Barrie's visit to the office, and of her demand that her entire fortune be converted into cash and deposited in the bank so that it would be subject to withdrawal by check. Bernie's eyes closed as he listened. His big, broad face was expressionless.

At the end of the recital he looked up and said, "Thanks, Scott. That might help. It's like I told you at the beginning of all this trouble: I'm a friend and I'm a cop. But I don't play 'em against each other."

"I'm not asking you to."

"I know, kid; I know." He did some more thinking. "Could be we have part of the answer. Suppose Miss Barrie got messed up with Kinkaid before she ever fell for you, Scott. Suppose she was fixing to buy her way out. Then suppose she got sore at you and decided to hell with it. How do you like that theory?"

Scott shook his head. "I wouldn't buy it," he said.

"Why not?"

"Plenty of reasons. First, I can't imagine her getting mixed up that deeply with Kinkaid or any other man. Second, Kinkaid wouldn't make his pitch for a million dollars on the strength of that. He'd try for a reasonable amount. Third, an intelligent, well-bred girl doesn't rush into marriage with a man like that just because she's mad at somebody else." He turned to Barbara. "Which one of us is right?"

She said, "You are, Scott. Bernie's ideas would sound better if we didn't know that Gail is a different sort of person from the one he has in mind."

"Is she?" Bernie's voice was flat.

"Of course..."

"Try again, Barbara. You never even saw her until about two and a half months ago. She's sweet, she's pretty, you like her. But you don't know a thing about her. You don't know what kind of life she led in Cuba..."

"I do," said Scott. "Paul Innes—manager at the Country Club—lived down there with the Barries for a year. I started thinking the way you're thinking, Bernie, right after Doris was killed. I had a talk with Paul. I asked him all about Gail's life in Cuba. Everything he said makes her out a nice, normal girl."

Bernie shrugged. "So what's one year out of twenty? Maybe Innes was right about her for that year. She must have been a kid then, anyway. Lots of things could have happened since."

Scott nodded. Plenty of logic there. Too much logic, perhaps.

Bernie spoke again. "Forget the sweet, wholesome angles, you two. There's something else here, and you know it. Two people have been killed. So far we haven't got a lick of evidence that would stand up in any court. The two of them getting married ain't any crime, either. If she gives all her dough to her husband when she reaches twenty-one, nobody can do a thing about it. But adding everything up, you can't make me believe that everything is clear and pretty. And you don't believe it, either."

"You're right," said Scott. "But all the common sense in the world doesn't change the instinctive feeling I have."

"Hell, kid—you're in love with her. So your instinct doesn't mean a thing."

"Mine does." Barbara was leaning forward. "You can guess how I felt about my father, Bernie. Whoever killed him…no matter who… But that doesn't make it Gail. I think she knows something, yes. But I'm sure there's an answer to this whole mess that would put her in the clear. I realize she's being foolish…"

"Lady! you said it."

Bernie announced that he had to be going. He refused Barbara's invitation to have dinner with them. He promised to keep in touch with them. He waved goodbye from the curb and spluttered off in the wreckage that he called his town car.

Dinner was a rather ghastly affair. Scott and Barbara toyed with their food, and made a valiant effort to keep up a casual conversation. Leander, hovering over them, was perturbed. He made his report to Oleander on one of his many trips to the kitchen:

"Them chillun sho' worry me," he confided. "Messin' aroun' but not absorbin' nothin'. Smilin' at each other like'n you smile at the dentist when he says to open your mouth so's he can pull your tooth. An' all the time they don't say one word 'bouten Miss Gail. Now I's askin' you, Oleander—where at is Miss Gail?"

Oleander shook her head. "You always talk wrong," she said sternly. "Askin' things I don't know. Fum now on, it seems like the best thing would be fo' you to gimme a lot of answers, an' leave me find the questions to fit 'em."

Scott and Barbara went for a walk after dinner. They walked along beautiful, curving roads lined with handsome homes and fragrant with summer blooms. They walked silently, and after a while they were holding hands. It was a gesture of friendship and of mutual understanding. It was Barbara's way of telling Scott that she sympathized and Scott's way of saying "Thanks."

Shortly after nine, pink-cheeked Lieutenant Homer appeared. Barbara's face lighted; no question that she was fond of the kid. Scott sat with them for a while, then said goodnight and went home.

He hated being alone. It was all right to tell yourself that you could control your thoughts…but you couldn't. You couldn't help thinking of the Cherokee Hotel and of Gail and Tony, now Mr. and Mrs. Anthony Kinkaid.

He undressed and flung himself on the bed. He lay there rigidly, staring up at the ceiling, begging for sleep and knowing that it wouldn't come. He started being sorry for himself and snapped out of that by getting up, lighting a cigarette and standing at the window. Then he went back to bed and slept fitfully.

He was awakened by the clamor of his telephone. It sounded too shrill, too loud, against the background of early morning silence.

As he reached for the telephone, he glanced at the mantel clock. Five minutes before six. He was wide awake when he said "Hello," Then he was sitting up on the edge of the bed, every muscle tensed.

Gail!

She said, "You heard about...about..."

Her voice was unsteady. Frightened. He said, "Yes, Gail. Yes, I heard."

"Scott! I need you. Can you come down here right away?"

"Of course. But what...?"

"I can't tell you now. I'm in 1001. It would be better if no one saw you come up."

He said, "Right away," and she said, "Thanks, Scott. For God's sake—hurry!"

He jumped into his clothes. He whipped his car out of the garage and tooled it downtown at top speed. The city was silent and peaceful in the dull light of early morning.

The lobby of the Cherokee Hotel was a dozen steps higher than the street. He went down a few steps to the lower level where the barbershop and lunchroom were located. He took an elevator there. He got off at eight. He walked up two flights to the tenth floor.

At the touch of his fingers on the panel of 1001, the door opened. Gail must have been waiting for him. He walked inside. She closed the door and stood with her back against it.

She looked lovely and she looked terrible. She was wearing a housecoat and slippers. She seemed on the verge of a crack-up. He took a tight grip on himself.

This was a sitting room: the average, unimaginative sitting room of the average first-class hotel. There was a door on either side.

Each led to a bedroom. Even under stress of what was happening, Scott wondered about that. It didn't look very much like a honeymoon.

He said, "What's wrong, Gail?"

She pressed her hand against her lips. He'd seen her do that once before; once when things were pretty bad. She gestured toward the bedroom on the left.

"In there, Scott... Tony... He's been murdered."

CHAPTER SIXTEEN

SCOTT HENDERSON looked around. What he saw was just another hotel sitting room: sofa and two club chairs covered with cretonne, which matched the summer drapes; two straight chairs, two end tables shoved against the couch, a table hard against the opposite wall beneath a mirror with a fancy frame. The carpet had been worn by thousands of guests; there were spots here and there where things had spilled. It wasn't dingy. It had probably been rather fine, at first, but now the room showed signs of wear and of weariness.

There was a haze outside through which the morning sun had not yet succeeded in breaking. There were two doors, both open. One gave access to a room at the right and the other opened into a room at the left.

Scott and Gail stood looking at one another. Her gray eyes were wide, and there were dark shadows in them. She wasn't crying, but he could tell that she wanted to cry. Her face was haggard. She looked lonely and forlorn, and a great wave of pity and tenderness welled up in him. For this moment he forgot his own misery; he forgot the emptiness she had created in his life by marrying another man. He forgot everything except that she desperately needed him.

After a while she stopped trembling. He said, "Good going. You've got a grip on yourself. Keep it."

He took her hand and led her to a chair. It was a big, overstuffed creation, and there was a little round hole burned in the covering of the right arm where some forgotten hotel guest had placed a cigarette and forgotten about it. He tried to smile, "Relax," he ordered. "It won't be easy, but you've got to do it."

Her gray eyes were clearer now. She said, "I won't crack up on you, Scott."

"Fine. That's fine. Sit steady while I look around."

That wasn't what he wanted to do, really. He wanted to ask a thousand questions which were hammering in his brain. But she needed time, time to get a tighter rein on herself, time to realize that she was going to be asked a lot of questions and that she had to have the right answers. Not for the questions he would ask. There were going to be a lot of police around pretty soon. That had to be. And maybe a couple of smart boys from the D. A.'s office or the D. A. himself.

Scott went through the door at the right. Twin beds. Only one had been used. Gail's room. He knew that from the wispy garments on the chair, by the intimate things on the French dresser, by the shoes that sat on the floor in front of an easy chair. Everything was as one might expect to find it, except that it didn't spell honeymoon.

He walked into the living room and across it. He approached the other bedroom door, which was open. He saw Gail's hand go to her lips, hold there for an instant, and then drop. It was as though she knew what he was going to see and was sorry for him.

He saw it, all right. A man's bedroom. Coat on the back of a chair. Trousers folded neatly on the bench in front of the dresser. Underwear on another chair. Shoes and sox on the floor near the bed. A summerweight dressing gown across the footboard. An open suitcase on the floor near the radiator.

Again: twin beds. Only one of them had been slept in. Only one of them had been died in.

The body of Tony Kinkaid was on the bed. He was wearing silk pajamas. Broad stripes of gray and navy blue. Plus an ugly splotch of crimson near the heart. Blood on the bed, too. Not very much blood, but enough for Scott to understand.

Everything was in order. Just as neat as an average man would have his room if he didn't expect to be murdered. No sign of a struggle. The bedclothes were no more disarranged than they would have been any night by any man. No furniture overturned.

Nothing smashed. "Now I lay me down to sleep…" That was it. And what was next? "If I should die before I wake…"

He stood at the foot of Tony's bed. Last night he had been angry and hurt. This morning he was shocked and afraid. Afraid for Gail. Afraid of what lay there on the bed, and of the part she had played.

He experienced a depressing moment of futility. He had so wanted to help before it was too late, and she hadn't let him. She had entered into this incredible marriage for reasons that she wouldn't tell him, and now tragedy had again intruded. This time more terribly, more intimately, than before.

He shrank from the ordeal that lay ahead. Questions. Endless questions. Questions that would probe and probe and probe. Questions that Gail must answer. He wondered whether she fully understood what she was in for. He returned to the sitting room.

He pulled a straight chair across and sat in front of her. He took one of her cold hands in his. He said gently, "Listen, Gail—the police will have to be notified. They're going to do a lot of questioning. Do you mind if I ask you a few things first?"

Her voice was tight. She said, "You can ask me anything, Scott."

"I may sound brutal. Maybe I'll hurt you. I don't mean to."

"You couldn't hurt me."

"Did you…" He choked over the words.

She looked at him steadily and shook her head. She said, "No, Scott—I didn't kill him."

"When did it happen?"

"I don't know."

"Explain that, honey."

"I woke up just a little while before I called you. It was like coming out of a nightmare. You know…when you first wake up and don't know whether you've dreamed something or whether it has happened. I was frightened."

"Of what?"

"I don't know. Maybe something happened while I was asleep…what I mean is, maybe I heard something and didn't know I heard it. I lay there trembling. I didn't know why I was trembling. I tried to make myself believe it was all nonsense. But I knew it wasn't. I got up and went into the living room. Everything was just as you see it. Tony's door was still shut. I hesitated to go in. Then I had to. That same fear kept driving me to do something I didn't want to do. I opened the door. I saw…I saw what you just saw…"

She clasped her hands tightly. Her voice had taken on an edge of panic, but she fought against it.

"I came back in here," she went on. "I felt sick and frightened and alone. I didn't know what to do. I called you. It was a rotten, selfish thing to do. I was sorry afterward, and I called again to tell you not to come. I didn't get any answer, and so I knew you had left." She unclasped her hands and spread them, palms up, in her lap. "That's all."

He turned it over in his mind. He wished Chris Peterson could have heard her story…just that way. Before she'd had time to rehearse. It might have convinced him of something. No matter how crazy it was, it had the ring of truth. Or maybe he just wanted desperately to believe her. Maybe she'd already had all the time she required. Maybe she had planned just that effect.

"I'm no expert on these things," said Scott, "but Tony seems to have been shot."

She nodded, and he went on:

"Did you find a gun?"

"No. I didn't find anything."

His voice tightened. "This is important, Gail. Have you got a gun? Here? With you?"

"No."

"They'll look for one. If there's one here, they'll find it. If the person who killed him threw the gun out of the window, they'll know it pretty quick. This is a tough spot. No matter what you tell anybody else, you've got to tell me the truth."

"I'm telling the truth."

"All of it?"

"Yes."

Henderson continued gently. "The cops are going to ask about the three rooms, Gail. It doesn't seem to fit in with yesterday's marriage."

She flushed. "I told Tony it had to be that way."

"You mean…?"

She didn't evade. "You're asking me whether Tony and I were together last night. As husband and wife. The answer is that we were not."

Something did a somersault inside him. It was just another fantastic element in a fantastic pattern, but it could be the truth. That was the trouble with everything she was telling him or had told him in the past: It could all be truth. It could all be a lie.

He said, "You mean you and Tony agreed when you married that you were not going to be his wife?"

"Yes."

"Then why did you marry him?"

Instinctively her right hand started for her lips in the little gesture he had come to recognize as marking a moment of uncertainty and stress. But it never got there. She said, "You won't understand this, Scott—and I can't explain. But I had to marry him."

He felt angry and embarrassed. "You mean that you and Tony…"

"No." She was hitting straight. "I've never had an affair with Tony, nor with any other man."

"But there must have been something between you, something you've never told me."

She nodded and said, "Yes."

"What was it?"

"I can't tell you."

He said, "You've got to tell me. Get that, Gail—you've *got* to! Me or the police. Maybe you think you can stall them, but you can't. They'll drag it out of you. They're smart. They're a lot smarter than you think. Because Peterson's grammar isn't polished, it's easy to think he doesn't know what the score is. But he does, honey. So you've got to tell me what the set-up is. Then we can decide what's best to do."

She said earnestly, "Look, Scott…I know what I'm doing. I know why I'm doing it. I know I'm in danger. None of that matters. I still can't tell you why I married Tony."

"But he's dead, Gail. He's been murdered. You were afraid of him...maybe that's why you married him. But you can't be afraid of a dead man."

She started to say something, then changed her mind. He wanted to shake the stubbornness out of her. He tried a different angle:

"Did our little scene of the other day—at my office—have anything to do with your marriage?"

"No."

"I thought you might have been sore..."

She shook her head. "Can't you understand, Scott, that I couldn't be angry at anything you might do? Can't you understand that, after all this tragedy, I wasn't concerned about trivial things like having my feelings hurt? No, dear. Believe me, it wasn't anything like that."

He said thoughtfully, "I don't get it, Gail. You've only known Kinkaid for a couple of months..."

She reached out and touched his arm. "That's not so, Scott. I met him in Cuba two years ago."

"Oh!" He let that sink in. "Then meeting him in Cherokee...?"

"That was accidental. I didn't even remember him until he reminded me. I'd been visiting in Havana with Dad and Margaret Allen for a couple of weeks. I met Tony at the Jockey Club. We ran into him again at the Casino Nacional a couple of nights later. We danced a couple of times. He didn't register very strongly. I forgot him until we met shortly after I came back here to Cherokee."

"And yet there was enough between you... Hell! Can't you see how screwy it sounds? How do you think the police will react to a story like that?"

"I don't know. But that is what I'm going to tell them."

He got up and walked to the window. Cherokee was waking up, getting to work. More traffic on the street, the sun was breaking through the haze. Business as usual. Normal life in a normal American city. Except that it wasn't normal in suite 1001. There was a dead man in 1001, and a bride who hadn't been a bride.

He came back and stood in front of her chair. He said, "I'd like to help you, Gail. But you won't let me. What you tell the police is up to you."

He was studying her, weighing everything he knew against all the things he didn't know. He said sharply, "You can't play it this way. You haven't the faintest idea what you're letting yourself in for."

She said, "It's the way I've got to do it."

He felt a deep, fierce anger—anger against what he considered her stupidity, her blindness. It had an overtone of bitterness because she had refused to trust him when there was some possibility that he might have been able to help. Suddenly his calm deserted him. He doubled his right fist and smashed it into the palm of his left hand.

"Damn it!" he exploded, "you've got to understand that you're wrong. Nothing could justify what has happened. Look at it straight, Gail. Doris is dead. You were there. There was that bruise on your arm. You were alone in the house the night Mr. Mathews got back from Washington. Kinkaid drove him home. Even before that you'd been running around with Kinkaid. You came to me with that fantastic request to convert your inheritance into cash. Why, Gail—why? And then this marriage. This sort of a honeymoon. Kinkaid killed. No witnesses. Nobody here but you. Oh yes…I know there are such things as skeleton keys. Somebody could have come in here and killed him and gotten away easily enough. But why? You've got to give me some sort of a reason—any sort of a reason."

She put out her hand. It was a tiny gesture; a pleading gesture. She said unsteadily, "Please don't go on, Scott. It won't do any good. And now I've dragged you into it. I wish I hadn't."

"But I *am* in it. I'm trying to help. And you can take my word for it that by refusing to trust me you're making your greatest mistake."

"I'm not!" The sharpness, the suddenness, of her protest startled him. "I know I'm not making a mistake, Scott. I warned you to keep out of this. Maybe I even married Tony to force you out…" She bit her lip and looked away, as though she had said too much.

He said, "That still doesn't make sense. But I won't try pushing you around." He reached for a cigarette and lighted it. "Sooner or later we'll have to call the police. Shall I do it now?"

"No!" She spoke vehemently. "You get out. I'll call them. I don't want them to find you here."

"That's no good," he said. "Even if I wanted to leave, I wouldn't dare. Somebody might have seen me. The elevator boy might remember. But even if I knew that part of it was all right, I'd stick around anyway."

He went to the telephone and called Bernie Williams' home. Bernie answered promptly, his voice bright and cheerful.

Scott spoke softly. He said, "Play this cute, Bernie. It's important. Don't say anything at your end. I'm in suite 1001 at the Cherokee Hotel…" He heard Bernie splutter at the other end of the phone. "I want you to come here right away. I'd suggest that you bring Peterson with you."

He hung up. He moved away from the telephone and sat on the arm of Gail's chair. He said, "This is going to take a lot of courage, honey."

She didn't say anything. She reached up and put her hand over his and let it stay there.

They looked at the brilliant sunshine. But their thoughts were in the next room where Tony Kinkaid lay dead.

CHAPTER SEVENTEEN

BERNIE WILLIAMS followed Chris Peterson into the room. He closed the door and stood with his back against it. His face was slightly less than expressionless. In it Scott saw worry and apprehension. But he didn't say anything. He left that to Peterson.

The wiry little sergeant advanced a few steps into the room, his keen eyes observing everything. If he felt any surprise, he didn't show it. "All right," he snapped, "what's it about?"

Scott gave him the highlights in a few words. Chris stood where he was, still saying nothing. Scott fancied that there was a gleam of triumph in Chris's eyes, and this was confirmed by the fact that Bernie Williams looked momentarily more and more miserable.

Peterson went into Kinkaid's bedroom. He stayed there quite a while. Then he went into Gail's room. They heard him telephoning headquarters, making a brief preliminary report and asking that the technical staff be hurried to the hotel, along with two additional plainclothesmen and some uniformed cops.

When he rejoined the others, it was not to talk immediately. He searched the room with devastating thoroughness. That done, he said, "You two better relax. This is gonna take a long time."

Peterson stood in front of Scott and Gail. He wasn't excited. He looked cold as ice and incalculably shrewd. He addressed himself to Henderson. He said, "You keep turning up in the wrong places, don't you?"

Scott didn't answer.

Chris's next question was an accusation. He said, "Where's the gun?"

"I haven't seen any gun."

"Did Mrs. Kinkaid get rid of it before you got here?"

Scott flushed. But he controlled himself. No sense playing into Peterson's hands.

Chris turned his hard eyes on Gail. "Let's have your story," he ordered. "And it better be good."

She told it, just as she had told Scott. And, listening for the second time, he knew that the story wasn't good. It wasn't good at all.

Chris said, "Cozy little honeymoon, huh? How come?"

She waited for him to make the question clearer.

"You marry this collar ad," he went on coldly. "Quick—like that. You take a three-room suite. It's all fixed up so it looks like you slept in yonder and he slept where he is now. Is that the way it was?"

"Yes..." Her voice was so low that Scott could scarcely hear it. "Why?"

"That's the way we both wanted it."

"I'm still asking why?"

She looked at him, but didn't elaborate on what she had said.

"I'm supposed to believe that on your wedding night you slept apart, is that it?"

"Yes."

"Both bedroom doors closed?"

"Yes."

"He didn't even make a pass at you?"

Gail flushed. Scott half rose from his chair, but Chris waved him down.

"You keep your lip buttoned, Henderson. You're in this up to your belt. What went on here, I don't know, but whatever it was, you loused it up good. She finds the body—she says. She thinks things over and then phones you. You come down and have a nice long talk with her. Maybe there was a gun, and maybe you took it out somewhere and got rid of it. You don't call the police until you get damned good and ready. I'm just drawing a picture so you'll know you're in a hell of a mess."

Gail said, "It was my fault…"

"I don't care whose fault it was. I'm figuring what I'm up against. The pair of you had time to cook up a neat story. You been playing it smart. What you've got is so screwy nobody would figure you'd make it up." He snapped back to Gail. "Was them two bedroom doors locked?"

"Mine wasn't. Obviously his wasn't either."

"You figured he was a gent, huh? Wouldn't change his mind during the night and walk in on his blushing bride?" Chris waited for the answer that was not forthcoming. "So how do I know you didn't change your mind and go in to see him? Or maybe he went in your room and you didn't like it, so you chased him back to his room with the gun and then killed him. How do I know it wasn't that way?"

Gail said steadily, "It wasn't—that's all."

"Why did you marry him if you didn't want to play house?"

No answer.

"What'd he have on you?"

Her body stiffened, then relaxed with a visible effort. She said, "Nothing."

"I must look like an awful dope," stated Peterson bitterly. "Just a poor dumb cop who's gotta believe everything he hears. That's why they made me a sergeant—so I wouldn't cause trouble to nobody who always happens to be around when people get bumped off," He made a gesture of disgust. "Just so you'll understand, Mrs. Kinkaid…" He emphasized the name unpleasantly, and Gail winced. "Just so you'll understand what's going on, lemme say that I don't believe none of this. Not a word."

There was a knock on the door. Bernie opened it and admitted a swarm of men from headquarters. Some were in uniform, some not. Two of the men were detailed to search for the gun, to interview the elevator boys who had been on duty from the time Gail and Tony had registered until this moment, to talk to the clerks who had been behind the desk, to the manager and assistant manager. The assistant coroner was directed to get busy on his chief's job, and to arrange for a post mortem. The fingerprint men were turned loose. So were the photographer and the engineer. Two uniformed men were left on duty in the hall. Nobody was to be admitted: friends, reporters…nobody.

Peterson picked up with Gail where he had left off.

"Too many things against you, Mrs. Kinkaid. A lot too many. Having a raft of dough ain't gonna help you none, either. Not in this town. I'm advising you to come clean. I'll forget all the lies you told me if you'll dish out just one thing I can believe."

She said, "I've told the truth."

"Sure. Sure, it's the truth, until we prove otherwise. Especially that idea about the two doors being closed. Nifty way of explainin' why you didn't hear no shot. Everything fits in just dandy." His eyes narrowed. "If you was so set on bein' a virgin bride, why did you go in his room early this morning?"

She repeated that part of the story: the waking up as though from a bad dream; the feeling that part of it was real—that something had happened. Peterson bestowed upon her a dry, mirthless smile. "You gotta do better, Mrs. Kinkaid. You gotta do a heap better than that."

"That's how it happened."

"Okay. I'll make like I believe you. Why did you telephone Henderson instead of the police?"

"He's a friend…"

"So I've heard. I've heard you and him was even closer than that. How about it?"

"He's also the trustee of my estate."

"That still ain't enough. Let's quit kidding. I got it straight that you and Henderson were falling for each other. Did he know in advance you was gonna marry Kinkaid?"

"No."

"You just thought it'd be a cute little surprise, huh?"

Scott said quietly, "Do you have to act so tough, Peterson?"

"Me? Sure. Police regulations. Detective in charge of a murder investigation has gotta be tough. So you just keep your shirt on, sonny. If you don't like the way I'm handlin' things, go find yourself another murder."

Chris gave a sharp, brittle laugh. "You really love stickin' your neck out, don't you, Henderson? Big shot! Got friends in high places, huh? Brother, you're gonna need 'em. Lemme see..."

He started checking things on his fingers:

"You drove the former Miss Barrie to the spot where Doris Colby was killed. Of course you didn't have nothing to do with it. You don't know a thing.

"Mathews gets back to Cherokee unexpectedly and chases all around town looking for you. But you ain't there. You're somewhere else. Maybe waiting for him to get home. Him cashing in doesn't hurt you none, you know. I read his will. Pretty soft for Scotty Henderson.

"Your girl marries a good-looking grifter. Yeh, I know all about him. High class and beautiful, but still a grifter. You wouldn't be liking that, would you, big shot? You'd maybe stay up and brood about it—maybe decide to do something about it. You'd maybe come to the hotel and plug the guy. Then you and her could cook up this silly story. Maybe it didn't happen that way, but it could be."

"You're trying to sell yourself a bill of goods, aren't you, Peterson?"

"You ain't just kiddin'. I got so much to go on, I don't know where to begin. But I know where to end, all right. And that's in the death house."

"Why not make an arrest?" inquired Scott wearily.

Peterson turned toward Bernie. "Now he's teaching me my business," he said unhappily. "It ain't enough he should obstruct justice...he's gotta instruct me how to be a cop. Look, you..." He was back to Scott again. "You don't need to worry that somebody ain't gonna sweat. You or her. Maybe both."

"Except that you haven't got anything to go on. No evidence that isn't circumstantial. You're not scaring me, Peterson. Not a bit. As a matter of fact, I'd also like to find out who did these killings."

"Oh, yeah? Suppose it come up Mrs. Kinkaid?"

"I'd still like to know," Scott's voice was level. "I'd like to help. You're making that rather difficult."

"Sweet of you. On behalf of the Department, I thank you." Peterson took off his hat and tossed it across the room. It hit the couch and bounced off. He said, "Lemme explain something. A murder is committed; it's my job to find out who done it. I ain't interested in building up a case against anybody innocent. If your nose is clean, it's clean. That puts you on my side. If it ain't, you're playing on the other team. Right now I figure you in. Mrs. Kinkaid is definitely in. She knows things she ain't telling. Maybe she told you, Henderson. I wouldn't be knowing that. But I will know before I'm finished."

"Are you arresting either of us?"

"Nope. You called it a minute ago. I couldn't make it stick. Throwing a couple people in the cooler wouldn't get me nowhere. Maybe I couldn't even get an indictment from the Grand Jury on what I could tell 'em. So I ain't grabbing you this minute. But that doesn't mean I ain't got ideas."

"If you think we did it..."

"Look, sonny—don't go kidding yourself. You and the lady couldn't get away, even if you wanted. Not these days when we got science on our side. Radio and all that stuff."

He looked down at the toes of his shoes. Scott noticed that he had tiny feet, amazingly small for a man.

"It's this way," stated Peterson reasonably, "I'm looking for the gimmick. I think all three of these murders are tied up. But what ties 'em, I don't know. Not yet I don't. Once I figure that gimmick, I got a good case."

Scott said, "Gail's story could be true, you know."

"Yeah. Or you wouldn't have cooked it up. Real bright folks, I'd say. Skeleton keys that would fit any door in this hotel are a dime a dozen. I looked already. I know there are three entrances into the hall from this suite: one from this room and one from each bedroom. It could of happened just like she said. But you tell me this...just gimme an idea to chew on...why the hell would anybody in Cherokee, except you or Mrs. Kinkaid, want to kill that guy?"

Scott said earnestly, "I haven't the faintest idea." He was surprised at the way he said it. It was so true that his words carried the ring of truth.

Peterson didn't miss it. Peterson didn't miss anything much. He said softly, "Maybe you told me something, sonny. Maybe you did."

He strolled into the other room and they heard him talking with the technical boys. From his post at the door, Bernie looked appealingly at his friend. He said, "He's confused, Scott. But Chris doesn't stay confused long."

"That's all right with me."

"What's more," Bernie went on, "he's got his teeth into something. Miss Barrie hasn't come clean. We all know that. If I was you, I'd try to get her to change her mind."

They sat there for a long time. They could hear people milling about in the hall. They could hear strident, insistent voices, which Scott correctly guessed belonged to reporters. The news was out all right...and it was definitely on the sensational side. Scott heard another voice, too: the close-clipped voice of David Gardel, his lawyer, demanding to see Scott. And that was as far as Gardel got.

Time dragged. Peterson sat and looked at them and walked around and sat down and looked at them some more. Then the telephone rang in Gail's bedroom. Peterson answered it. They couldn't tell from his end of the conversation what was going on, except that he liked it.

He rejoined them in the sitting room.

"At least," he stated, "we ain't standing still. That was HQ. They just finished testing the bullet that was dug out of Kinkaid's body," He bowed to Gail. "It seems that your late husband was killed with the same gun that was used on Fletcher Mathews."

CHAPTER EIGHTEEN

NEVER, IN ALL THE HISTORY OF CHEROKEE, had there been so much food for gossip. Speculation ranged from the wildest impossibility to the simplest probability.

The three local newspapers made the most of what they had—and they had plenty. But Scott Henderson knew they didn't have it all. Neither did the police. Nor did he, for that matter. Only Gail Barrie knew the answer—and she wasn't talking.

All through the first few days after Tony Kinkaid's death, Gail remained at home. There were innumerable official details that could not be avoided, but—because of her intimacy with the Mathews family, and the high esteem in which her father had been held these were made as simple as possible.

There was the funeral, which was a solemn and drab affair. There were hundreds who would like to have attended, but they were barred. There was an inquest, which declared blithely that Anthony Kinkaid had come to his death at the hands of a person or persons unknown. There was a police examination of his effects, which yielded nothing except the enormous and flashy wardrobe of a vain and handsome man, a bank account of less than one thousand dollars, and an address book that Bernie Williams ventured to guess contained many interesting numbers. There was nothing that linked his past with Gail's, or with anything else that might provide a motive for murder.

The loyalty of Barbara Mathews to Gail remained steadfast. She was stubborn in her refusal to believe that Gail had anything to do with any of the three murders. Scott was content enough to let that ride. It was pleasant to talk to someone who didn't continually fire unanswerable questions at him. And, without doubt, the effect of Barbara's loyalty on Gail was good.

There were long periods of time when she looked and acted like a person who has been stunned by a physical blow. There were other times when, in the privacy of the Mathews home, she was almost herself.

Her relationship with Scott remained inexplicable. She tried to be natural and made no effort to conceal the fact that she cared for him. But she also gave no indication that she was even considering taking him into her confidence.

At first it annoyed him. He spent restless days and sleepless nights. But he was young and healthy, and before long normalcy asserted itself. He was no less horrified by what happened, but the initial reaction of stunned incredulity was beginning to pass off. Life was like that: adjustments that at first seemed impossible were made.

But the fog remained no less dense.

Thus far, Chris Peterson had made no arrests. Without playing false to his duties as a member of the Cherokee police force, Bernie Williams kept Scott posted.

Sax Bailey, owner and operator of the semi-disreputable Valley View Lodge, was grilled. He stated that he knew nothing about the affair except what he read in the papers. Yes, Fern Meredith was a friend of his; yes, he was off the deep end about her; yes, he was glad that Kinkaid wasn't underfoot anymore. He made no pretense of being sorry, but he argued reasonably that if he hadn't done anything about the situation while Tony was single, he certainly wouldn't want to mess it up once Kinkaid had gotten himself married.

Fern Meredith yielded no more satisfactory results. She wasn't too fond of Sax Bailey, despite their intimate relationship, but she couldn't figure why Sax would have wanted to kill Tony on his wedding night…or any night after his marriage, for that matter. As for herself: Nuts! She had no alibi; she was sore as a goat, but she didn't do it. "Another thing," she argued: "Supposing Gail Barrie's story is true. At five o'clock in the morning a man might have gone up in the elevator and never been noticed. He could have walked up the fire stairs. But me?" She indicated her golden hair, her voluptuous figure… "Angle it for yourself, Copper. In a hamlet like this, where virtue is always triumphant, what chance would I have of getting up there and away again without being spotted?"

Peterson said he was satisfied. He wasn't—not entirely, but if he'd been compelled to make a decision, he'd have checked Fern out.

The elevator boys on duty between one and seven in the morning didn't remember anybody who looked as though he was about to commit a murder or had committed one. They'd each ridden the normal number of passengers up and down. One guy more or less didn't mean a thing. They didn't even remember Scott Henderson.

The manager and assistant manager yielded even less than that between them. Sure, they knew Kinkaid. Off the record they admitted that occasionally Tony had stayed there with a casual friend…invariably of the opposite sex. Always within the law, of course, because he'd used suites, and there wasn't any rule that said a gentleman couldn't entertain a lady in his apartment. Never just a room! Heavens, No! Chris Peterson smiled thinly at that and uttered a profane ejaculation, which was calculated to inform them that he knew what went on occasionally in the Cherokee...or in any other hotel, for that matter.

They found plenty of fingerprints. These were tied up with Gail, with Scott Henderson, with Tony Kinkaid, with the bellboy who had brought their luggage upstairs and with the maid who— with some bewilderment—had fixed up the two bedrooms for the honeymoon couple. It all checked, and it all added up to zero.

On the Tuesday following Kinkaid's death, Scott got a telephone call from Fern Meredith. He left his work and went to her apartment. He stared at her as she closed the door behind him, and she caught what he meant. She said, "Yeah, I know. I look like I'd been hit by an atomic bomb. Well, I have. I don't give a damn what I look like."

Her face was drawn. It was hard. There was a cold, bitter light in her blue eyes. She said, "Maybe you want to hear what I got to say; maybe you don't."

"I think I do."

"Okay. So I'm asking a question. Do you want to know who killed Tony, or are you covering for somebody?"

He said, "I want to find out."

"Suppose it turned out to be Gail Barrie?"

"I'd still want to know."

He was afraid. Afraid that she had discovered something that had escaped him, something that might tie Gail up too tight.

Fern said, "I got nothing to go on. Just intuition—whatever that means. I can't figure Gail in it."

Scott exhaled. Until that instant, he didn't know he had been holding his breath.

"If I did," she went on, "I'd talk so fast it'd make your hair curl. The thing I want most in this world is to find the person who killed Tony. Reason I don't check Gail in is because it doesn't fit. Tony was making a play for her. A million bucks would look good to any man. You know something the cop's don't: I wasn't jealous. He liked to play around with me. He had no conscience and no scruples. He wasn't afraid of billy-be-damned. I was nuts about him so it's a cinch for me to figure another dame feeling the same way. Even a classy one like Barrie. I'll admit I don't understand the two bedrooms for a honeymoon. The more I think of that, the queerer it strikes me. It ain't Tony. He wouldn't play it that way. I think once you get the answer to that, you've maybe got the answer to everything."

Scott watched her through a haze of cigarette smoke. Even with the ravages of grief showing on her face, she was a seductive creature. What was more, she was shrewd. Hard, perhaps, and uncultured—but smart. She said, "Somebody killed Tony. Maybe Gail Barrie—maybe somebody else. I'm keeping after it until I know. I sent for you to find out if we're on the same team."

Scott said simply, "We are."

"I'll take that as it lays. And I'll ask you another question: How do you figure it?"

"I don't."

"You think it was Gail?"

"No."

"Why?"

"No logical reason. No reason anybody would credit. The same sort of reason you have: I just don't see it that way."

She nodded. "You said it. We can reach out and touch the answer. Only we don't know which way to reach."

He said, "You and Tony were pretty close. He must have told you a good deal about himself. Did he ever mention..."

"Enemies? Hell, yes. But not the killing kind. There was lots of muggs who hated his guts. But Tony played everything smart. He liked it that way. He'd tackle anything that had to be tackled, but he never led with his chin. Get it?"

"Yes..."

"Maybe you can tell me this. Dames always went walleyed about him. I did. Gail Barrie did. What I'm wondering is...was there somebody else? Perhaps some babe in the Country Club set he'd been giving the works? Maybe somebody who would blow her top when she found out he'd up and married another girl?"

Henderson nodded. "I hadn't thought of that angle. It's plausible. But I don't know of any such affair."

She hesitated before speaking. Then: "You won't fly off the handle if I snap one at you?"

"No."

"How about Miss Mathews?"

"Barbara?" He leaned back in his chair and smiled.

"That's the silliest idea I ever heard. Good Lord! She's only a kid…"

"Just a year or so younger than Gail Barrie."

"And she's got a half dozen boyfriends…"

"Maybe you got something right there. A half dozen means she hasn't got any. If there was one…an exclusive one…see what I mean?"

"Yes. But Barbara didn't even like Tony. She kidded about how handsome he was and how he loved himself. She couldn't see why Gail wasted time on him…"

Fern Meredith was gazing at Scott with an odd intentness. She said gently, "Think back over what you've just been saying, Mr. Henderson. Maybe you'll see it could point two ways."

"It's ridiculous! You've let your imagination run away with you…"

"Try again. And I ain't taking it the easy way, either. I'm even checking out Gail until I know different. But there's one thing I can't check out. Tony is dead. Somebody killed him. They didn't do it for money, because the poor lug didn't have any. So what have you got left? Answer me that." She laughed harshly. "You got love; that's what you got. It could be Gail Barrie's kind of love. She could have been sore because he married her and then gave her the brush-off. Maybe the guy didn't tell her the real score until he was married to her."

"But you said you didn't think that."

"I still don't. I'm thinking of the other kind of love. The love that's been kicked in the teeth. I know how a woman could feel. If I hadn't known just where I stood with Tony…if I hadn't seen this coming and been rooting for it…if I'd been suddenly slapped down by his marriage…hell! I could have played a swell Frankie to his Johnny. Don't kid yourself, Mister. When a dame's overboard about a man, she's like any other woman. 'He was her man, and he done her wrong…' That's old stuff. It's always been good and it's good now."

She got up, and he followed suit. She said, "I had a hell of a nerve asking you to come over. I know you're busy. But you're the one guy I know can be trusted. I wanted to find out if we were looking for the same thing."

"You've found out."

"Yeah... And you're playing it that way, even if Gail Barrie gets hurt?"

"No matter who gets hurt."

She followed him to the door. She held out her hand—rather timidly—and he took it. She smiled: the first real smile he'd seen since he came in.

"I wonder what it'd be like," she said, "to be tied up with a regular guy like you? Somebody who might worry about you once in a while, who might be gentle..." She tore her hand away from his. "I'm a dope," she snapped. "I always was a dope..."

He went out. The door closed behind him. Gently. He walked to his office. He got there a little after three o'clock. The girl at the PBX looked at him peculiarly and said, "Mrs. Kinkaid is in your office, Mr. Henderson."

"Mrs. Kinkaid!" The name didn't fit, somehow. And he was aware that all of his employees studiously refrained from looking at him. He went inside and closed the ground glass door.

Gail got up and held out her hand. She was smiling, but her gray eyes looked worried. They chatted inconsequentially for a moment. Then he asked what was on her mind.

She told him. She told him in a tense voice that demanded no interruption. She said:

"This is something I don't want to argue about, Scott. It isn't an impulse. I know what I'm doing and why I'm doing it."

She went on. "I need twenty-five thousand dollars, Scott. I've got to have it. Right away. Today if possible. Tomorrow at the latest. I haven't anything like that amount in the bank. But you can lend it to me. You can advance it against what I'll be getting soon from the estate."

He was saying nothing, thinking hard.

"I want it in reasonably small bills. Nothing over fifty dollars. I want your word of honor that the money will not be marked."

He said, "Suppose I refuse?"

Her eyes darkened. "You'd be making a mistake, Scott. This is the most important thing I've ever asked you. You've got to do it!"

He met her gaze levelly. Then, to her obvious surprise, he nodded. He said, "Okay, Gail. I'll get it for you. But not today. The banks are closed. Will tomorrow morning be all right?"

"Yes..." Then her eyes filled with tears. She had won her point with unexpected ease. She said, "Thank you, Scott... thank you. You don't know how much you've helped. You haven't any idea how important this is."

He walked around the desk and patted her on the shoulder. He led her through the office and stood in the corridor until the elevator arrived.

Then he went back to his desk. He knew just exactly what he intended to do.

He asked his switchboard operator for a line. He dialed the number of police headquarters. He asked for Bernie Williams.

A half minute later Bernie's heavy, lazy voice came to him. They exchanged hellos, and Scott said, "Busy?"

"Nope."

"Can you come over to my office right away?"

"Important?"

"Yes."

"Okay, kid. Look out the window and the guy you see comin' around the corner is me."

Scott Henderson put down the telephone and stared thoughtfully at the blank wall. "Maybe," he said to himself, "maybe this is it."

CHAPTER NINETEEN

SCOTT HENDERSON talked and Bernie Williams listened. He was slumped in a big leather chair, big feet stretched out halfway across the rug and thumbs hooked in his belt. His eyes were half closed, his face expressionless. Only the tiny trace of a frown gave any hint of the intentness with which he was listening.

Not once did he interrupt. When Scott finished talking, he hitched himself upright, shook his head and said, "Well, whaddaya know."

It wasn't a question. It was merely an indication that he was properly impressed.

Scott opened a cigar humidor and shoved it across the desk in the direction of the big detective who had been his friend since high school days. Between these two men there was warmth and understanding and mutual admiration. What was more, they trusted each other.

Scott said, "How do you figure it, Bernie?"

"It's easy, kid. You got exactly two guesses. One's got to be right."

"I'm listening."

"First, things have gotten too tough, and she's taking a powder."

Scott thought that one over, then shook his head. "I'll probably like the other one better."

"Me, too. I'd say that somebody had turned on the heat and she was fixing to pay 'em off."

"Who—and why?"

"If I knew that, kid—I'd be a sergeant myself." Bernie lighted the cigar with meticulous care. He said, "Good smoke. Too rich for my blood. It'll spoil me. What're you fixin' to do, Scott?"

"I'm just about to ask your help."

"You got it already."

"I thought I'd give her the money—just exactly as she asked for it. If it fits in with your plans, I'd give it to her at eleven o'clock tomorrow morning. You could pick her up when she left here with the package. Follow her, and see what she does."

Bernie was thoughtful. He said, "If she tried to get out of town, Scott, I'd be bound to stop her. That wouldn't help her situation any."

Henderson nodded. "That's all right with me."

"She could maybe get hurt. I don't mean hurt, really…but surprised and shocked. That sort of thing. If she figured you had spilled, she wouldn't be too happy."

"I'll take the chance. But frankly, I don't peg it that way. I think she's planning to give the money to somebody. I haven't the faintest idea why. But if you could see her deliver the package, then let her get clear, then pick up the person she gives it to…it might give us the answer to a lot of questions."

"It still wouldn't make her position too healthy."

Scott spoke earnestly. "Listen, Bernie," he said. "I'm in love with Gail. I've never been in love before. What this might lead to could hit me hard. But Fletcher Mathews' death hit me hard, too."

"You're afraid she's right in the middle of it, ain't you?"

"I know she is. But dammit! Bernie, I can't believe that she had anything to do with any of these murders."

"Don't bank on that too strong, kid. I think you're right. I dope it out the same way you do. But it could be worse than you think. Putting together just the things you've told me, and speculatin' on the things you haven't spilled...you gotta remember that if people conspire to commit any sort of a felony and that if one of the conspirators, in the commission of that felony, commits a greater crime...murder, we'll say...both or all the conspirators are principals in the crime." Bernie inhaled deeply, blew out a cloud of fragrant smoke and grinned across at his friend. "Jeez! Imagine all them ten-dollar phrases from me, who was the prize dope in high school. I reckon the only thing I ever studied was police stuff. I like being a cop. That's how come I can spout all them fancy things."

Scott was smiling. "You did have me walking on my heels for a minute, Bernie. And thanks. I know what you're driving at. It's a risk that's got to be taken."

"Keeno! So you hand the package of money to Gail. I follow her. I see her give it to someone. We'll say she goes off and leaves him—if it is a him. I let her go. I tail this lug, and when he gets to some place where she couldn't know—I pick him up. That it?"

"Yes."

"Then what gives?"

"What would you suggest?"

"You'd like to talk to him, wouldn't you? Real private?"

"I certainly would. I'd also like you to be there. Can it be done?"

"Hell, yes. I can slap him in the can without making an entry on the blotter. Under the laws of this State, he can be held for three days. If we need him any longer than that, you'll have to start throwing your weight around."

"What does that mean?"

"Well, under the law, we either got to charge a guy with something or let him go. But when a felony's been committed, there's all kinds of ways to get around that. You got influence with the chief and the D. A. If we got this figured right, and if we needed to hold him out longer than three days, you'd have to fix it up."

"Peterson?"

"Yeah. The guy ain't sociable. He ain't too happy about you and me being friends. He wants this case to stay right in his own pocket. If he found out I was pulling a fast one, he'd carry his howl right up to the Chief."

"I get it. But I think I can handle things. If I can't, then David Gardel can."

"We all set then?"

"Yes."

"I'll be outside the bank tomorrow morning long before eleven. If anything slips, you lemme know." Bernie hoisted himself from the chair. "Anything else?"

"How about having dinner with me?"

"Chop suey?"

"Right."

"You're on."

It was a nice dinner. Not that Scott was too passionate about chop suey, but because this seemed like old times...as though they were kids again. Bernie helped Scott to forget things he wanted to forget and to remember things that were pleasant. They talked football mostly. They didn't discuss murder very much.

The following morning Scott telephoned Gail. She asked him whether he'd gotten the money. Her voice sounded eager. Too eager. He told her the bank was fixing it up, and that if she'd meet him there at a few minutes before eleven, he'd turn it over to her.

She was in his office by ten-thirty. Her eyes were unnaturally bright, her color too high. She looked excited, rather than afraid. He tried to act as though he had nothing up his sleeve. He asked again what it was all about, knowing that she wouldn't tell him...and not caring.

They went to the bank together. George Keyes, one of the assistant cashiers, hailed them. He said, "I got it fixed up for you, Scott."

Henderson took the package. He was surprised by its lack of bulk. Keyes was smiling. He said, "What's cookin', feller? You figurin' on promotin' a crap game?"

"You never can tell."

"If you do—an' it starts sizzlin'—you know my phone number. I want in."

They left the bank together. Scott glanced across the street and saw the big shoulders of Bernie Williams blotting out half the window of a jewelry store. He didn't look too hard. He didn't want Gail to suspect that he had an iron in the fire.

"How'd you get downtown?" he asked.

"In Barbara's car. I'm parked on State."

He walked to the car with her. She slipped under the wheel and he handed her the package of money. She put it on the seat beside her; and then, to give Bernie plenty of time, he stood talking for a while.

She had a forced, brittle gaiety this morning. But she was obviously impatient. She was the one who ended the conversation. She pulled away from the curb and headed east toward an area of sprawling middle-class suburbs. Scott watched her go. He felt excited and apprehensive. The chips were down. Nothing he could do about it now.

Before Gail had progressed two blocks, Bernie Williams' car passed the spot where Scott was standing. Bernie didn't look in his direction. He was intent on keeping Gail's car in sight without being seen. He was sticking close because traffic was heavy. Later, he'd widen the distance between them, so that even if she looked into the rear-view mirror, she wouldn't suspect that she was being tailed.

Scott went back to his office. Important matters were popping; important men were waiting to confer with him. He wasn't much interested. Outwardly, he was all right. Inside, he was seething.

The more he thought about the set-up, the more convinced he became that the gimmick that thus far had eluded all of them was about to be brought to light. He didn't know where that would put Gail Barrie; he didn't know what repercussions it would have on him. He was doing this because he had to—because he wanted to. But that didn't keep him from being afraid.

He told himself that love was a hell of a thing. He could consider all the angles with complete detachment. He could even figure the unpleasant possibility that Gail was criminally involved.

He knew he'd follow through on what he had started because there was in him an uncompromising decency. But he also knew that he was deeply in love with Gail Barrie and was going to stay that way.

Eventually he got rid of his clients. The noon hour struck and the office help started streaming out. Scott didn't leave. He sat at his desk, thumbing through papers that meant nothing at the moment. The door was open and he could see the big electric clock on the opposite wall. The hands didn't seem to move. He was becoming magnificently jittery.

The phone rang and he lunged for it. He said Hello and Bernie's voice answered: "Scott?"

"Yes."

"How's about meeting me at the hot dog stand on Maple in ten minutes?"

"Make it five."

"Five it is."

The stand was a mere hole-in-the-wall. It was crowded. The odor was violent but appetizing. Bernie ordered two, all the way, and pressed one into Scott's hand. He said, "Chew on it, kid. It'll make things look good."

They sidled into a corner and talked in whispers.

"Any luck?" asked Scott.

"And how."

"She gave the money to someone?"

"Yeah. A man."

"Who?"

"Nobody you know. Or me, either. I got him in the cooler now, incognito."

Scott smiled in spite of himself. "Incommunicado?"

"Jeez! I'm always gettin' 'em mixed up."

"Tell me about it."

"She drove out through Woodhaven. Turned right at 58th Street. Went beyond the houses. Just vacant lots there. A few trees and a hell of a lot of weeds. She pulled over and parked. After about ten minutes a little guy came strollin' along. Funny little duck. He went up to the car; they talked for two-three minutes. She handed him the package of money. She asked him something...maybe could she ride him somewhere... I wouldn't be knowing for sure. He shook his head no. She made a U-turn and started back in the general direction of where I was. I got behind a tree. She zipped by me without ever lookin'.

"I gave her plenty of time. Then I got into my jeep and tooled along after this guy. He couldn't have gone far, I figured. I was right. I pulled up alongside and said, 'Hey, mister...' At first I thought he was going to run for it. Then he changed his mind.

"I got out and flashed my badge. He looked kinda unhappy. He asked what it was all about. I said he'd find out soon enough. I told him to climb in, and he climbed. I frisked him to make sure he wasn't rodded. No gun on him. No blackjack. No brass knucks. We drove into town.

"He tried to talk his way out. No luck. He asked if he was being arrested for anything. I said, 'Hell no...what would we want to arrest you for?' He didn't have no good answer to that one. I said I just wanted to talk to him a while, private like. With that he clammed up. Not another peep out of him all the way in. I got him past the desk sergeant, Doyle. Him and me are good friends. He ain't talking. Maybe because I also winked and mentioned that this would be okay with the chief and the D. A. I shoved my little partridge into a nice, clean cell. I went through him. Nothing on him that meant anything. Less than twenty dollars cash, not counting the package of money Gail had given him. No identification cards. I said if he'd play nice, there wouldn't be any trouble. He thought that one over and finally gave me a name and address...I suppose he figured I could find out easy enough, so he might as well make like he was playing ball. He's registered at the Grainger...and what a joint that is. He says his name is Ollie Drucker. It mean anything to you?"

"No."

"I thought not. This guy is small, but he looks tough. Real tough. It ain't the first time he's been picked up by police. You can tell that by the way they act."

Scott said, "What do we do next?"

"We can case his room at the Grainger. Or we can talk to him."

Scott drew a deep breath, as a high diver does just before leaving the springboard.

"Okay," he said, "let's look at his room first."

CHAPTER TWENTY

THE GRAINGER was the second oldest hotel in Cherokee, and even when new, it hadn't been the best. Now it was dingy, furtive, down-at-the-heels. It was built of red brick and was six stories high. It had a gloomy lobby, a set of ancient chairs, and a young, hard-eyed clerk who had seen so many things that nothing could surprise him.

He took a look at Bernie Williams' badge and didn't turn a hair. He glanced at his registry cards and said, "Three-seventeen." He tossed a big brass ring with a passkey on it across the counter. He asked, "Want a bell boy?"

"No, thanks. How long has Drucker been here?"

"August first, the books say."

"Owe anything?"

"Nobody owes anything here. If they don't pay, they get pitched out."

Two young ladies, wearing profuse make-up and summer dresses that didn't conceal what they obviously fancied were voluptuous figures, swayed across the lobby and demanded keys from the clerk. He tossed them over. They looked with professional interest at Bernie and Scott. The clerk said, "Nix on that. These guys is dicks."

The young ladies immediately tried to make themselves look less voluptuous. They made speed across the lobby and disappeared into the rickety elevator. The room clerk said, "Coupla tramps," and Bernie exclaimed, "Imagine that!"

He and Scott waited until the cage returned. The operator was old and almost as rickety as the elevator. He was chewing tobacco, and seemed to have no interest in anything whatsoever. He let them off at the third floor, languidly closed his door, and dropped from sight.

Bernie said, "You get it, Scott? This Drucker checked in August first. That was three days before Doris was killed."

Henderson nodded. The very thought of Gail Barrie knowing anyone who would live here was more than incongruous. He said, "I've never been in this hotel before. It's quite a dump."

"Brother, you ain't kiddin'. A few decent folks from the country come here because it's cheap. But mostly it's the hangout for every hustler and floozie in town."

They entered 317. It was a big room. All the rooms in the Grainger were big. But when you had said that, you'd said it all. The plaster was cracked and dirty. There was a big, white-enameled double bed, which showed black scars where the enamel had chipped off. There was an old dresser of the type that was called a bureau in its day, a wardrobe, a closet, a large but unkempt bathroom, a straight chair and another chair that was supposed to be easy but wasn't.

The bed looked as though it had been made that morning, but meanwhile had been lain on. The closet door was open. There was a suitcase on the floor. Inside the closet a single suit was hanging. Bernie didn't waste time. He started searching the room.

The search didn't take long, nor did it yield anything to get excited about. The room contained the sparse and threadbare possessions of a man who had been pretty close to the financial rocks—a minimum of everything, and most of that cheap and shoddy. "Just one thing interestin'," stated Bernie. "The name of the store where that suit was bought has been snipped out. You usually find it inside the coat, by the pocket. Some laundry marks have been cut out. Looks like Brother Drucker was kind of precautious about bein' checked."

He finished with the closet, the bathroom, the suitcase. On the dresser he found a pencil stub, a brush and comb—both slightly the worse for wear—a comic supplement from last Sunday's local paper, a racing form and two magazines. He opened the drawers and discovered a minimum of undershirts and shorts, half a dozen neckties, two suits of clean pajamas and seven assorted shirts. He probed through the clothing and came up with a little notebook in his hand. He said, "Maybe we got something here."

Scott wasn't optimistic. If Mr. Ollie Drucker had left a notebook in his dresser drawer, the chances were that it wasn't important.

Bernie thumbed through it. He said, "Hell! Nothin'. Mostly telephone numbers. Broads, I reckon. You wouldn't think it of the little guy. Garages. Stores. Looks like he musta traveled a lot. There's telephone exchanges from all over the country."

He handed the book to Scott. That young man studied it. He said, "Doesn't look very interesting, does it?"

"Naaah! Nothin' to it."

Scott turned several pages. He said, "I wonder who F. O. is?"

"Whaddaya mean, 'F. O.?'"

"Drucker apparently has the habit of writing out telephone exchanges in full. In front of three of these numbers are the initials 'F. O.' Look! Here's one number repeated...FO 4779. Could be a lead."

Bernie shrugged, "Not much to go on, Scott."

Henderson seated himself at the dresser. He took a fountain pen from his pocket and a sheet of paper from the drawer. He said, "Mind if I copy down what's in this book?"

"Go ahead, Kid. But it ain't gonna get you nowhere."

Scott worked carefully, checking back with each page. He finished finally and looked down at his handiwork. It wasn't very impressive:

Walnut 3715 (Mirtle)
Agnes (call 8:30)—Ellinder 2146
Repairing blowout—$3.50 (Tip 25 cents)
FO 4779
Mable—10—Vista Club.
Yancey & Co.
Lv. 10:38. Arr. N. Y. 8:30 (See Joe at Wallie's)
Ethel—Main 8199 (married)
Clover 1245
41732
FO 4779
River 4231 (got a friend)
Jake owes $3.75
FO 1295

Bernie took Scott's list, read that far and said, "Nuts! It'd take the whole department a year to check everything you got down there. Unless that 'FO' business really means something." He scratched his head. "I'd like to know why he put down 4779 twice?"

"That's what I'm wondering." Scott folded the paper and slipped it into the inside pocket of his coat. He put the notebook back with the shirts, where they had found it. He said, "We may as well mosey along to the jail, don't you think?"

The City Hall was Cherokee's pride. It was an impressive white building twenty stories high. The city jail occupied the three top floors. That meant that the prisoners could enjoy the view but didn't have much chance of getting to it.

Bernie chatted with Doyle, who was still on the desk. He conducted Scott to the office of the jailer and said he wanted to talk privately with Ollie Drucker. The man grinned and said, "There ain't no such person here, Bernie. But you can see him."

He unlocked the door and led the two young men down a forbidding but immaculately clean corridor. He inserted a key in a barred door and let them into a cubicle that looked more like a room than a cell. The jailer said, "We keep this special for nice folks. Mister Drucker is nice folks. He don't bother nobody. Maybe that's on account he ain't here, really," He laughed loudly at his own jest, and Bernie said, "You slay me, Pete."

Pete rolled off, still chortling. Scott whispered to Bernie, "What did you do with the package of money?"

"In the safe downstairs."

Ollie Drucker was sitting on his cot. Scott regarded him curiously. He saw a small, wiry man of perhaps forty years of age. Ollie was partly bald. He was wearing a gray suit, which was sadly in need of pressing, and a gray shirt that was open at the throat. He had cold gray eyes, but Scott gathered the impression that those eyes were not without fear.

The little man tried to appear disinterested. He sat staring at them, and only the fact that his fingers were interlaced so tightly that the knuckles showed white gave any indication that he was under a strain.

Bernie waved at his friend. He said, "Go ahead, kid. See if you can make him sing."

Scott tried to talk like an average man on an average social visit. He said, "Why did Miss Barrie give you that package, Drucker?"

Drucker didn't say anything.

"Where did you meet Miss Barrie?"

He could see Ollie's brain working. The man was badly frightened, and trying not to show it. At length he said, "I don't know nobody by that name."

"Who do you know in Cherokee?"

"Few guys at a poolroom."

"You've been here since the first of August, haven't you?"

"I forget."

"What have you been doing all that time?"

"Looking for a job."

"What kind of a job?"

"Anything. They say they don't want no old men now the war's over. Hell, I ain't old. I'm forty-three."

"Planning to leave town?"

"Sure, if I can't get a job here."

"Who's been giving you the money to live on since August first?"

"I had some when I got here. It's run out now."

"Do you know what was in that package Miss Barrie gave you?"

"Nobody gave me no package."

"But you had a package when Detective Williams picked you up."

"Yeah, sure. I found it in a vacant lot."

"Didn't it strike you as funny, finding a package in a vacant lot?"

"Look—what's this all about? I ain't done nothing."

"Suppose I told you that we know you're lying. Williams saw Miss Barrie give you that package."

"I'm telling you," said the little man with desperate earnestness, "nobody gave me no package."

Bernie snapped, "Wise guy, huh?"

Ollie looked up at him. He said, "That's the truth. Honest."

"Do you know what was in the package?" persisted Scott.

"I told you—"

"There was $25,000 in that bundle. Small bills. Not marked. That money belonged to Miss Barrie. She had a right to do anything with it she wanted to do. If she gave it to you—and we know she did—it's yours. We'll give it back to you."

There was the faintest sort of a glitter in Ollie's eyes. He said, "Then why don't you leave me be?"

"So far as we know, you're in the clear. But we need to know two more things. First, what is the connection between you and Miss Barrie? Second, why did she voluntarily give you twenty-five thousand dollars?"

Ollie was fighting against temptation and fear. He said, "I don't know anybody named Barrie. Nobody gave me no $25,000."

Henderson sighed. He wasn't getting anywhere. Fast. "You're just not talking, is that it?"

"I can't talk when I don't know nothin'."

"I'll try something else. Did you ever hear of a man named Anthony Kinkaid?"

Ollie's eyelids drooped. He seemed to be badly scared. "I read about him in the papers," he said cautiously. "Somebody killed him."

"Was it you?"

Ollie made a gesture of weariness. He said, "Look—supposin' I did kill the guy—which I didn't—would I say so?"

"I suppose not. But you knew him, didn't you?"

"Never heard of him until I read about it in the papers."

Scott's voice tightened. "Did you ever hear of a man named Fletcher Mathews?"

"Same way as I heard about Kinkaid."

"Or about a girl named Doris Treadway Colby?"

Ollie said, "What goes on here? Three people that got bumped off. Why should I know any more about them than anybody else?"

"I've got an idea. Mrs. Colby was a friend of Miss Barrie's. Mr. Mathews was her trustee and guardian. She had become Kinkaid's wife a few hours before he was murdered."

"Kinda makes her look like the patsy, doesn't it?"

"Yes. Except for you. You were in town when those murders were committed. A little while ago, Miss Barrie—or Mrs. Kinkaid, whichever way you want to think of her—gave you a package containing a lot of money. That puts you right in the middle. If you'll come clean, I know that the police will meet you half way."

"They will like hell. Guys like me are sirloin steak for cops. So I ain't changing what I already said. I found a bundle in a vacant lot. I got no idea what was in it."

"You're lying."

"Prove it."

"That's easy enough. Miss Barrie could identify you and—"

Drucker said, "If she was mixed up in this, and if she was willing to talk, you wouldn't be here askin' me questions."

Scott looked helplessly at Bernie. He'd gone as far as he could go—which was no distance. Bernie said, "How's it feel to have three murder raps hangin' over you?"

There was a whine in Drucker's voice when he said, "You can't get anywhere that way. It ain't no crime for a guy to find something, is it?"

"Maybe. What were you planning to do with it?"

"I'd have opened the package, and if it had money in it, I'd have turned it in to the cops."

"Jeez! Are you a card. You find twenty-five thousand smackers an' you're gonna give it to the police."

"Yeah. Like any honest citizen is supposed to do."

Bernie said, "We've sent your fingerprints to the FBI for checking. Maybe that'll tell us something."

Ollie shook his head. "I got no criminal record."

Bernie gathered from the way he said it that Drucker was telling the truth. He said, "No dividends, Scott. Why should we waste any more time?"

"Just a minute." Drucker got up from the cot. "You got no right to keep me here. Not without a charge you ain't."

"You ain't here," stated Bernie calmly. "The blotter says so."

"How about habeas corpus?"

"It's swell. I like mine with chocolate sauce."

"You gotta charge me with something."

"So what? If that time comes, we'll make it vagrancy. Or suspicion of murder. Or nothing. It's in your lap. When you make up your mind to do a little talking, ask the jailer to send for Detective Williams. That's me."

Drucker watched them close the door, heard them walk down the hall. Standing at the elevators, Bernie said, "The runt is full of pay dirt, Scott…but he ain't distributin' any of it. He's scared stiff, and sometimes it's hard to make a scared guy talk. I'll work on him a little. Nothing rough. Just persuasive. But I wouldn't be hopeful, if I was you. My advice is you see the Chief and the D. A. or get your lawyers on the job. That's so if Chris Peterson finds out what we're doing, he can't mess it up."

Scott nodded. He said, "If we had one thing to break him down with…"

"He was lying about Gail Barrie and the money. But what the hell, the dope you handed him was straight. It was her dough. If she wanted to slip it to a small-time grifter, that was her business. He knows it, and he's playing cute."

"He's afraid of something."

"Uh-huh. And that's where we came in. We knew that before we began."

Scott started back for the office. Halfway there, he changed his mind. He drove to Brookside and pulled up in front of the Mathews home.

Leander was putting fresh covers on the veranda chairs. "Yes," he said, "Miss Gail is home, an' I sho' will be happy to leave her know that you's callin'."

Scott knew exactly what he was going to do. He realized that Gail mustn't suspect that her contact with Ollie Drucker had been observed. But there was something else that intrigued him.

In spite of all she'd been through recently, she made his heart jump. She was prettier than he remembered her. And sweeter. And more desirable. No matter what happened, that was the way she affected him.

They seated themselves side by side. He said, "I want to ask you something, honey…"

He could see that she was instantly on guard. She said, "Yes…?"

"I want you to think carefully. Do you know anybody whose initials are F. O.?"

She shook her head. "Not that I can remember, Scott." He felt that she was telling the truth. He was disappointed. "Think carefully," he urged. "Don't those initials mean anything to you?"

"F. O." She was turning it over in her mind. Then she looked up and smiled. "F. O. means something," she said, "but not as initials."

"As what, then?"

"There's a telephone exchange in Havana that's called FO."

"What does it stand for?"

"Nothing. The Havana exchanges are all letters. In Havana proper there are A and U. In Vedada—that's the chief residential section—it's F. In Marianao, the exchange is FO." She looked at him oddly. "Why do you ask?"

"Nothing... Just curious."

They talked a few minutes more. Then he got up and said he'd be going. She put her hand in his, and he smiled down at her.

On the way downtown he started thinking again. He was toying with a new thought.

So FO was a Havana telephone exchange. It appeared three times in Ollie Drucker's little notebook.

That tied Ollie up with Cuba. Gail had lived most of her life in Cuba.

Ollie—Gail—Cuba—$25,000. They made a pattern of some sort.

"I don't know what it means," Scott Henderson told himself, "but at least it's something to work on."

CHAPTER TWENTY-ONE

SCOTT HENDERSON stopped to look at the poster that a most attractive young lady had left in his office with the request that it be prominently displayed. She explained that similar posters would blossom all over Cherokee within a few hours, and that it was the civic duty of all firms to contribute to the success of the enterprise.

The placard announced that on Monday, September second, Labor Day, the Executive Committee of the Community Chest was sponsoring a fiesta at the Country Club—a bazaar, a la carte meals, music, dancing and entertainment. Grateful acknowledgment was made for the cooperative spirit shown by the Board of Governors of the Club, and thanks were extended individually to Mr. Paul Innes for his indefatigable efforts in behalf of the venture. But all that was of small interest to young Mr. Henderson.

What did interest him—the thing that started an idea simmering—was the list of entertainers, recruited from local amateur talent and professional performers who were at the moment playing local theaters and nightclubs. The name of one of them stood out in bold type:

"FERN MEREDITH—The Songstress With A Soul." Henderson plunged into the routine duties of a routine day. Shortly before noon he was visited by Bernie Williams, who invited him to lunch.

Bernie was definitely discouraged. "That Ollie Drucker," he said, "he still hasn't changed his story."

Scott said, "We know he's lying."

"Sure we know it. But what good does that do?" Bernie drummed on the table with his big, spatulate fingers. "There's a feller for you," he stated. "I never saw so much bluff wrapped up in such a small package. The little guy is scared green. He's jittery as all get-out. But there's something else that scares him worse than the police."

"I know..." Scott was thoughtful. "I got that idea when we first talked to him. He gave the impression of a kid whistling in the dark."

Bernie said, "Peterson knows about him. He's sore as hell."

"Don't worry about Peterson. He got orders straight from the Chief. The D. A. is letting us play it this way."

"For how long? What happens if Drucker never sings?"

"We can prove that Gail handed him the money..."

"And that we jumped at conclusions. Taking money from a dame ain't no crime. If this flops, you'll look silly and I'll be in the doghouse."

"It can't go on much longer. Gail's twenty-first birthday is the seventh of September. She hasn't changed her ideas."

Bernie sighed. "It's been fun stringin' along with you, kid. I just hope we haven't made a bum play."

"Me, too. I'm beginning to get another idea..."

"What?"

"It isn't worth telling right now. It sounds absurd even to me."

They separated outside the cafeteria. Cherokee sizzled in a blistering August hot spell. Heat waves danced above the pavement. Men walked around without coats, mopping their faces. Air-cooled movie houses, stores, and restaurants did capacity business. Municipal swimming pools were jammed. The torrid heat was the outstanding topic of conversation.

Even in the well-ventilated offices of Mathews, Henderson & Company the staff worked with difficulty. The heat radiated up from the pavements. The building was like an oven.

At four o'clock Scott called it a day. There was plenty of unfinished business, but that would have to wait. The employees staggered out. They were grateful but discouraged. The paper said that there was no prospect of a break, no sign of rain.

At 4:30 the door of the main office opened. A man in the uniform of an army officer walked in. He was tall and thin, and he wore the silver leaves of a Lieutenant Colonel. Over his left breast he carried the ribbon of the Asiatic theater with three battle stars, the Purple Heart, and the Bronze Star with oak leaf cluster.

He glanced hesitantly around the deserted office. Scott introduced himself, and the visitor shifted a big package he was carrying from his right hand to his left and held out his hand. "Lieutenant Colonel Fraser," he said.

"How do you do, Colonel." Scott led the way into his private office. He explained why the office was deserted. Fraser smiled. He said, "It doesn't seem that hot to me. Where I've been it really gets warm."

He put the big bundle on Scott's desk, accepted a cigarette and a chair. He said, "Is Mr. Mathews in?"

"Mathews?" The casual inquiry came like a dash of cold water. Scott explained briefly that Fletcher Mathews was dead. He didn't call it murder. Colonel Fraser was properly, if impersonally, sympathetic. He said, "I suppose, then, that you are the firm?"

"More or less."

"I brought this…" He gestured toward the bundle. "I brought it from Okinawa. It's got a lot of Major Barrie's personal stuff in it. His watch, his ring, some memos, a packet of letters from his daughter, his decorations and insignia… He asked—long before he was killed—that if anything ever happened to him, I was to have them delivered to Mr. Mathews, who would forward them to his daughter. I think he said she was still in Cuba."

"She's here in Cherokee now. She came up as soon as she got news of her father's death."

"Barrie and I were rather close. We'd made the same request of each other. Kidding along, you know. You never really think you're going to get it yourself. And right after he did...well, I was being sent back here and I routed myself home via Cherokee..."

Scott thanked him. He liked the tall, serious man; liked his diffidence. He invited him for dinner, but Fraser said "No," that he was leaving that night. He talked about Barrie, and while he talked Scott gazed at the bundle and a new idea commenced to take shape.

It occurred to him that the package on his desk might contain the answer to his problem. Fraser had mentioned that there was a packet of letters from Gail to her father. Maybe Gail had written something that would explain her incredible actions of the past six weeks. Of course, when she had written those letters it had been to a father whom she believed to be alive. But whatever it was she was involved in now, it must have been part of her life when the letters were written. It was not too much to hope that she had confided. If she had needed money desperately, she might well have asked her father for it and have given some sort of an explanation.

Scott didn't have to do much thinking to arrive at a decision. Ethics was of slight importance in view of what he was up against. What he wanted now was to get rid of the Colonel and to inspect the contents of that package. He felt that the end would justify any means.

Colonel Fraser rose and said that he must be going. But he didn't go. He started talking about Major Barrie again. And while he was doing that, the door opened and Gail walked in.

She stopped short at sight of the two men. She said, "Sorry, Scott... I'll wait here..."

He was on the spot. Fraser was looking from Scott to Gail and back again. And so Scott did the only thing he could do under the circumstances. He introduced them. He explained the purpose of Colonel Fraser's visit.

The two started talking. Gail was asking questions and Fraser answering—in great detail. Scott couldn't think of anything except his disappointment. His new scheme had been knocked silly. He knew that Gail would walk off with the bundle.

He was right. She picked it up off the desk as a matter of course. She insisted on driving Colonel Fraser to his hotel. It was all very nice and natural...and tough on Scott.

Eventually there was the usual handshaking and thanks and best wishes. Gail and Colonel Fraser went out together. Scott dropped into his swivel chair, stared at the door and said, "Damn!" Then he dialed the number of the Mathews home. Barbara answered.

"This is Scott," he said. "I'll make it brief—but it's important." He told about what had just happened. He confessed what he had planned to do and why. He said, "Fraser's got a train to catch. Gail won't be with him long. She'll bring the bundle home. I want you, if possible, to be with her when she opens it. I want to know where she puts the things that are in it."

"I understand..." Barbara seemed hesitant. "Suppose I can't, Scott? Suppose she simply goes to her room and opens the package there?"

"Barge in on her. Peep through the keyhole if you've got to. You haven't any idea how important this might be. Whatever's wrong must have been brewing for a long time. It's a ten to one bet that if she was in any jam she would have written to her father for advice."

"You don't really mean that I'm to spy on her?"

"I definitely *do* mean that. It's rotten, sure. But that's the way it's got to be."

There was silence for a moment. Then she said, "Okay, Scott."

"I'll stay here in the office. As soon as you find out what's what, telephone me. If you can't phone from your house, go next door. But don't miss anything, Barbara. No matter what you have to do...do it."

The wait seemed interminable. Scott telephoned down to the drugstore for a sandwich and a cup of coffee. Six o'clock. Seven. Seven-thirty. He'd been chain-smoking since he talked to Barbara. His nerves were jumpy. He knew that he might draw a blank, but at least this was a new angle.

At 7:35 the telephone rang. It was Barbara. She sounded breathless.

She said, "Bad news. Gail got home an hour ago. She went straight to her room and locked the door. I peeped through the keyhole. I felt like a criminal. She took the things out one by one. She was crying. They were the usual things, Scott—just what you'd expect in a package like that. There was a bundle of letters. A dozen or so, I'd guess. Tied with a piece of string. She read them over one by one. She looked completely miserable. Then she put all the mementos away...in a dresser drawer."

"What did she do with the letters?"

"That's where the bad news comes in. She burned them."

Henderson's heart sank. "Burned them?" he repeated inanely.

"Yes. Put them in the fireplace and touched a match to them. She stood watching the little fire, and crying...a sort of grisly ceremonial, Scott. She waited until the last spark had gone out. Then she scattered the ashes around with her foot. It was a pretty thorough job, Scott."

"And then...?"

"She lay down on the bed."

Henderson began to click. His lips tightened. Barbara's voice said, "Scott...?"

"Hold on. I haven't cut off." He slammed his fist against the desk. "I'll talk fast, Barbara. I'm handing you another job. I don't know how you're going to do it...but it's got to be done. Where are you phoning from?"

"The McIntyres'."

"Okay. Go back home. Tell the servants you're taking Gail out for a little while. Tell them not to go near her room while you're out. Tell them I'll be there pretty soon and that I'll go to her room. They're not to say anything to anyone. Especially to Gail. Got that?"

"Yes. But Scott..."

"On your toes, kid. It's got to be this way."

He hung up and waited twenty minutes. Then he telephoned the Mathews home again. Leander answered.

"This is Mr. Henderson. Is Miss Barbara there?"

"Nossuh, Mistuh Scott. She done went out."

"Did Miss Gail go with her?"

"Yassuh. She sho' did, Mistuh Scott."

"Did she tell you I was coming over?"

"Well, yassuh. She tol' me an' Oleander."

141

"Right. I'm on the way. Don't let anyone go in Miss Gail's room before I get there."

He put down the telephone, picked it up again, got the dial tone, and fingered the number of police headquarters. He asked for Bernie Williams and got him. "Lucky guy, you," said Bernie. "I was on my way to Green Lake for a swim. Want to come along?"

"No. And you're not going, either."

"Something?"

"Something. Be at the corner in two minutes. I'm picking you up."

Bernie was waiting when Scott drove up. He climbed in beside him, and they started south toward The Ridge. Bernie said, "All right, feller...spill it."

Scott handed it to him in capsule form. Bernie whistled and said, "You had it and lost it."

"Maybe."

"What do you mean: Maybe?"

Scott said, "This town has spent a fortune on its police laboratory. If it's half as good as they said it is..."

"It's good, all right."

"If it is, I want to scrape up the ashes of those letters Gail burned. Isn't there some sort of a process by which they can restore 'em and then make photographs of what they get?"

Bernie shook his head. "That's a toughie, kid. Sure, there's such a process. They do a lot of technical stuff I don't understand, and then they photograph the results and blow 'em up...you know, like enlarging a picture. But I guess it depends on how thoroughly they were burned..." If you think you can restore the letters complete..."

"I want the best I can get. How long would the job take?"

"Can you give us forty-eight hours?"

"If I have to."

"I'll see you get action. But if I was you, I wouldn't point my hopes too high."

They reached the Mathews house and went upstairs. Bernie picked up the charred ashes carefully and put them in a little pasteboard box. He overflowed with pessimism. He said, "Science is a swell thing...but it ain't this swell."

Scott drove him downtown. He waited until one of the best technicians had been contacted. Then he started a wait that made all other waits look like rapid transit.

During the following day Bernie telephoned. He announced that they'd need another twenty-four hours. He said, "I ain't hopeful, Scott...I ain't hopeful."

Forty-six hours after the ashes had been taken downtown Bernie called on Scott. They locked the door of the private office and Bernie unwrapped a big, flat package. He said mournfully, "We drew a blank, kid."

He displayed fourteen pieces of glazed paper on each of which there were reproductions of handwriting. Snatches. Pieces of words. Nothing intelligible. Nothing that made any sense. Each piece had been blown up so that the letters looked as though they'd been written by a giant.

"It comes up zero," confessed Bernie, "She sure did a good job of burning the stuff. That's all we could get. Nothing fits."

Henderson slumped in his chair, staring at the disconnected bits of handwriting. His first reaction was of a disappointment more profound, more bitter, than any that had previously come to him.

He said, in a flat, hopeless voice, "Can you leave these with me?"

"Yeah. I wish they meant somethin', kid. Only they don't. Our nice lead turned out to be a dud. But there ain't no reason to get whipped down. We'll figure a new angle."

Scott was staring helplessly at the bits of enlarged handwriting.

He said, "I hope you're right, Bernie. But I'm beginning to think I'm running out of angles."

CHAPTER TWENTY-TWO

SCOTT HENDERSON tried to turn off his brain. It wasn't that he was opposed to thinking, as such, but rather that it didn't seem to get him anywhere.

He had smoked until his throat was raw. He had stood at his window staring into the night until he saw nothing. He was thinking of Gail Barrie and of Barbara Mathews. He was thinking of a frightened little man named Ollie Drucker. He was thinking of

Doris Colby and Fletcher Mathews and Tony Kinkaid, all of whom were dead. He was thinking of the connection between Gail and Drucker, and of her insistence on having her fortune converted into cash for reasons that she would not explain. He was remembering that Kinkaid and Fletcher Mathews had been killed with bullets from the same gun, and that it was the same type of gun that had been used to kill Doris. He was remembering—although it hurt—that the letters from Gail to her father had been destroyed so completely that, despite the best efforts of a modem police laboratory, only tiny bits of them could be restored.

He tried to blank everything out—to start over. He tried to concentrate on himself—and Gail. He knew she had been holding out on him and the police. He wondered why he was still in love with her, why he wanted to protect her. It was all wrong. But, right or wrong, that's the way it was.

He stretched out on the bed. He lay there with his eyes closed. Sleep did not come, but sheer exhaustion brought a certain relaxation.

It was four o'clock in the morning when he leaped out of bed, his brain blazing with an idea. He didn't know where it had come from, or why. He didn't care. He was trembling. Here was an idea. Here was a fresh angle.

He again tried the bed, and this time was more successful. He didn't know when he went to sleep, but whenever it was, he slept soundly. The alarm clock roused him at eight. He started the percolator going and stepped under a cool shower. He drank two cups of coffee and some orange juice. He shaved and smoked. He considered the idea that had come to him in the early morning, and it still looked good. He called Bernie Williams at headquarters. Bernie was waiting downstairs when he got there. They drove into the country where they could talk without fear of interruption.

Scott said, "I've got an idea, Bernie. It may be lousy, but I don't think so. I don't want to start the ball rolling until I found out whether you'd help. And even then I'm not going to tell you everything."

"Why?"

"Personal reasons. And because it may not work."

"Let's have it."

"First, let me ask you a question. Do you still think Drucker is the panicky type?"

"I still think so. He's been in the can a long time now. Nothing to do but think. He doesn't know how much we know. One little push in the right direction, and he'd crack wide open."

"Good…" Henderson gave Bernie a cigarette, took one himself, and held the match for both of them. He said, "There's big doings at the Country Club Monday night. That Community Chest shindig. Everybody and his uncle will be there if the weather's good. I think Ollie Drucker might find it interesting."

"How interesting?"

"That depends. Suppose you picked out a nice, quiet-looking detective friend of yours…plainclothes, of course…and had him escort Ollie to the carnival Monday night. Not a word of explanation. Just take him there and stick close enough to see what goes on. You'd be there, too, but not near enough for anybody to connect you with Ollie. Now suppose you were Ollie, and that happened, what would you be thinking?"

"I'd be nervous as a cat," stated Bernie without hesitation. "I'd know somethin' was cookin', but I wouldn't be able to figure what."

"And if anything *did* happen, it would hit you pretty hard, wouldn't it?"

"Brother, you said it…"

"Will you do it? Blind?"

Bernie hesitated. "Have you really got something, Scott?"

"I don't know. I won't know until Monday night."

"You insist on playing it your way?"

Scott was apologetic. "It isn't that, Bernie. If things come out like I hope, I'd rather you were in the dark. Then nothing you can do will give Ollie any hint as to what's stewing."

"I always pegged you for smart," stated Bernie. "I still think that way. So maybe this will make more sense later than it does now."

"Good. No word to Drucker in advance, then. Monday evening get him shaved and washed up. Be sure he doesn't know where he's headed until he gets there. See that he watches the floor show. I checked with Paul Innes. He tells me the show will start promptly at 10:00 in the ballroom. You might get Drucker to the Club about 9:30."

"What else?"

"Nothing." Scott pressed the starter and drove his friend back to police headquarters. Bernie got out with a wave of his hand. He'd checked in with Scott's play and that was that. He wasn't arguing.

Henderson went to a telephone. He called Fern Meredith. She answered in a heavy voice, as though she'd been aroused from a sound sleep. Sure, she said, Scott could come right over. Just give her fifteen minutes.

She accomplished a lot in fifteen minutes. The sleep had vanished from her violet eyes. She had fixed her yellow hair attractively. She was wearing a gay housecoat over what was most obviously a sheer nightgown.

Scott didn't waste time. He said, "You're still keen on finding out who killed Tony Kinkaid, aren't you, Fern?"

She nodded emphatically.

"You're singing at the Country Club Monday night?"

"Yes... What's that got to do with it?"

"Plenty." Scott hitched his chair closer and started talking. He talked steadily for perhaps twenty minutes. At first, she looked more than a trifle bewildered; then, as the idea commenced to seep in, she started nodding and her eyes took on a new luster. He said, "I'm playing a wild hunch. Shooting the works on a single roll of the dice. It may not work. Are you willing to help?"

"You know damn well I am."

"Good." He smiled. "It'll take a bit of acting."

"What that takes, I got. It's hammy, and that fits me." She regarded him levelly. "You're sticking your neck out," she said.

"How?"

"Gail Barrie."

He nodded. "I'm taking that chance, too."

At the door she said, "You're quite a guy, Mister Henderson."

He shook his head and said, "We'll know more Monday night."

"Thirty hours," she commented. "That's a long time to wait."

That afternoon—Saturday—Henderson got in touch with Barbara Mathews. She met him at the Country Club. Apparently it was a casual meeting. They took an outside table near the swimming pool and ordered drinks.

"I have a new job for you, Barbara," he said. "It may turn out to be the most important job you've ever had. You've got to sell Gail the idea of attending the Community Chest party here Monday night."

She shook her head. "That'll take a lot of doing, Scott."

"It's got to be arranged. Make any approach you want: Charity...anything."

"She's not exactly in the mood for a fiesta."

"Neither are you. Maybe that's an idea. Put it up to her that you think you should go. Civic duty and all that sort of thing. Make it plain that you want to, but that you won't unless she does. Insist on it."

"All right. I'll insist. Now may I confess that you've got me curious."

"I don't doubt it. But I can't explain. The important thing is to get Gail to the Club. Secondly, leave her alone as much as possible. Third, don't keep too close an eye on her. Is that clear?"

"Clear as mud. Whatever you've got up your sleeve, I'm pulling for it."

"Good kid." He sipped at his drink. "One more thing: Don't mention me in connection with this. It's all your idea. They've been urging you to attend. You won't go alone. Make it strong. I'll drift over to supper tomorrow night. I'll spend the evening. You can tip me off whether it's all set. If not, I'll try my hand. But if you've managed to work it, I'd prefer to keep out."

She said, "You make it sound interesting."

"When it's over," he said, "I may look like a complete sap. And no wise cracks out of you on that, either."

He got to the Mathews house at six-thirty Sunday afternoon. Barbara had evidently been watching for him because she met him on the veranda. "All set," she whispered. "I had to do a heap of arguing, but she gave in finally."

"No slip-up?"

"Listen, dope, I've done the hard part. I promise you nothing will slip now."

One of Barbara's numerous boyfriends dropped in a few minutes later. Barbara and Gail served a cold supper. It was pleasant, without being gay. After they had cleared off and rinsed and stacked the dishes, Barbara and the young man disappeared. Scott dragged two chairs around the corner of the veranda. It was pleasantly dark. Moonlight filtered through wisteria vines and etched a golden pattern on the tiles. He shoved the chairs close together and seated himself beside Gail.

He was trying to forget all the yesterdays and the tomorrow that were so close at hand. He smoked silently, then flipped his cigarette onto the lawn.

He took Gail's hand. He said, "I don't mean this to sound silly, but I want you to do something."

"Yes, Scott..."

"Let's pretend that there's no trouble in the world; that there never has been any."

Her fingers tightened over his. She said simply, "I'd like that."

He sat on the arm of her chair. He bent over, and she turned her face up to his. Their lips met.

It was easier than either of them would have believed possible. It was good not to think. It was good to hold Gail in his arms without wondering and fearing.

Through all of it, one thought kept pounding. She loved him. There was more than passion in her kisses. There was an infinite tenderness in the way her fingers caressed him.

It didn't check, he told himself. None of it checked. But he shoved those thoughts into the back of his brain and kept them there. For a few hours they could be young and in love; they could pretend that the future was bright. They made the most of their moment. They made it to be unforgettably lovely...

Shortly before midnight, he rose and held her tight against him.

He said, "Goodnight, sweetheart."

She leaned back in his arms and looked long into his eyes. She said, "Goodbye, darling."

He turned then, and was gone. He drove home. It was not until he was in his apartment that her words came back to him.

"Goodbye, darling," she had said. "Goodbye..."

CHAPTER TWENTY-THREE

WHEN SCOTT HENDERSON reached the Country Club Monday night with Gail and Barbara, the fiesta was in full swing.

The chairman of the Community Chest, with the assistance of Paul Innes, had done himself proud. The huge, sprawling, graystone clubhouse was ablaze with light. The lawn was studded with little booths, each of which was presided over by a young lady of considerable pulchritude.

The public had been invited. The party wasn't limited to members of the Club, which was smart, because those who hadn't ever before been within the socially sacred precincts flocked out by auto and bus to see what it was all about. There was an admission charge of a dollar; the price tags on everything—soft drinks, refreshments, souvenirs—were more than adequate. The articles that were for sale had all been contributed; the entire proceeds were earmarked for the Chest.

Four local bands had volunteered their services, and in the big ballroom, as well as on the broad veranda near the swimming pool, dancing had been continuously in progress since eight o'clock.

For this night all social barriers were down. The public was in a mood to make merry in a large way. The rigors of wartime restrictions were forgotten; the future looked bright and prosperous. Even those who were working hardest looked like celebrants.

Scott was making a valiant effort to be gay, but the life-of-the-party role he had assumed was difficult. True, Barbara was helping, but it was still hard sledding.

Even yet he didn't know how Barbara had won her fight with Gail. He knew it had been difficult; he knew that she had been discouraged until almost the last minute. And then Gail had given in only because Barbara's pressure was relentless. So here she was, slightly dazed at finding herself in this gala atmosphere, knowing she would be talked about, and determined to take it in stride. Scott squeezed Gail's arm as they walked into the clubhouse. He said, "Atta gal! This is just what the doctor ordered."

She gave him a quick, forced smile. He knew she didn't entirely agree with him. He knew that she'd come only because Barbara had made it a personal issue. But that was unimportant. The important thing was that Gail Barrie was here...and that things were about to happen.

Scott was apprehensive. He was about to make his pitch, test his theory, shoot the works. No chance to alter his plan. For better or for worse, the chips were down.

In the lobby they encountered a full-bosomed, big-voiced matron who was explaining to Paul Innes how much more efficiently things could have been handled if she had been put in complete charge. Innes, his tall body stooped under the strain, his habitually grave countenance more solemn than ever, was gazing wildly about for a chance to get away from his tormentor. He saw Scott and the girls, and practically leaped at them. He shook hands all around, sternly informed the pursuing matron that he was too busy to talk to her anymore, and suggested—with the tact that had come to him as manager of the club—that she'd better take a look around to make sure everything was operating smoothly.

She sailed majestically away, not entirely sure whether she had been complimented or given the brush-off. Paul waited until she was out of earshot and then proceeded to express his opinion of her and her ancestry. Barbara broke into a laugh, and patted him consolingly on the arm. She advised him to forget his troubles and to remember only that he had performed miracles in a worthy cause. Innes looked over her head at Scott and shrugged. "Every time I think I've gotten completely case-hardened," he said, "something like this pops up."

Two harassed and bewildered committee members swooped down on him and dragged him off. Three young men spotted Barbara and descended on her in a cloud. Scott and Gail made an appropriate effort, and the little group began to give the appearance of enjoying itself.

A few minutes later some of the younger crowd captured Gail. She wasn't particularly enthused over being towed away, but there was nothing she could do about it. They were kids, and they meant well—which left her helpless. They were delighted to see her; they knew what she'd been through; they appreciated her presence at the Club...and they wanted her to understand that she was one of them.

Scott walked off by himself. He circulated through the grounds. Things were progressing beautifully. This was the sort of party he could have enjoyed had his brain not been in such a turmoil. Everybody seemed to be in the groove. He stopped to watch a few jitterbugging couples on the veranda. They were going through wild gyrations while the orchestra beat it out solidly.

Shortly before nine-thirty he saw his friend, Bernie Williams. Bernie caught Scott's eye and winked. He glanced toward the right, and Scott followed the direction of his gaze.

He saw Ollie Drucker. Mr. Drucker's bald spot was shining. His rather shabby suit had been freshly pressed. He was wearing a gray shirt and a new necktie. It was readily apparent that Ollie was aware that something was happening to him and also that he was trying—without success—to figure what it was.

A casual observer might have thought Ollie was alone. But Scott knew better. There was a short, stocky man with keen eyes, curly hair and an efficient manner, who kept within three steps of Drucker at all times. It wasn't noticeable, but two looks at Ollie and you couldn't doubt that he was only too keenly aware of his police escort.

Scott studied Ollie from a distance. He didn't know what Ollie was thinking, but he knew what he'd be thinking under similar circumstances. To be kept incommunicado in the city jail for more than a week, to be dolled up prettily without explanation, to be taken by a cop to a Community Chest party at the Country Club...

Ollie Drucker couldn't fail to understand that this was a trap of some sort. He was noticeably on guard. Yet his face was expressionless, except that there was fear in his eyes.

Yes, Ollie was nervous. And that was one of the prime factors in Scott Henderson's plan.

The show in the ballroom was scheduled for ten o'clock. A loudspeaker blared that information and stated that this one was strictly for free. People started moving in from the grounds, away from the booths. The plainclothesman who was chaperoning Drucker moved up a couple of steps and whispered something. His words didn't appear to fill Ollie with glee. For a second it seemed that he was going to balk—but then he thought better of it, and started slowly toward the ballroom. He looked like a forlorn little man who didn't belong and wasn't having any part of a good time.

The ballroom was already bulging. The arrangement was that of a big nightclub, with chairs lined up on all four sides of the polished floor. The bandstand was at one end, and the musicians were throwing away their cigarettes and picking up their instruments to play the show.

Ollie came in with his one-man convoy. He was trying valiantly to look impassive, and all he succeeded in doing was to appear abysmally unhappy.

And as he came through the door, something happened. It was something that Scott saw only because he was watching Gail Barrie even more closely than he was watching Ollie.

Gail's group surged into the ballroom. Gail was right in the middle. She got inside the door. She saw Ollie Drucker.

Her eyes met the blank stare of Mr. Drucker. His expression didn't change, but hers did. Scott saw the color leave her cheeks, saw that little unconscious gesture of her hand being pressed against her lips. He saw in Gail's eyes a look of bewilderment, and—he felt—of fear.

Gail's friends grabbed her arm and hustled her toward a vantage spot by the wall. The trumpet gave out with a shrill, unmusical blast, and the crowd fell silent. The master of ceremonies made a little speech and introduced the first act, an exceedingly juvenile brother and sister dance team. They were local talent, and definitely amateur, but the crowd was in a holiday mood and anything looked good.

Ollie was standing rigidly, his watchdog within a couple of feet of him. A few yards away the big figure of Bernie Williams was visible. A slim, middle-aged man with cold, gray eyes spoke to Bernie and moved a little closer to where Ollie Drucker was standing. Henderson spotted him as another cop. He liked that. It meant that Ollie was fenced in, but good.

The second act wasn't exciting. It consisted of a buxom local lady who gave out with a loud soprano. The applause was merely polite, but it was all the needling she required. She was off again. She finished on a high, triumphant note and waddled off convinced that she had been a riot.

The third act was also juvenile and also amateur, but it was good. The three daughters of the physical director of the Cherokee Athletic Club danced out in tights and went through an excellent routine of gymnastics and tumbling. And it was during this act that Gail Barrie detached herself from her friends and moved toward the door leading to the lobby.

Scott shifted his position so that he could watch her. She looked frightened and worried. She made her exit unobtrusively. Scott was cautious. He didn't want her to know that she was being watched. He didn't dare to follow her into the lobby. He was relieved when, after the little gymnasts had finished and a blackface comedian (local amateur radio talent) had taken over the spotlight, Gail came back into the room. He saw her look at Ollie Drucker as though still refusing to credit the evidence of her senses.

She obviously was scared. And that put her all even with Scott Henderson, because he was frightened, too.

Gail was coming through the crowd. But she wasn't moving in the direction of the people she had been with. It didn't take Scott more than a moment to realize that she was headed toward Ollie.

He caught Bernie Williams' eye. A glance of understanding, a warning, passed between them. Gail was getting closer. Her eyes were big and bright, her manner tense.

Scott saw Ollie look up. He saw the glance that passed between the little man and Gail Barrie. He saw panic in Ollie's eyes.

Ollie looked around. The detective who had brought him was standing close. Too close. The officer didn't appear to be watching Ollie...but that didn't fool the frightened little man.

He stood rigidly. Gail came closer and closer and closer. She was standing right next to Ollie now. She pretended not to notice him. She was looking toward the floor where the performers were trying to entertain the crowd.

Gail backed up against Ollie. Scott saw her shove a note into Ollie's hand.

Then she moved away toward the group she'd been with. Scott could no longer see her face. But she could see Ollie's expression.

Drucker looked like a man into whose hands a hot coal has been put. He glanced around furtively. Scott knew what he was thinking. He dared not drop the note. And he dared not keep it. But the latter alternative was less dangerous than the first.

Scott saw him shove the note into his coat pocket. He knew that Drucker was hoping the little byplay hadn't been noticed.

Scott edged backward into the crowd. Bernie Williams was moving toward him. They finally stood shoulder to shoulder.

Bernie said, "You see that?"

"Yes."

"She slipped Drucker a note."

"Yes..."

There was concern in Bernie's voice. He said, "Looks bad, kid."

"I know..."

"Do we go through with it?"

Scott felt miserable. But his voice was steady.

"Yes," he said, "we go through with it."

The show went on. The next act was a professional who was currently on the bill at the Cherokee, the city's foremost movie palace, which played unit shows along with its cinematic entertainment. After him came a ballroom dance team from the same bill. Then a first-rate male comedian who stopped the show.

And then half the lights in the room went out. The immediate effect was to quiet the crowd, to give that air of hushed expectancy that portends something really worthwhile.

The M. C. walked out to the microphone. He announced that he wanted to introduce a girl who had been long in Cherokee and had become a great favorite. He gestured toward the darkness.

"Fern Meredith," he said.

The spotlight beamed to a place at the right of the bandstand. The last murmurs of the crowd were stilled. The orchestra played softly, so that the music furnished an unobtrusive background to a big moment.

And then Fern appeared in the circle of light. There was a spontaneous, audible in-drawing of breath.

She looked like all the sex and seductiveness of the world capsuled into one body. She was wearing a gown of black, shiny material. It was cut low in front, and it had no back at all. The creamy skin of her shoulders and throat rose from the unadorned black line. Her hair looked more gold than gold. She carried a black chiffon handkerchief. She wore no jewelry.

She moved into the spotlight. It was the slow, sinuous walk of the trained showgirl, but it didn't look like that. She didn't raise her eyes. She glided to the microphone. The music swelled. The breathless silence of the crowd was the most sincere tribute it could pay.

And then she sang. Her voice was low and husky. It wasn't a good voice, technically, but it was blue. It was as blue as all the depths of the bluest ocean. It was as blue as all the grief and sadness of the world. She sang intensely, making no gestures. There was no movement at all except the almost imperceptible swaying of the gorgeous body.

Scott had heard her sing at Valley View. But this was different. It took his breath away. At the Lodge she had been a torcher—hot and suggestive. Here it seemed as though the song was being torn from inside of her.

The crowd was under a spell. They knew this woman's story. They knew the gossip. They knew—at least they had heard, and now they believed—that she had been in love with the man who had married Gail Barrie and who had been murdered on his wedding night.

The obvious words of the lyrics she was singing did not now seem tawdry. It was a wail, a chant…a plea for the happiness that could never be.

She finished her first number. There were women in the ballroom who were crying. The very absence of conventional handclapping was tremendous in its impact.

And then the orchestra, itself under the spell, swung into the classic of all blue numbers. They played the opening measures of "My Man."

Fern Meredith had made this magic, and she was now caught up in it. Her voice took on a deeper, more intimate, nuance. It was as though she was parading her grief, naked and unashamed, for everybody to see.

She sang slowly. You couldn't hear the orchestra. It was there and it was playing…but it was background, it was color, it was part of that husky voice that brought heartache into the open. She sang with terrible, devastating sincerity:

> Oh, my man, I love him so—he'll never know
> How my life is just despair…

The voice broke. The sobbing of a woman came from somewhere in the crowd. The orchestra stopped playing. The musicians looked at Fern…waiting…

She swayed. She was fighting an emotion that she was not strong enough to fight. This was real now. It was real and terrible.

Then, suddenly, her head went back.

"I can't go on..." Her voice broke. "I can't..."

There was an instant of awful expectancy.

"I can't do it!" she cried. "I can't do it...knowing that I'll never see my man again, knowing he's been murdered..." The voice was clearer. It carried to the farthest corner of the crowded room, carried deep into the consciousness of every horrified spectator.

"I'll tell you why I can't do it," she said. "It's because the person who murdered my man is in this room... He's there!"

She raised her arm. She pointed at a little bald-headed terrified man.

She pointed at Ollie Drucker.

CHAPTER TWENTY-FOUR

UNEXPECTED THINGS HAPPEN in moments of stark drama. This time it was a kid from a downtown theater who did it. With the uncanny precision of an electrician in a popular night club, the lad swung his spot light on Ollie Ducker.

An instant before, you couldn't have picked him out—not unless you knew him and had been watching him. Now his fear stood forth nakedly. His semi-bald head gleamed under the blinding glare of the spot, his thin lips twitched, his sharp little eyes were filled with fear.

Bernie Williams stepped closer. The cop who had been nearest moved in until Ollie's shoulder touched the other's arm. Another policeman—the slim one—came up on the other flank. It was done neatly, unostentatiously, efficiently. Scott Henderson watched the byplay and felt a sense of admiration. He wanted to say "Nice work." They had Ollie hemmed in tight, and that was good, because Ollie's natural aptitude for panic seemed to be on the upswing.

They had brought him here, and hadn't told him anything. He had known—he must have known—that it was a trap. But things had moved so placidly that the topper had caught him completely by surprise. Never had the cornered rat cliché seemed less like a cliché.

Scott could almost see him making up his mind to take a desperate chance. The crowd was beginning to murmur. Fern Meredith had handed them their emotions on a platter. Some of the male guests were closing in. The murmur had an angry undertone. It was threatening, and not at all reasonable. It broke what was left of Ollie's courage.

He made a break for it. He dived toward the door. But he didn't get anywhere. The quiet cop alongside him saw to that. Bernie came up with astonishing speed. They were holding Ollie by both arms and Bernie was ordering the crowd to stand back.

The music had wailed off into nothingness. In the huge ballroom there was anger and a premonition of hysteria. Bernie said, "Take it easy, folks. We're police." That helped. The immediate threat of mob violence was gone, but Ollie didn't look any happier.

The crowd surged in and formed a ring around Ollie. A crowd always forms a ring when something terrible is happening: when two men are pounding each other with their bare fists, when someone has been run over by an automobile, when any human being has been overhauled by fate and is suffering.

Bernie Williams dipped his hand into the side pocket of Ollie's coat and came up with a bit of folded paper. It was the note that Gail Barrie had slipped into Mr. Drucker's reluctant hand not too long ago. Bernie stared at it. His expression was one of utter disgust. He said, "What the hell," and handed it to Henderson.

Scott didn't look any too enlightened, either. He frowned at the words that had been scrawled in pencil on a bit of notepaper:

No podemos hablar aqui. Vete enseguida y llamame por telefono en cuanto puedas.

Bernie said, "What is it?"

"Spanish, I believe," answered Scott.

"You savvy it?"

Scott shook his head. Bernie raised his voice and asked whether anyone in the room understood Spanish. A young man with an old face, pale eyes and sparse, colorless hair edged forward apologetically. "I'm Arthur McNab," he stated. "I teach Spanish at Southside High."

Bernie shoved the note at him. "What's it add up to, Professor?"

The little teacher was having his moment of greatness. The crowd was staring at him expectantly. He was embarrassed, but you could see that he thought it was wonderful, too. The *"podemos"* stumped him for a moment and so did the *"cuanto puedas,"* but they didn't stump him for as long as he waited. He could translate the note for them, but then he'd drop into the background where he'd spent all of his thirty-three years.

"What's it mean?" inquired Bernie with some impatience.

McNab cleared his throat. He was back in the classroom again, his voice even and precise. He said, "I'll have to give a rather literal translation," he started, but Bernie cut in. He said, "Okay—let's have it, Professor—any kind of way."

McNab translated:

"We cannot talk here. Leave right away and call me on the telephone as soon as you can."

Bernie looked disappointed. "That's all it says?"

"That's all."

"Thanks…"

Bernie looked at the spot where Scott Henderson had been standing. But Scott wasn't standing there now.

Young Mr. Henderson was shoving through the crowd in the direction of the spacious lobby. And he wasn't being too polite about it. It was apparent to Bernie that wherever Scott was headed, he meant to get there in a hurry. Bernie said something to the two other detectives and started after his friend. The crowd was dense, and his progress slow.

He was only halfway through the jam of humanity when he saw Henderson race across the lobby and smash into a door that was in the process of closing. The door banged open, and when it finally closed Scott was on the other side. Bernie shoved forward and eventually reached the lobby. On his side of the door through which Scott had gone was a single word, neatly inscribed in chaste gold lettering. The word was "Manager."

On the far side of the door two men faced each other: Scott Henderson and Paul Innes. Innes looked taller and more gaunt than usual. He was standing behind his desk. He was holding a revolver. He said, "That'll be all. Scott."

Henderson stayed where he was. Innes didn't have to spell it out for him.

Scott said, "Put it down, Paul."

"In a minute. Meanwhile, stay right there."

Innes backed toward the window. Below the window was the parking lot. He relaxed for just an instant and Henderson made his play.

He'd been a good broken-field runner once. He hoped he hadn't forgotten his swivel-hipped technique. He twisted as he sprang forward. The crack of the gun was vicious. But Paul Innes had missed.

Scott hit him hard. His shoulder caught Innes just above the waist as the Country Club manager fired again and missed again. Scott's arms went around the tall, sinewy figure. They crashed to the floor and started rolling over, flailing at each other.

Henderson found the going tough. He was heavier than Paul Innes and stronger, but the other man fought with a desperate fury that multiplied his strength. He gouged and butted and tried bringing his knee up into the groin. Scott felt a stab of pain and relaxed his grip for an instant. Innes tore loose and made another leap for the window, but Henderson grabbed one foot and hauled him back, and once again they were threshing around on the floor.

It was a brief battle and not a pretty one. A world of action was compressed into an unbelievably short space of time. Scott swung wildly but hard. He brought his head up sharply. It smashed against Innes' jaw. He felt the lean body relax.

The office door opened and Bernie Williams barged in. He was across the room in three steps. He wrapped his big, powerful hands in the neckband of Paul Innes's shirt and dragged the man to his feet.

The crowd had followed. The two other policemen came into the room, dragging Ollie Drucker. Fern Meredith appeared, and they let her through. Scott spoke with difficulty; his lips were torn, the inside of his mouth was bleeding. He said, "Where is Gail?"

The crowd milled around. A few seconds later a path was cleared and Gail Barrie came in. Barbara Mathews was with her. Behind them was the ubiquitous Bill Daggett of the *News-Herald*. He was more than a trifle drunk, but, as usual, he was on the ball. He said, "What goes on here?" and Bernie told him to get out.

Daggett protested. His protests didn't get him anywhere. Bernie pushed him outside, shoved the crowd back, slammed and locked the door. Daggett lurched to a telephone booth and started dialing his office. No matter what was going on in Paul Innes's office, he already had a wow of a story. He'd give what he had and tell 'em to hold it open. More coming. Lots more.

Inside the room, Bernie Williams stared at the faces of the others. It was a study in contrast, but one thing was unmistakable: there was fear in that room, a new sort of fear.

Bernie said, "All right. Let's have it."

He looked at Scott Henderson. It was the look of a policeman, not that of a friend.

Scott dabbed at his bleeding lips. He said, "It worked, Bernie."

"Give out some more, kid."

"We've got the person who murdered Doris Colby and Fletcher Mathews and Tony Kinkaid."

"All right," said Bernie, "who is it?" Scott Henderson pointed.

"Paul Innes," he said.

There was a low, wailing cry from Fern Meredith. She started forward, but one of the detectives grabbed her arm. He said, "Take it easy, Sister; take it easy."

Bernie was trying to drink it in. He said, incredulously "Paul Innes?"

"Yes."

Innes said hoarsely, "That's a lie..."

Scott didn't bother to argue with him. His manner held nothing of triumph.

Bernie said, "You're sure of that, kid?"

"I'm sure."

Bernie was staring at his friend. He had a feeling that this wasn't all, that there was more coming. He started to ask a question, hesitated, then blurted it out.

He said, "What about Gail Barrie?"

Scott Henderson looked across the room at the face of the girl he loved. He said, "This isn't easy, Bernie—but I've got to do it."

There was an instant of silence. It seemed an eternity. Then Scott Henderson spoke again.

"That girl," he said, pointing across the room, "is not Gail Barrie. She's an impostor."

CHAPTER TWENTY-FIVE

THERE WAS NO MUSIC, no spotlights, no husky voice moaning the blues...but the impact of Scott Henderson's accusation was even greater than that of the one Fern Meredith had made only a little while before.

The group in Paul Innes's office was shocked into silence. Nobody said anything because, in that first incredible moment, there seemed nothing to say.

The first person to move was Barbara Mathews. She faced the girl who was known as Gail Barrie, took her hand and said over her shoulder, "I don't believe you, Scott."

Henderson was miserable. He was staring at the girl he had just accused. She seemed stunned, and yet there was a certain dignity about her. Bernie Williams looked at her and then at Scott. He said, "Well, I'll be damned," and let it go at that.

Another voice broke in. It was the voice of Paul Innes and it trembled with outrage. He said, "The man is crazy."

"I'm not crazy, Paul." Henderson was sure of himself now. "I haven't said anything I can't prove."

Innes's gaze moved about the room. He encountered hostility, but he saw also that there was considerable disbelief. His tone changed. He spoke in a quiet, reasonable voice. He said, "You had the right man the first time, Scott. Ollie Drucker committed those murders."

Drucker tore loose from the policeman who was holding him. He shook his fist at Paul Innes.

"Liar!" he shouted. "You're a lousy liar! You know I never killed nobody."

"You didn't?" Innes had regained his poise, "Suppose you tell them what happened to the real Gail Barrie." He smiled coldly at

Scott. "There's your answer to the whole thing," he said, "Ollie Drucker killed Gail Barrie. He kidnapped her in Cuba, and then murdered her when she tried to escape. Ask him."

Drucker started to say something. But no one heard him because the girl who was known as Gail Barrie moved swiftly to the center of the room and confronted Innes. "Is Gail dead?" she asked.

Innes nodded. "Yes. Drucker shot her. That's why he left Cuba. That's why he came to Cherokee. That's why he killed Doris and Fletcher Mathews and Kinkaid...because he was afraid it would catch up with him."

Everybody started to talk at once, but the girl silenced them. She said, "Let me talk to him," and there was something in her manner that compelled obedience.

She faced the frightened Drucker. She asked, "Where is Gail?"

He shook his head and made weak, futile gestures. He said, "I don't know. Honest, I don't. She got away."

Paul Innes broke in. "Can't you see he's lying?"

The girl stared at Ollie. Then she faced Scott Henderson.

"I believe Paul Innes," she said. "I should have known something like this had happened. I should have known it the minute Drucker showed up in Cherokee." She was talking calmly. "Things have turned out miserably," she said. "But because I believe that Gail is dead, I can talk." She hesitated briefly and then went on. "Up to this minute my hands were tied. I was trying to protect Gail."

Innes said, "Keep your mouth shut! This is no time to talk! Think what you're doing."

"There's nothing to think about any more, Paul. They may as well know the entire truth."

She addressed herself to Bernie Williams. "I don't know where Gail is. But if she's dead—or if she can't be found—then I believe that Drucker killed her. I know that Paul Innes killed Doris. I saw it happen. I'm sure he killed Mr. Mathews and Tony Kinkaid...although I can't prove either of those charges."

"One murder charge is enough," said Bernie. "If you can make it stick. But suppose you give us the rest of it."

She spoke slowly. Her voice was flat and dead and hopeless.

She said, "My name is Margaret Allen. I've been like a sister to Gail since we were children. I was raised in her home. Mr. Barrie wanted to adopt me after my parents died. There wasn't anything I wouldn't have done for Gail. There wasn't anything I didn't try to do."

There was a terrible simplicity, a terrible honesty, in her words.

"When Mr. Barrie received his army commission, Gail and I decided to stay on in Miramonte. That had always been her home. It had been my home for a long time.

"In January, 1944," she continued, "right after Mr. Barrie had been sent to the Far East, Paul Innes visited us in Miramonte. I suppose that's easy enough to check.

The State Department is certain to have the passport records. We were glad to see him. Neither of us had liked him much when he was living there, but at least he was someone we knew.

"He was very solicitous. He said if we insisted on remaining in Miramonte we should have a protector. He seemed to think that two girls living alone in a little Cuban town needed some sort of a bodyguard. He went to Havana and returned with Ollie Drucker. He said he'd known Drucker for years, and that he was trustworthy. We weren't in any mood to argue…especially about something that seemed logical and friendly. Ollie went to work for us. Among other things, he was our chauffeur.

"Near the end of May—this year—Gail got a telegram from the War Department saying that her father had been killed in action…" She choked, but managed to keep going. "Gail cabled Mr. Mathews that she was leaving for Cherokee immediately. I was to come with her. We closed the house, closed our little school, told everybody goodbye. You can see what that would mean: that no one in Miramonte would miss us. We were to stay in Havana until we got our passports through the American Embassy. Except that we never got to Havana.

"The distance from Miramonte to Havana is about 175 miles. The town itself is about thirty miles south of the main highway. That thirty miles is in pretty poor condition. Even on the highway, it isn't advisable to make speed. The road is all right, but narrow. We paid no attention to what Ollie was doing. We had too many other things to talk about.

"Shortly after dark, we had trouble with the car. Ollie didn't seem to be able to fix it. He said he knew a place off the road where it could be done. He drove us to a *finca*—a little farm. I don't yet know its exact location except that it is in Matanzas Province. The country around there is wild and sparsely settled. The farm was owned by a man named Pancho Mendoza. He lived there with his wife, Carmita.

"A little while after we got to the farmhouse, Ollie walked into the room where Gail and I were washing up. He had a gun. He told us what was happening. He said if we didn't play things his way, we'd both be killed. He explained that he had Pancho Mendoza under his thumb. He said the Havana police had been looking for Mendoza for a long time. Mendoza later admitted this. He seemed to be afraid of what he was being compelled to do, but even more afraid that Ollie would turn him over to the Cuban police. Anyway, Ollie made it plain that this wasn't any sudden idea. He told us that the entire scheme had been planned by Paul Innes during his last visit…that it was the real reason why Paul had come to see us in Miramonte."

"Wait a minute…" Innes's voice was harsh. "Don't you see what's happening? She believes she's telling the truth. But she's only telling you what Ollie Drucker told her."

The girl's eyes flicked him contemptuously. "I'll get to that in a moment," she said. "Mr. Innes seems to forget that I saw him kill Doris."

Innes tried to say something else, but the policeman next to him grabbed his arm, "Pipe down, you," he growled. "Leave the lady talk."

"Ollie explained the scheme," she went on. "He said that Paul Innes had told him that if anything ever happened to Major Barrie, Gail would be his sole heir. Barrie had been sent to the Far East with a combat engineering outfit. Innes figured from the first that there was always a strong chance he wouldn't come back. If he survived…nothing would ever be known about what had been planned. If he didn't…Ollie was under orders to act fast.

"I was to proceed to Havana. Alone. I was told to get a passport under my own name. Ollie and Pancho were to stay at the *finca*, guarding Gail. Ollie told me—and I believed him—that if

I talked, if I betrayed them—even by accident—Gail would be killed. And that's what I had on my mind from the first. That's why I wouldn't trust anybody. If it had been only myself, it wouldn't have mattered. But I had Gail's life in my hands. I know that sounds melodramatic. The truth often does.

"The plan was simple enough. Nobody in Cherokee knew me. Nobody knew Gail. Nobody except Paul Innes. The very fact that he vouched for me would keep anybody from suspecting that I wasn't Gail. And he did exactly that. If he hadn't been in on this, he would have told someone that I was Margaret Allen.

"I was to insist that Major Barrie's estate be converted into cash. As soon as it came into my possession, I was to start turning it over to Paul Innes. He and Drucker were playing for a million dollars. I know that murders have been committed with a lot less incentive than that. Anyway, the agreement was that when Innes had the money, he and Drucker would drop out of the picture; Pancho Mendoza and his wife would be paid off, and Gail would be free.

"Gail and I talked it over. There was only one decision possible. We believed that Ollie would kill Gail if she refused. The money didn't seem very important. Gail begged me to do what they wanted. She insisted. If she were alive, she'd verify that. I hated everything about it. But I agreed to do what she wanted. I agreed because otherwise I felt certain that she'd be killed."

Margaret Allen paused. Someone brought her a glass of water. She looked as though she might go to pieces. Then she controlled herself and continued.

"I'd never been to Cherokee, but I knew as much about it as Gail did. I knew as much about her as she did. And Paul Innes knew just about that much, because he'd made it his business to find out. He even knew about Doris Treadway."

Bernie Williams said, "That's the one I never could peg. About where she fitted in."

"When Gail was three years old, she lived next door to Doris. Doris was six at that time. She was a combination of big sister and nurse. One day Doris was riding Gail in a little wagon. She thought it would be fun to coast down the hill in front of the house. But Gail got frightened and didn't steer very well. The wagon crashed into a fireplug. Gail got a nasty cut on her head, just above the hairline. Doris became hysterical. There was a lot of blood. A doctor was called, and some stitches were taken. Gail came out of it with a permanent scar.

"That wouldn't mean anything to anybody else. But it had made an impression on Doris that would probably never be forgotten. It was a certainty that if they ever met again, Doris would inquire about it. After all, it was about all they had in common. It was the one topic of conversation that was inevitable. Paul Innes knew everything I'm telling you. He had even told it to Drucker in explaining how safe his scheme was. He told Drucker that there wasn't a soul in Cherokee who could possibly remember Gail...except Doris, and she wasn't even living there anymore. Doris had married and was living in Los Angeles.

"Then, on the evening of the day that Doris was killed, I heard that she was in town. Paul Innes heard it, too. I didn't think about him then. But I wanted to see Doris. I wanted to tell her the truth, to explain what was happening. I knew we'd have to meet and that it wouldn't take her long to find out that I didn't have any scar and therefore that I wasn't Gail. Unless I warned her in advance, she'd be certain to tell someone. The story would get out. Innes's only protection would be to notify Drucker, which meant that Ollie would kill Gail. Nobody would know she had been killed. And that was what I was afraid of. That was why I had to see Doris immediately.

"Scott Henderson drove me to her house. We took too long. Paul Innes knew where I was going. He must have suspected why. I saw him shoot Doris. I ran out the back door after him. I was horrified. He grabbed my arm and held it while he threatened me." She looked at Henderson. "That's where I got the bruise, Scott."

He smiled at her. It wasn't a very bright smile because he was all torn up inside, but he hoped it would encourage her.

"I knew that I was talking to a murderer. Instead of making me feel that I should tell the police, it made me more afraid to tell them. Having seen a murder committed, I didn't need any further proof that Gail's life was in danger. Paul argued that Doris was dead. There wasn't anything I could do to bring her back. All I could accomplish was to cause Gail's death. And he threatened me with something else…" She bit her lip, and then hurried on, as though afraid she might not be able to finish. "Paul knew that I had fallen in love with Scott Henderson. He said if I talked, Scott would be killed. Scott and Gail. I didn't seem to have a choice. Rightly or wrongly, I kept my mouth shut. I'd do the same thing again." She made a simple, appealing little gesture. She said, "I thought that was all. If I'd dreamed that anyone else might be hurt—Mr. Mathews, for instance—I might have talked. I don't really know what I'd have done. I couldn't even tell the police where Gail was. I didn't have the faintest idea."

Bernie said, "This Kinkaid guy: Was he in with Paul Innes?"

"I don't know. But I don't believe he was."

"Then how come you chose to marry him?"

She drew a deep breath. "He was the only other thing that went wrong with Paul's scheme. Actually, I didn't know Tony. He met me one night and reminded me of our meeting in Havana. He knew I was Margaret Allen. He figured something was happening. He had everything right, except that he thought I was working with Innes. He didn't seem to know what really had happened in Cuba.

"All Tony knew was that I was apparently on the way to dishonestly acquiring a million dollars. He said if I didn't marry him, he'd talk. And there I was up against the same problem. I couldn't even warn him. He had the power to ruin everything—to practically sentence Gail to death…and then it occurred to me that marriage with him might be a good idea."

"Why?"

"Two reasons. If he was my husband, Paul Innes would be up against a situation he hadn't counted on. I had heard stories about Tony. I knew he was fearless and competent. I didn't like him, yet—in a certain odd way he seemed like a protector. Even if it didn't do anything more than to give me time…I knew that would help. And then…"

"Keep going…please…"

Her voice was low. "I was more in love with Scott Henderson than ever. I was afraid for him. Mr. Mathews had been killed, too, by that time. I had plenty of evidence that Paul wouldn't draw the line anywhere. It seemed to me that if I married Tony, it might disgust Scott. He might wash his hands of me. It seemed that if I married Tony, Scott would be in less danger."

Bernie said, "Did you see Innes kill Kinkaid?"

"No. I told you the truth about that. I also told Scott that I had known Tony in Cuba."

"How about Mr. Mathews?"

"I didn't see that, either. But I knew that Mr. Mathews was worried. He had been worried ever since the day I told him about wanting the estate converted into cash."

"Why didn't you trust him?"

"The same reason. I was thinking of Gail. I was always thinking about her."

"Why do you think Innes killed Mathews?"

"Mr. Mathews went from the airport to the Country Club, looking for Scott. He talked to Paul Innes. He might have talked about me. And if Paul had gotten the idea that Mr. Mathews had discovered anything wrong…"

She turned toward Barbara. She was fighting hard to keep the tears back. "Maybe I should have known it was coming, Barbara…but I didn't know. Believe me, I didn't."

And this time there was no holding back her grief. Barbara put her arms around the sobbing girl.

"You poor kid," she said gently. "You poor, poor kid…"

CHAPTER TWENTY-SIX

BERNIE Williams fidgeted, not knowing quite what to do about it. But since affirmative action of some sort seemed to be in order, he suggested that the two other policemen snap the cuffs on Paul Innes and Ollie Drucker, and take them downtown to the city jail.

Drucker was frightened, Innes resentful. The latter started to say something, but Bernie stopped him. "It ain't outrageous," he stated firmly. "And no matter what you said now, it wouldn't make no difference." He grinned at the other cops. "On your way, boys. Take good care of 'em."

The two prisoners were marched through the lobby. The crowd saw handcuffs on Paul Innes and started firing questions. The unpleasant, inquisitive voice of the efficient Bill Daggett of the

News-Herald was heard demanding to know what the hell had been going on. Bernie closed the door and locked it. He said, "That guy is a good reporter, but he gets in my hair."

Margaret Allen had regained some small measure of composure. Henderson was holding her hand, talking gently. He said, "I still think of you as Gail Barrie…" It wasn't a particularly brilliant remark, but it was the best he could think of at the moment. He was trying to steady her. It didn't really matter what he said, so long as it sounded casual.

Bernie was solicitous, too. He said, "Feeling better, Miss Allen?"

"Yes…"

"You've been swell. I wonder could you tell us just one more thing. What about that $25,000 you gave to Ollie Drucker?"

She spoke in a low, clear voice. "I had thought Ollie was in Cuba. I saw him in Cherokee for the first time two days after Tony was killed. I met him by appointment. He told me he'd just gotten to town.

"He said Gail was all right. He said he had brought her in from Cuba and that he had her hidden out, and that even Paul Innes didn't know where she was. He told me that he had been willing enough to check in with Paul in the first place because the plan looked foolproof. It was a gamble, but a million dollars was a lot of money.

"He told me that he knew Innes had committed all three of those murders. He said that was something he hadn't counted on, and didn't like. He said frankly that he was afraid. What he wanted was to save himself.

"He made me a proposition. He said if I'd give him $25,000 in cash, he'd clear out. As soon as he got clear, he'd write me full details about where Gail could be found. He said it wasn't far from here. The idea was that as soon as she was free and safe, I'd be at liberty to talk. I didn't see anything wrong with his story. I didn't suspect that Gail was dead…" Her voice broke, but she hesitated only a moment. I knew he might be lying, but I didn't dare take a chance. Gail's safety had always been the most important thing in my mind. Fear for her was all that kept me from talking.

"I gave Ollie the money. I thought he had left town with it. I was waiting for word from him. I was amazed to see him here tonight."

Bernie explained briefly what had happened to Ollie. Then he turned to Scott Henderson. He said, "You sure pulled this out of the hat, kid. But I'm damned if I know how."

Scott felt awkward and embarrassed. He said, "I wasn't very smart, Bernie. Things just sort of fell into place."

"Yeah...but how!"

"Frankly," said Scott, "I was bewildered. Nothing seemed to make any sense. The answer was right there, and I couldn't get hold of it. For a long time I figured Tony Kinkaid must be at the bottom of whatever was going on. But when he died and Gail—Miss Allen—didn't confide in me, I knew I had missed out somewhere along the line. She was still in the middle of something, and yet I couldn't convince myself that she was a criminal.

"On account of my connection with the firm...that is because I had access to all the details of the inheritance... I had information that no one else had. And then I learned that she had asked Fletcher Mathews to convert her estate into cash, and that he had argued against it. He had gone to Washington shortly after that. I believe now he must have suspected that something was wrong, and didn't want to tell me until he was sure. Whatever it was, he must have found out—which would explain why he rushed from the airport to the Club the day he got back to town. He probably intended to tell me all about it. But he got to the wrong man first. Knowing now where Paul Innes fits in, it doesn't take a lot of imagination to figure that Innes knew the fat was in the fire. He must have gotten to Mr. Mathews' house before Mathews and Kinkaid got there. The rest we know."

Bernie nodded. "That's good so far. But it ain't far enough. All you got there is guesswork."

"Ollie put me on the right track. When we checked the contents of his notebook, I found out that he had some Cuban telephone numbers. That made sense. It also reminded me again that Paul Innes had lived in Cuba with the Barries for a year.

"I had a funny feeling that I had missed something. You remember the list I copied from Drucker's notebook, Bernie?"

"I remember."

"I studied it again. The answer was sitting right there, only I had been too dumb to see it."

"That doesn't make me too bright, either, Scott. Even now I don't get it."

"In the middle of that list," explained Henderson, "was the number 41732. It struck me as familiar. At first I couldn't spot it. Then it hit. That is the number of Paul Innes' private telephone right here in this office. It doesn't come through the switchboard.

"I couldn't peg it. How would Drucker know Innes' private number? Why would it be important enough to write down in his book? The answer had to be that they were in something together. But that presented a fresh problem. Hunches were a dime a dozen right about then. What we needed was proof.

"At that time I was feeling definitely unhappy. Anyway I looked at it, Gail was in the middle. I still thought it was really Gail. I figured Innes must have some sort of a grip on her, something dating back to the year he lived in Cuba.

"Then came my next idea. You remember Major Barrie's letters that came back from Okinawa, and which were burned?"

"I should forget that! But the laboratory couldn't fix 'em up the way you wanted."

"You're wrong there, Bernie. Of course I had hoped to have at least one letter restored completely. What I got was some blown-up samples of the handwriting. It was Gail's handwriting, all right. It had to be. But I had seen a lot of the handwriting of the girl who said she was Gail Barrie. She had signed dozens of papers in my office. It wasn't the same handwriting. I was sure then—for the first time—that the person we were dealing with was an impostor.

"I got in touch with our attorney in Washington. He contacted the State Department. Their passport records showed that no Gail Barrie had come into the United States. But on May thirty-first, Miss Margaret Allen arrived in Miami by plane from Havana.

"That helped make me more certain. Remember that Innes lived in Miramonte with the Barries for a year. Miss Allen was living there, too. So Innes knew that this was not Gail Barrie, yet he accepted her as Gail. Whatever was cooking, they were in it together. I was afraid to move too fast. I had messed things up before, and I was scared of doing it again. My job seemed to be to set a trap and to hope that Paul Innes would betray himself. I had connected Innes and Miss Allen, Innes and Drucker, Miss Allen and Drucker. But it still wasn't enough. It was you who gave me the lead, Bernie."

"I'm glad I done something."

"You planted the idea that Drucker would crack under pressure. I got Miss Meredith to supply that pressure by accusing him of a murder that I was reasonably sure he hadn't committed. You're a marvelous actress, Fern."

She nodded, but didn't say anything.

"I tried putting myself in the place of Paul Innes. If I was right in presuming that he was mixed up in this thing with Drucker, it was logical to presume that he'd be panicked if Ollie showed up at the Club tonight. He wouldn't dare to talk to Ollie openly, and he wouldn't dare not to talk to him. Any way you look at it, he'd be under a strain.

"I watched Innes all evening. I saw his face when he first spotted Drucker. From then on, he was plenty worried. He had to figure that Drucker had come there to see him, and the last thing he wanted was to be connected publicly with Ollie.

"I saw Innes call Gail into his office. I saw him give Gail a note. We all saw her hand that note to Ollie."

"You mean," asked Bernie, "that the note to Ollie was from Innes, not Miss Barrie?"

"Yes. It's easy enough to prove. You'll find a hundred samples of his handwriting here in this office. But it was only when I saw the note itself that I knew I had him. I knew then that I'd been lucky enough to connect Innes and Drucker so that neither of them could wiggle out of it."

Bernie said, "Okay, buddy. You tell me."

"If we had confronted Innes with Drucker, both men would have denied knowing each other. We'd still have been up against a tough proposition. But the minute I saw that note..." Scott shrugged. "Figure it for yourself, Bernie. Ollie Drucker was supposedly a stranger. I'm asking you this: How would Paul Innes know that this stranger understood Spanish?"

Bernie said, "Not bad, Scott—not bad at all. So what else?"

"Nothing. That's all." Scott had a moment of apprehension. "Isn't it enough?"

"And how it is. There's also the chance that a ballistics test will show that the bullets that killed Mathews and Kinkaid came out of that same little pop gun Innes tried to plug you with just now. It'd be neat, but not necessary."

Henderson asked, "What's the next move?"

"I'm gonna go home with you-all. I'll get in touch with the Chief, the D. A., and Chris Peterson. Maybe they'll look at it my way, and maybe they won't."

"What does that mean?"

"I think the young lady has given us a straight story. Me, I'm willing to buy it. But it could be that she was doing some fast thinking. It could be she figured her way out. It's all according to how the big boys rate it. My guess is they'll let her stay at the house and put a guard there until they check with the Cuban police.

Margaret Allen, Scott Henderson and Bernie left the Club by the service door. They reached the Mathews home in advance of the District Attorney, the police Chief and Chris Peterson. Then there was a lot more questioning and a complete recapitulation by Henderson. They permitted Margaret to remain at home with one policeman on duty in front of the house and another in the rear.

"Keep everybody out," ordered Bernie. "And that goes double for Bill Daggett."

And then they were alone: Margaret Allen—whom Scott still thought of as Gail—Barbara Mathews and Scott. Barbara was magnificent. She had been magnificent throughout the evening. She said, "I'm afraid Margaret isn't far from a crack-up, Scott. Maybe you'd better go."

He went out of the house, climbed into his car and drove home.

He knew what was happening back yonder. He knew what it must mean to Margaret to realize that her mission had ended in disaster. Scott was feeling low himself. But he was exhausted, and because of that, he slept.

He telephoned the house at intervals during the next day. Barbara reported that everything was under control. Margaret hadn't cracked. She'd put up a good fight, and she had won. But the knowledge that Gail Barrie was dead preyed on her. That news had robbed her of any feeling of accomplishment.

At nine o'clock that night, Scott got a telephone call from Bernie Williams.

"I'm over at the Mathews' house," said Bernie, and his voice was exultant. "Better come over. *Pronto!* How you like my Spanish?"

Scott needed no urging. Fifteen minutes later he walked into the brilliantly lighted sitting room. One glance and he knew the news was good.

Bernie Williams was still there. So was the District Attorney. The latter started talking immediately.

"I'll hand it to you the quick way, Scott," he said. "We just got a detailed report from the Cuban police, via the American Embassy in Havana. Gail Barrie is alive."

It came as a shock. A delightful shock, but a shock just the same.

"Tell me more," he urged.

"They found Miss Barrie in a hospital in the city of Santa Clara. She has been there for about six weeks. She's getting well and will be all right, but she had a close call.

"At first she wouldn't talk. Then when she was told that Innes and Drucker were under arrest, she opened up. The story checks in every detail. She did urge Miss Allen to take her place and carry out Innes' orders. During the time she was being held prisoner on the farm, she became friendly with Carmita Mendoza, Pancho's wife.

"Carmita was afraid. She helped Gail. Ollie Drucker caught her. He shot Gail twice. Bad abdominal wounds. He wasn't stretching a point too much to believe she was dead.

"He got panicky and cleared out. We figured he came to Cherokee and spilled everything to Innes. That put them both behind the eight-ball, but they were still reasonably safe so long as nobody suspected that Gail was dead. The hospital in Santa Clara reported that there were no identification marks on Gail when she was brought in. Incidentally, they checked on the scar she got when she was three years old. It's there all right.

"Unless I'm all wrong, the supposed murder in Cuba made Innes desperate. He was smart enough to realize that if conspiracy could be proven, he was as guilty as Drucker. They were making their pitch for a million dollars. With a good part of that in their hands, they had an excellent chance of getting away.

"Evidently Drucker got scared. Too many murders, too fast. Maybe he figured he might be next. That's undoubtedly why he made his deal with the young lady.

"But getting back to the Cuban set-up. Carmita followed Ollie. She saw him shoot Gail Barrie. She saw that Gail was alive, and stayed with her. She was afraid to carry her into Havana or even Matanzas. She took her to Santa Clara, and simply said she had found her lying beside the road. Even then she was trying to shield her husband, who, by the way, has disappeared.

"Miss Barrie had two bad wounds. Peritonitis developed. There was an operation. She was suffering from shock. Until a week ago she was on the ragged edge. Then she began to get better. But she wouldn't talk, evidently because she was afraid of what might happen to Miss Allen if she did.

"And that's the story. We'll want Miss Allen as a witness, but that's all."

There was a little more conversation, and then the visitors left. Barbara went upstairs, leaving Margaret Allen alone with Scott.

They walked out on the veranda together. They stood by the rail and gazed across the valley. They didn't say anything.

Then they turned and faced each other. Scott put his arms around her. She pressed close against him and started to cry softly.

He soothed her as best he could. He whispered a lot of things…things that only lovers find important. And then she raised her head, and he kissed her.

It was a long kiss. They forgot everything except themselves. They did not see the police car that whizzed down the road and jerked to a halt in front of the house.

They were still wrapped up in each other when the voice of Chris Peterson sounded in their ears.

The tough, wiry little police sergeant looked straight at Scott Henderson.

"Smart guy, huh?" he said, with a broad, friendly grin. "And this time I really mean it."

THE END

If you've enjoyed this book, you will not want to miss these terrific titles…

ARMCHAIR MYSTERY-CRIME DOUBLE NOVELS, $12.95 each

B-16   **KISS AND KILL** by Richard Deming
THE DEAD STAND-IN by Frank Kane

B-17   **DANGEROUS LADY** by Octavus Roy Cohen
ONE HOUR LATE by William O'Farrell

B-18   **LOVE ME AND DIE!** by Day Keene
YOU'LL GET YOURS by Thomas Wills

B-19   **EVERYBODY'S WATCHING ME** by Mickey Spillane
A BULLET FOR CINDERELLA by John D. MacDonald

B-20   **WILD OATS** by Harry Whittington
MAKE WAY FOR MURDER by A. A. Marcus

B-21   **THE ART STUDIO MURDERS** by Edward Ronns
THE CASE OF JENNIE BRICE by Mary Roberts Rinehart

B-22   **THE LUSTFUL APE** by Bruno Fisher
KISS THE BABE GOODBYE by Bob McKnight

B-23   **SARATOGA MANTRAP** by Dexter St. Claire
CLASSIFICATION: HOMICIDE by Jonathan Craig

ARMCHAIR SCI-FI & HORROR DOUBLE NOVELS, $12.95 each

E-5   **THE IDOLS OF WULD** by Milton Lesser
PLANET OF THE DAMNED by Harry Harrison

E-6   **BETWEEN WORLDS** by Garret Smith
PLANET OF THE DEAD by Rog Phillips

E-7   **DAUGHTER OF THOR** by Edmond Hamilton
TALENTS, INCORPORATED by Murray Leinster

E-8   **ALL ABOARD FOR THE MOON** by Harold M. Sherman
THE METAL EMPEROR by Raymond A. Palmer

E-9   **DEATH HUNT** by Robert Gilbert
THE BEST MADE PLANS by Everett B. Cole

E-10   **GIANT KILLER** by Dwight V. Swain
GOLDEN AMAZONS OF VENUS by John Murray Reynolds

ARMCHAIR SCI-FI & HORROR GEMS SERIES, $12.95 each

G-21   **SCIENCE FICTION GEMS, Vol. Eleven**
Gordon R. Dickson and others

G-22   **HORROR GEMS, Vol. Eleven**
Thorp McClusky and others

BEACHFRONT MAYHEM AND MURDER

The young girl down by the beach was going to mean a lot of trouble for the little community of Palisades City. Thelma was her name. Beautiful, blonde, and young (only sixteen), she attracted men the way honey attracts flies. She was "visiting" her landlord "cousin," Lu Warren in his beachfront duplex. But in this case it seemed that flesh was thicker than blood. Dave Russell was another man who had caught her eye. As a commercial artist Dave could see the kid's potential and that her youthful image was meant to be splashed onto a professional canvas in a most provocative way. Then there was the local cop, Tommy Riggs, who tried to patch his troubled marriage during the day, while dallying with Thelma at night. But all this didn't add up to much more than the sordid exploits of another underage hussy on the make—until she turned up stone cold dead on a southern California beach.

POLICE LINEUP:

DAVE RUSSELL

He was an artist by trade, but his new subject, a hot young blonde, had him contemplating more than just his next brush stroke.

TOMMY RIGGS

A scoundrel of a cop whose inner corruption was matched only by his unabashed willingness to defile the ones he loved.

HELEN RUSSELL

This beautiful professional woman had the awkward situation of being more successful than her starving-artist husband.

MILDRED RIGGS

She had her hands full keeping her small beach café afloat while staving off the advances of her no-good creep of a husband.

EARL BINGHAM

Not the smartest cop on the force, but a lot smarter than most people gave him credit for.

THELMA GRANT

Only sixteen years old, but her gorgeous body and her affinity for booze got her a lot more than she bargained for.

KEN HURLEY

You could hear the melody of his ice cream truck all over town—but one never expected to hear it at two o'clock in the morning.

ONE HOUR LATE

By
WILLIAM O'FARRELL

ARMCHAIR FICTION
PO Box 4369, Medford, Oregon 97504

*For more information about Armchair Books and products, visit our
website at…*

www.armchairfiction.com

Or email us at…

armchairfiction@yahoo.com

CHAPTER ONE

IT WAS late spring. The Southern California season had ended only the week before but the afternoon was hot. The prowl car from the sheriff's sub-station drove slowly down the beach road. It passed Point of Rocks, and a few miles farther south pulled off the road at the foot of Martinez Canyon. It parked there, facing the highway and partly hidden by a concrete bridge, in a position to observe traffic approaching from three directions. Cars came south from the sub-station and Point of Rocks, north from Palisades City, and from straight ahead down the winding canyon road. The location was a good one, from the point of view of the two deputies in the car. The shopping center on the far side of the road was a traffic focal point.

The parking spot had further advantages for one of the deputies, the man who sat erectly on the right. He was dark and good-looking, and his black eyes stared expectantly at the small cafe next to the supermarket. His name was Tommy Riggs. The big round face of the other deputy, the one who sat behind the wheel, was placidly expressionless. His name was Earl Bingham, and he didn't have the driving curiosity that Tommy had. Some people, and Tommy was among them, believed that when Earl was physically awake he was still half-asleep.

They sat there for twenty minutes, from two-thirty until ten minutes to three; and all that time Tommy watched the cafe. Customers came and went, but whomever or whatever he was waiting for did not appear. He gave an irritated glance at the Swiss cigarette lighter Earl was playing with, and turned his attention to the row of beach houses on his right.

There were fifteen or twenty of these, built close together in a straggling line along the road. The nearest was about twenty yards away. Tommy knew the weather-beaten, wooden house. It had recently been bought by a man named Warren, who had divided it into two apartments, one above the other. Warren lived in the lower level and rented the upper half to an artist and his wife. From where he sat, Tommy could see the upper bedroom window. The same look of irritation he had given the cigarette lighter crossed his face. He disliked and disapproved of artists. Tommy disapproved of any man, for that matter, who apparently had to work less hard than he did. He shifted his position, looked past the house down at the beach. He muttered an exclamation and leaned forward, watching the couple on the sand.

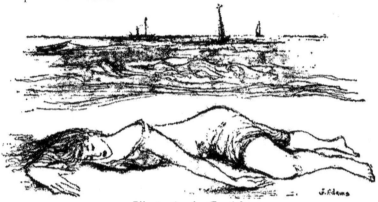

Illustration by G. Adams

There's no law forbidding a man and girl to make love in public, within reasonable limits. But when the man is married and at least thirty-five, and the girl a year or two below the age of consent—well, a thing like that, it makes a guy's blood boil. Tommy said so, in anger and disgust.

"What do you mean?"

"You saw those two down there!"

Earl nodded. "He kissed her. What do you mean, it makes your blood boil?"

Tommy, intent on what was happening delayed his answer. The man trotted across the sand and disappeared around a corner of the Warren house. The girl waited for a moment, then sauntered after him. She, too, disappeared, and Tommy turned back to stare at the cafe.

"I mean it makes you sick."

"Why?"

"You saw what happened. She's just a kid. You know what's happening right now?"

Earl thought about it. He nodded doubtfully. "I guess so," he said.

But he guessed wrong. What had actually happened and what was happening at the present moment, was not at all as Tommy had imagined. It was ten minutes before three. The motivation of the scene the deputies had just witnessed was only slightly tinged by sex, and it had no sexual outcome. Its beginnings lay in nothing more serious than a restlessness that had come over Dave Russell thirty-five minutes before...

At two-fifteen Dave had taken a half-hour break. The decision to knock off was not reached easily. He had to talk himself into it. He wasn't satisfied with the way his work was going. The magazine cover he was doing had a posed quality, lacking life.

He left his drawing board and went out on a narrow exterior stairway that climbed to the porch behind the kitchen. The porch was on a level with the beach road and, beyond it, he could see fast, thick traffic. This part of the beach was getting to be as cluttered as a business street in town.

He got his swimming trunks from the clothesline and turned back to the stairs. These descended to his own door, and then continued down to a sandy enclosure that served as both patio and front porch to the lower half of the duplex. The lower half was where Lu Warren—now that his wife, Amy, had gone home on a visit—lived alone. Dave went down the steps, his right shoulder brushing the side of the house, his left hand on the banister. If he had raised his hand he could have touched the wall of a similar but empty house next door. He returned to the living room to peel off his paint-smeared sweatshirt and khaki trousers.

After his swim, he would hang the trunks on the line exactly as they had been before. They would be dry when his wife came home at six; Helen need not know that he had taken time off from his work. The only thing lost would be a little more of his self-respect—which, it seemed to him, was already wearing pretty thin. Helen had made more money in the past year than he had.

This slump was not entirely Dave's own fault. The market for his stuff had been unsettled by the easy popularity of TV. These things happen and invariably adjust themselves in time. In time Dave also would adjust to changing conditions, but meanwhile his ebbing confidence was beginning to affect his work. He would gladly have taken a job, any job, except for the fact that his painting was the only thing that might pull them out of their present hole.

In a way, it was too bad that this was so. A job, if it accomplished nothing more, would at least have returned them to an equal, companionable level. Formerly they had swum together. Now Helen worked while he swam alone, and concealed the evidence of his loafing. It was an unpleasant, furtive situation all around.

Dressed for the beach, he wound a towel around his neck and frowned at the hand still holding it by one end. It was a strong hand with long, thin fingers. His fingers were as skillful as they had ever been. They had mastered their techniques so thoroughly that they could work without conscious direction from his mind. And there was certainly nothing the matter with his mind. His tanned body was well muscled, he was thirty-four years old and married to an attractive woman with whom he was in love. He had been a successful commercial artist for thirteen years. This was a period during which he should have been turning out the best work of his life, and he was doing nothing of the kind. He shrugged, and went to take a swim.

Barefoot, Dave ran down the rest of the wooden steps to the sandy enclosure at the bottom. He started across it to the beach, and stopped. A girl was blocking the way, sprawled out in a deck chair. She looked as though she were about sixteen. Her short blonde hair was so light that it was almost silver. She wore a tight, black strapless swimming suit, and stared up at him with sullen but curiously beautiful gray eyes.

The French windows at the far end of the patio were open, but this was Friday and Dave knew that his landlord was not at home. Lu worked at an aircraft plant inland and about ten miles away. The girl was probably a young friend of his wife.

Dave nodded, waiting for her to move her legs. They were stretched across the only gap in the low concrete wall. She did not move.

"Hi," she said.

Dave smiled. "Didn't know anyone was here."

She shrugged. "I'm here. All of me—two hands, two feet, ten fingers and ten toes." She wriggled them. "Got nothing else to do so I just finished counting 'em. You going someplace?"

"For a swim."

"I can't swim. Not much swimmin' where I come from," she said.

Her voice and diction were straight out of the Ozarks— nasal, high, and slurred. Lucius and Amy Warren had both come from Western Arkansas. The connection established itself in his mind as he waited for her to let him pass.

She continued to study him, lying motionless in the deck chair. He said, "Pardon, please," stepped across her outstretched legs and went out on the sand.

The tide was on the ebb. The waves had left behind them a small embankment about two feet high. He dropped his towel on the embankment and sat beside it, his feet on the wet sand. He did not know the girl had followed him until she appeared from behind and sat down at his side.

"Like the beach?" she asked. "I can't get used to the fishy way it smells."

She carried a bulging beach bag from which she was taking a pack of cigarettes. "Hey," she said. "It's okay. I'm a sort of cousin of Lu Warren's. Thelma. You're that artist, ain't you? Got a match?"

He shook his head.

"Never mind. I got one here." She found a box of matches and lit her cigarette.

There was no shade, and the hot sun had only declined slightly. Already there was a light film of perspiration on Dave's skin, but Thelma seemed unaffected by the heat. She sat on her heels, slender legs folded lithely underneath her, leaning back for balance on her right hand and arm. Her left forefinger drew concentric circles on the sand, but her gray eyes did not follow the motions of her finger. They rested fixedly on him. He noticed that the sullenness had left them. It had been replaced by an expression he found difficult to define. Her eyes were interested. They contained a hint of calculation, but this was overbalanced by a wistful quality. More than anything else, they were alive and aware of their aliveness. Her slightly parted lips disclosed good teeth. She had a short, straight nose with nostrils that pulsed in rhythm with her breathing. Her body was fully developed. There was a vaccination scar high on her right leg.

Dave got up quickly. "Think I'll take a dip," he said.

The wave broke as he plunged into it. The cool salt water buoyed him up to greenish light. He was facing seaward when his head broke surface, and he dived again to swim beneath a second wave. The ocean was relatively calm next time he came up. The backward toss of his head was unnecessary and done from force of habit; it had been years since he had worn his hair long enough to have it wash across his eyes. He swam straight out, and presently swerved to look back at the beach.

Thelma sat where he had left her. She was rummaging in her bag again, and had the settled appearance of a person who had found a place that suits her and intends to stay. His self-allotted thirty-minute break was nearly up, and he swam back slowly. She rose and carried his towel to him as he waded through the surf.

"You swim good," she said.

"Thanks." He saw that she was holding a pencil and a large pad of paper, evidently taken from her bag. "Writing letters?"

She shook her head. "Who'd I write to, and who'd bother to read my letter if I did? Got nothing and nobody. An hour late and a dollar short, that's me." She held out the pad with simulated coyness. "Draw my picture...Dave?"

He did not want to. That little pause before she spoke his name, and the soft way in which she'd drawn it out into two syllables, making it sound like "Day-yuv," warned him off. But he had learned that it often consumes less time to grant a small favor than to frame a plausible excuse.

"Okay." He accepted the pad and pencil, and wound the towel around his neck. "Sit down."

"Here? What's the matter with your studio?"

"I don't have a studio."

She sat down, disappointed. "Thought your wife was out."

"She is. Look straight at me. Now turn your head a little to the left." Dave sketched with rapid competence. The girl was stiff, too conscious of the fact that he was studying her as a subject rather than as a female. In an effort to relax her, "When did you come to California?" he asked.

"Six months ago." She was thinking about herself now, and her face was animated. "But I just ran into Lu last week. Lucky thing I did. I was working at the five-and-ten in Palisades City. I'd just got fired when he come ambling in."

"Why'd you get fired?"

"Well, they didn't exactly get a chance to fire me. I beat 'em to it. You know something? You're sort of cute," she said.

She was leaning forward, looking straight into his eyes. Dave, susceptible to her expression as a man, accepted it whole-heartedly as an artist. Something happened to his fingers. They took on independent life. He finished the rough sketch, put his initials at the bottom, and handed her the pad.

"Portrait of a promising young girl," he said.

She examined the sketch and got up very slowly. But her breathing was rapid and color tinged her cheeks. "Hey," she said in a low, wondering tone, "it's me, all right. It's the way I really am." Before he could guess what she intended, she ran forward, threw her arms around him and kissed him wetly on the lips. "Gee, thanks!"

Dave disentangled himself. "Glad you like it." He went away from her, trotting across the sand. He crossed the little patio, ran up the stairs. Without pausing to shower or dress, he went directly to his drawing board. He had recaptured something down there on the beach; it was a feeling he had mislaid what seemed a long, long time before. He wanted to get it down in line and color before it slipped away, if it did slip away. Maybe this time he would be able to hang on to it.

After he had gone, Thelma stood for a quarter of a minute, looking at the flight of stairs he had just climbed. Then she followed him as far as the patio, and went through the French windows into the lower section of the house.

But, of course, the two deputies in the prowl car got a totally different impression. And that impression gave rise to an idea in the deviously working mind of Riggs...

CHAPTER TWO

Anything that Tommy said or did was perfectly okay with Earl. He knew that he was—well, say inexperienced; and he admired his partner. Tommy had taught him practically everything he knew about his job. There were lots of little extras to be made; the trick was to make them without getting caught. Little by little, just by keeping his ears open, Earl was catching on. When Tommy told him to stop clicking his lighter, he stopped doing it. "Going to get this fixed tonight," he said, and put it in his pocket. When Tommy said the blonde girl was jailbait, and that a guy who'd take advantage of her like that ought to be jugged, Earl nodded in slow agreement.

"She's beautiful." He pronounced it *beauty-full*, reaching forward to turn on the ignition.

"The guy's one of these artists. Probably got a dozen models running after him. You and me, we get what's left." Tommy spat through the open window. "Where you going?"

Earl had started the motor. "Been an hour since we went down to the pier. Figure we got time for one more round. Okay. Tommy?"

"You're driving. Suit yourself."

The prowl car eased into the southbound traffic. Tommy studied the Warren house as they drove past. There was parking room for three cars beside a gate that opened on a flight of wooden steps. Near the gate was a small porch on a level with the road. A kitchen window opened on the porch, but it was screened. Tommy tried, but it was impossible to see inside.

They turned around at the pier, completing the southern leg of their tour, and were back at the foot of the canyon by three-thirty. There was still time for a trip to Point of Rocks before knocking off for the day. Tommy grunted affirmatively when Earl glanced at him. Ten minutes later Earl swung the car in a U-turn and parked off the road.

Tommy opened the car door and got out. The high tide had left ankle-deep pools of water on the beach fifty feet below. Children played in the pools, watched by their sunbathing parents. A zigzag path, starting at his feet, led down to where the children were. Beyond them was the gray mass of Point of Rocks, a pile of jagged boulders stretching out into the sea. A few fishermen had climbed out to the end. They sat stolidly on uncomfortable bare rock, exposed to sun and wind. Tommy was exasperated by a patience he could not understand. The poor morons would sit there all day long, and make a big production of it if they caught so much as a single fish—a fish that could, when you counted in the cost of their tackle, time and transportation, be got a lot cheaper in the market. It just went to prove what he had always known: that people, taken as a whole, were pretty stupid. A smart operator could always make out without breaking his back or even trying very hard.

The idea that had been churning in his mind this past half-hour took recognizable form and floated to the surface. There was a chance that cradle-snatching artist might be parted from a few coarse bills. But it would have to be worked smoothly, if it was worked at all, and the layout would have to be well cased first. Tommy grinned. Maybe he could talk the girl into cooperating. An investigation under such circumstances might turn out to be fun. Like Earl had said, the little blonde was beauty-full.

He turned to the right, looked north along the wide curve of the bay at the little settlement where the sub-station was located. The cluster of buildings was similar to the one at the foot of Martinez Canyon. There was a post office next to the sub-station, a grocery store, a restaurant and cocktail lounge, a service station. About a dozen houses were on the hill above the settlement. Tommy, since he had split up with his wife, lived in a rented room in one of these. The road north of Point of Rocks was relatively new. It had been chipped out of the palisades only six years before, and was shorter by ten miles than the old road winding inland over the mountains. There was no beach. The new road ran high above sea-pounded rocks.

Earl called diffidently, "How's about it, Tommy? Getting late."

Tommy got back in the car. They reached Martinez Canyon at quarter to four, fifteen minutes before the end of their shift. Earl parked on the beach side of the highway, as he always did, and Tommy resumed his alert surveillance of the cafe. Above the door of the cafe a sign, bright green on a white background, read, *MILDRED'S PLACE. GOOD EATS*. On the plate-glass window in frosted letters had been written, *TRUCKERS* WELCOME. Two trucks and an ice cream wagon had stopped in front of it. The ice cream man was doing a good business selling to people from the beach.

A woman came to the door of the cafe. Wiping her hands on her apron, she blinked at the declining sun. She was about thirty-five, a year or two younger than Tommy, and she was well-built and had good, regular features. Once she had been pretty, but her freshness was all gone. Her neat brown hair was gathered at the nape of her neck and tied with a ribbon, but the dull colored ribbon was strictly for utility. She looked harassed, and continuous worry had burned deep lines in her face.

Earl cleared his throat. "There's Mildred."

"Blow the horn."

The horn blared out. The woman shielded her eyes against the sun and turned toward the sound. Tommy waved. She looked directly at him and, without acknowledging his salutation, went back inside. The afternoon was still warm, but she closed the door.

Tommy chuckled. "She'll be sorry."

"You hadn't ought to treat her that way, Tommy. She's sort of nice."

"You married to her, or am I?"

"You are. I just—"

"You just shut up. I'll treat her any way I like."

Mildred walked through the opening in the counter, past the two truck drivers who were having early dinners, and went into the kitchen. Hazel, her white-haired helper, was busy at the stove. Hazel glanced at her as she walked silently to the window and sat down in a chair. From the window she could see the supermarket, Manny's beer joint and a good stretch of the highway, but nothing she saw stirred her interest. A person walking a tightrope doesn't pay much attention to the scenery. She's got all she can do to keep her balance and stay alive.

"What's the matter, honey?" Hazel asked. "Feeling punk?"

"I'll be all right."

"You'll get over it. You always feel punk every time you get a letter from the kid."

Ralph's letters arrived regularly once a week. One was like a carbon copy of another. He never complained. Complaints would have been edited by the reform school censor. On the other hand, he never really told her anything. "I'm well and hope you are the same." Nothing much to say except I wish I was home... They treat me pretty good... Your loving son." He never mentioned Tom Riggs. Not even when Mildred had written that she and Tom had separated and that she was considering a divorce. Ralph utterly rejected his stepfather. That's possible when hundreds of miles separate you from the person you reject. It's not so easy when every day you have to see, and sometimes talk to, the man you hate more than anything on earth.

Familiar sounds came in from the front. The cash register rang, the truckers slammed the door as they went out, a couple came in and ordered hamburgers and cans of beer. Mildred started to get up but Hazel said, "I got it, hon," and she sat down again. Hazel was nice. On days like this she did more than her fair share of the work.

There was a lull when no customers entered the cafe. Hazel came into the kitchen, stood beside her. She looked out the window, too. She said, "There's Lu Warren's cousin-or-whatever-she-is. Like to know what Amy thinks about her staying in the house. Going to the market," Hazel gasped audibly. "Well, I'll be—!"

The blonde girl, dressed in sandals, white shorts and a pink halter, had not been headed for the market. Passing the beer joint, she had suddenly turned in.

Hazel was indignant. "Got a mind to tell Lu Warren, just to see him burn!"

"It's not a saloon," Mildred said quietly. "Manny doesn't sell hard liquor. You drink beer yourself."

"There's a world of difference between sixteen and sixty, dearie. And she ain't a day older than sixteen."

Three-quarters of an hour went by. More customers arrived and left. Hazel took care of them. Mildred remained in her chair. Once she made an effort to rise, but sank back again. She felt incapable of movement, drained. But her mind was active, surveying her problem from every conceivable angle, and from every angle meeting the same high, barricaded wall. She did not see Thelma come out of Manny's place, but she probably would not have noticed if she had.

The front door was opened briskly and Tom Rigg's voice boomed through the cafe, "Mildred here?"

Hazel didn't answer. Mildred heard approaching footsteps. Then a moist hand was rested heavily on her shoulder.

"Hi."

She sat rigidly. "Take your hand off me, Tom. I don't want you to touch me, and I don't want you in my kitchen."

"Baby, why don't you give in?" He burlesqued a noisy sigh. "You know you're crazy for me. Why don't you break down and tell me so?"

But when she swung around to face him, he jerked his hand away. He went over to the icebox and got a can of beer. She studied him as he punctured it and drank.

She still held a physical fascination for him, and she despised herself for it. He was shallow, cheap, and cruel, but he was also strikingly handsome. One of his ancestors had been an Indian; it showed in his slightly Oriental features, dark coloring, and black hair. He had changed from his uniform at the station. In slacks and a loud sports shirt, he looked like what he had been before he'd joined the force: a salesman on a used car lot. A good but disappointed salesman. Tommy had been able to move jalopies as fast as anybody in the trade, but every time he tried his hand on new cars—especially expensive ones—he failed to make it. Folks who bought Lincolns, Cadillacs, and Jags seemed to prefer subtler pressure. They shied away from overbearing charm.

Mildred saw his amused eyes watching her above the tilted beer can. She stared back at him. "What're you doing here? You got anything to say, you can tell it to my lawyer."

"Hell with lawyers. You're my wife. Man's got a right to come in his own place."

"I'm not your wife. This restaurant belongs to me."

"We're still married. This is a community property state." He finished his can and tossed it in the wire receptacle beside the sink. "This is the day you're supposed to hear from Ralph. Get a letter?"

"Yes."

"They treating him all right?"

"He says so."

"You got me to thank for it. I got friends up there."

"You want me to thank you for something, Tom? Get out and don't come back."

He shrugged. "Of course, if you don't want him treated right I might be able to arrange that, too."

Mildred got up slowly. "You'd like to do that, wouldn't you? You've always hated Ralph."

"Now, hold on—" A flush crept from the collar of Tommy's shirt to spread across his face. "I did everything I could to help that punk. He was guilty—"

"Of what? He didn't even know that car was stolen." She walked toward him with purposeful, unnerving deliberation. "Guilty of trying to protect himself after you'd run the car off the road and killed his friend?" Her right hand dipped into her apron pocket. "Ralph never owned a switchblade in his life."

Tommy had backed up against the sink. He watched her pocket. "You gone crazy, woman?"

Hazel's head came through the open service panel. "Mildred, you okay?"

"I'm okay. Everything's okay." Mildred's hand was no longer hidden in her apron. Hazel glared at Tommy, withdrew her head.

"Like mother, like son. Screwy." Tommy edged away from the sink, went over to the window. "Switchblades! Getting so it ain't safe for a man to open his mouth."

"You're safe," Mildred told him. "You'll stay safe just as long as your friends are good to Ralph."

He grinned, his confidence restored. "You want that, why don't you try being nice to me? You ought to see my new room, Milly. Got a color TV, twenty-one inch. Private entrance, too. Feel like a short drive up the coast?"

"I don't feel like a drive of any kind with you."

"You will, one of these days. Can't hold out forever, baby. Let's have another beer."

Mildred got a can from the icebox punched it and held it out to him. But Tommy was no longer interested. Suddenly he had become intent on something on the far side of the window. Mildred looked past his shoulder. She saw the blonde girl, Lu Warren's cousin, standing in front of Manny's. Thelma was a little drunk. She was talking to Dave Russell, smirking and swishing herself around in a way she probably thought was cute.

Mr. Russell seemed to be listening politely, but he only took it for about twenty seconds. Then he went into the supermarket. Thelma wrinkled her nose as she turned toward the beach road. She was evidently going home.

Mildred was still holding out the can. "Take your beer, Tom. I got to go to work."

Tommy didn't take the can. He turned from the window, crossed quickly to the icebox, slipped out a six-pack, and hurried from the kitchen. He acted like a man with something on his mind. Mildred didn't ask him what it was. She was too glad to see him go.

But a moment later, when she saw his yellow convertible turn into the beach road, she nodded as though she'd known that he was up to something of the kind. And didn't care.

"Hazel, you want a can of beer?" she called.

A girl's got to have her kicks. Beer's all right but it wears off fast, and a girl is left feeling even lower than she was before. With nothing to do but sit on the beach and nothing to look at but the crazy ocean, and nothing to look forward to but Lu coming home and preaching at her like he was a shouting Holy Roller trying to get her to repent.

Give a girl a chance. First let me do something to be repentful for, Thelma told herself as she walked home. She giggled. I'll be as repentful later on as right now—I'm full of beer.

It wasn't easy walking alongside the road. There were all kinds of little hills and hollows. Her feet kept climbing up on one and slipping down into the other and once she sort of lost her balance just before she reached the gate. She was leaning against the gate when she saw the yellow convertible. It must have sneaked up on her; it was standing only a couple of feet away. A man was grinning at her from behind the wheel.

"Hi, honey. Want a lift?" he said.

He was good-looking. Not the way Dave Russell was. You had to study Dave close before you realized he was as good-looking a fellow as you could ever hope to meet. This fellow's crazy looks reached out and sort of slapped you in the eye.

"Don't need a lift," she told him. "I'm already home."

His teeth, set against the darkness of his face, were white as skimmed milk. The wider he grinned, the whiter his teeth got. "Home's a place to come back to. How're you going to come back if you don't go places first?"

"Now if that ain't just what I was thinking! Mister, it's the awful, lousy truth. You take me places?"

"I'll take you, honey, and bring you back again. Climb in."

Thelma climbed in. There was a cold six-pack on the seat. She lifted it to her lap. The car swung in a U-turn, drove past the supermarket, turned right into the canyon road.

"There's an opener in the glove compartment," the good-looking fellow said. "My name's Tommy. What's your pretty name?"

CHAPTER THREE

On this particular late afternoon, Dave Russell for a change did not resent the fact that, in a sense, he was doing his wife's work while his wife did his. The painting promised to turn out even better than he'd hoped. He was like a man who, having risked his last quarter on a slot machine, unexpectedly lines up the three jackpot symbols. Running into Thelma a second time had not especially disturbed him. He was sorry about what was happening to her, as he would have been sorry to see rust forming on a piece of gleaming, well-designed equipment. But, after all, he did not own the equipment. It was not his business if she let herself grow up to be a tramp.

He wheeled his groceries to the cashier's desk. They were whisked from the bag and put into a paper sack. He peered through the glass door before carrying the sack outside. Thelma was not in sight. He was on the sidewalk before he remembered that he hadn't bought dessert.

The ice cream man was getting ready to move on. Dave caught him as he closed the side-panel of his truck.

"Pint of chocolate, please." In surprise, he added, "Well, hello! When did you take on this job?"

It was Ken Hurley, a young man who had formerly worked in the service station. He and his wife lived about six houses south of the Warrens' place.

"Do it every year, soon as the warm weather starts. Pump gas during the winter months."

Dave paid him for the ice cream. "Like it?"

"Why not? Keeps me outside and not too far from home."

He slammed the side-panel, got into the driver's seat. He raised his hand in casual salute, let in the clutch. As the truck rolled away it automatically began to play a tinkling little tune. Dave smiled, listening. It was good advertising, that particular nostalgic number. It brought back memories of childhood. He hummed it, crossing toward the house. *Oh Where, Oh Where Has My Little Dog Gone?* It made him think of long, hot summer days—and cold ice cream.

He went through the gate and down the steps, entered the living room, and carried the groceries to the kitchen. The house was built in a manner conforming to the steep hillside; in order to get to the kitchen, he had to climb another flight of narrow stairs. He set the groceries on the sink, put the ice cream in the refrigerator, and glanced through the screened window at his trunks hanging on the line. They were quite dry now. On impulse, he returned to the living room and placed his almost finished picture where Helen would be sure to see it as she came in. She would like it. He told himself the pleasant things she would say about it, and went back to the kitchen where he made preliminary preparations for dinner. He was an indifferent cook, but Helen more than made up for his lack of skill. She always put the finishing touches to their meals.

A few minutes later, he heard their Rambler come to a stop beyond the window. He saw the car door open, and returned to the living room. Helen seemed unusually slow coming down the stairs. He opened the front door, stepped out and called.

"Need any help?"

Helen smiled, but it was a tired smile. Her left hand rested on the banister. "I'm a little beat. Hard day at the shop and the traffic's tough."

Dave felt quick concern. He climbed to take her hand. It was an extremely feminine hand but he sensed resistance in it, as he had sensed resistance in many of Helen's reactions during the past few months. He let go immediately, a little hurt.

But that, he knew, was behaving immaturely. When a man's wife comes home tired he doesn't, or shouldn't, sulk. He held the door open, turned back with a smile.

"Little surprise for you," he said.

Helen entered the living room. She hesitated when she saw the picture. Dave shut the door.

"Well—like it?"

"It's good," she said, with no particular enthusiasm. "Quite good. Mind if I rest a few minutes? Then I'll fix dinner. I have to work tomorrow."

"Tomorrow's Saturday!"

"Maybe it'll only be for a few hours in the morning. I'm lucky Victor doesn't have me working Sundays, too."

She walked to the little stairway that mounted to their bedroom. Dave lifted his hand uncertainly as though to stop her. But he let her go.

Helen resisted an impulse to slam the bedroom door. She eased it shut, crossed to the dressing table and grimly inspected her reflection in the mirror. It had happened, as she had known it would happen the first time Dave caught sight of that little blonde girl from downstairs. Helen had only seen her once herself, the night before when they'd passed each other on the outside staircase. But even that small encounter had been enough to put her on her guard. There are females who regard all marriages other than their own as personal challenges; their own they usually regard as unavoidable inconveniences. Thelma—that was the name Lu Warren had used when he had called her from below—was one of these. Okay. Helen could accept that. What she could not accept was the fact that Dave—who was *her* husband!—had proved himself to be in no way different from any other husband, any other man. Susceptible? He could not possibly have met that predatory child before this very morning—and already he had painted her portrait, had the damn thing nearly finished!

Helen went to the closet, got out a pair of white silk lounging pajamas, and dropped them on the bed. She started taking off her clothes. She was a smart woman, in several senses of the word. She dressed smartly; as buyer for a woman's shop, that was an essential part of her business. She was beautiful, but she was also clever. It was her cleverness that she would have to call on now. Thelma might have her teenage freshness and resiliency, but she—Helen reminded herself—had experience, self-control, and brains.

Furthermore, it was entirely possible that she was allowing herself to become agitated over a trifle. Dave might have seen in the girl an interesting subject for a picture, nothing more. Very likely, during the course of the evening, he would mention having spoken to her—politely, casually—and having noted her pictorial possibilities. That would be Helen's cue to compliment him, slip him the happy needle, tell him what a really fine job he had done.

Helen sat on the foot of the bed, reached for the pajamas, started to pull them on. With one foot lifted to plunge into the trousers she abruptly paused.

If only the damned picture didn't absolutely reek of sex!

His wife was the only woman Dave had ever known who felt about good, natural things—the sun, the sea, music and the correct proportions of vermouth and gin—as he did, and did not think it incumbent on her to chatter about them. But now, when it came to a critical appraisal of his painting, she was carrying taciturnity too far. "Quite good," she had said. If there was one word he hated, it was that affected adverb. *Quite.* He sat on the couch and lit a cigarette.

Before he had time to finish it, there were footsteps on the stairs and she was back again. She had changed to white silk pajamas. They set off her brown hair and dark suntan, and she stood before him in an attitude of amused contrition. Dave frowned, knowing that she was not contrite, but unable even as he frowned to keep from thinking how her long legs and perfect figure could do anything she liked with any kind of clothes.

"Your picture's wonderful, Dave. It's the best thing you've ever done."

Dave got up and kissed her warmly. "Sit down, working woman. I'll fix dinner."

"Oh, no you won't! I'm hungry. Whip up a couple of martinis, if you like."

Getting his mixing implements together, he had an impulse to tell her about Thelma. But he repressed it. He would find a more suitable occasion later on—make a joke of how he had met, and talked to, and drawn a quick sketch of Lu Warren's little cousin on the beach.

But of course he didn't do it. That would have called for an explanation of how he had happened to be on the beach in the first place, an explanation that would in effect have been a semi-apology. He didn't feel that an apology was indicated, and he saw no reason for ruining the tranquility of what had turned out to be a pleasant evening. Helen became oddly quiet about ten o'clock, and they went to bed at eleven. It was illogical but Dave, as he undressed, had all the symptoms of a queasy conscience.

It must have been the same symptoms, whatever caused them, that kept him awake. He lay still, waiting first for the little muscular spasm that always signified Helen's "jumping off to sleep," and then he lay still for another three-quarters of an hour, afraid that any movement might awaken her. He grew increasingly tense. He wanted a cigarette, he wanted a drink of water, and these two wants combined to make any immediate prospect of sleep unlikely. At last, with infinite care he slipped out of bed and tiptoed to the living room. He stopped there long enough to light a cigarette, then climbed to the kitchen, not having bothered to turn on the lights.

There was no light in the kitchen, either, but none was necessary. He went unerringly to the sink, felt for and found a glass, turned on the tap. He stood there for a moment, sipping water and discovering that he wasn't thirsty after all and had started back to the living room when he heard a car stop by the gate.

He would have paid no attention if, simultaneously, he had not heard Thelma's petulant, slurred voice.

"Home?" It came blurred through the window screen, and it was obvious that she was drunk. "Whatcha bring me here for, hon?"

"You change your mind too much." The man's voice was heavy with resentment. "Say you'll go to a motel, then say you won't. Now you can go to bed by yourself."

"See you tomorrow?"

"I'll think about it. Go on now—scram!"

There was a pause, followed by the sound of a scuffle. A car door slammed. Dave heard the motor accelerate, then fade away. All this happened before the girl began to scream.

"*You* scram! Hear me, you old goat? Scram! Scram..." Her anger dwindled as quickly as it had risen. She chuckled, talking softly to herself. "Should of asked Dexter when you had the chance, old goat. He could of told you. Knows all, sees all—sees it in the stars." The gate creaked and Dave moved closer to the window. He looked out.

He could just make out her figure, a shadow darker and more opaque than the shadows that surrounded it. She wavered past the window and beyond his line of vision, but he heard a soft thud as she sat down abruptly on the steps. She started humming to herself.

It was no recognizable tune she hummed, and it was interrupted after only a few seconds by a man who came running up the stairs.

"Drunk!" It was Lu Warren, whispering furiously. "You get down to bed!"

Thelma laughed. "Whose bed? How you, Cousin Lu?"

"Shut up!" There was a sharp crack; he must have slapped her face. "You're no kin of mine, you little wench!"

Her protest ended in an unintelligible gurgle. It sounded as though Lu had clamped his hand across her mouth. Dave heard her heels thump as he half-dragged, half-carried her down the steps.

She broke loose once and screamed, "Le' me go, you ol' devil! I'll tell Amy—"

He silenced her again. Her heels bumped rapidly for a moment, then there was nothing to be heard except diminished traffic on the road and surf breaking on the beach. Dave let out pent-up breath, grateful that Lu had been able to handle her without awakening Helen. He returned to the living room and was halfway across it, tiptoeing toward the bedroom, when the lights switched on.

Helen stood by the light switch. Her hair was disheveled but she was wide-awake.

"What time is it?"

"About twelve. Sorry you woke up," he said. "Lu Warren had a little trouble with his cousin."

"His what?"

"Girl who seems to be visiting him. Supposed to be a relative but, from what I overheard, could be she isn't. She came home swacked."

"I heard that much," Helen said. "In fact, I heard too much. Why on earth are you up wandering around the house at this hour?"

"I got up to go to the kitchen—"

"This is hardly a time of night to start a long discussion about nothing. Are you coming to bed?"

Dave said huffily, "I don't want to disturb you. I'll stay here on the couch."

"Well, really—!" Helen would have said more, but she caught sight of his expression. She shrugged, switched off the light, and climbed the bedroom stairs. Dave stretched out on the couch. It was lumpy and the pillow had been designed for purely decorative purposes. He blamed Helen for what he knew would be a long, uncomfortable night.

In the morning, as usual he awakened first. He dropped his feet to the floor and sat up stiffly. There was a crick in his neck, and he was tempted to let Helen fix her own breakfast for a change. But his better nature joined with his own need for a cup of coffee, and he went to the kitchen to fill the percolator and put it on the stove.

Waiting for the first beige spurtings to turn brown, he reviewed the little tiff. The danger of such a misunderstanding, and even of a serious argument, seemed to be always with them lately. It lay just below the surface, as a shark might swim around and under a small boat. He would have to watch himself. He didn't know why it should be, but under the present unnatural conditions, responsibility for domestic peace seemed to be all his.

He opened a can of orange juice, poured coffee and arranged a breakfast tray. He braced his shoulders and carried the tray into the bedroom. Helen was still sleeping. But her face looked fresh and rested, and her sleep could not have been very sound. As he placed the tray on the bedside table, her hand reached out and touched his lightly. That was all. No more was necessary. He sat on the bed, handed her the orange juice and watched her fondly as she sipped.

CHAPTER FOUR

It was a bright morning with a blue sky and no smog, and Dave was interrupted only once. There was a knock on the door about ten-thirty. He opened it, and experienced something like psychic panic when he recognized his visitor. It was Thelma. The girl showed no signs of a hangover. Her bright hair was covered by a red babushka. She wore her strapless swimming suit and had assumed a model's pose—hand on hip, weight on her right leg, left knee forward and slightly bent. Her provocative gray eyes were amazingly innocent.

"Hi, Dave. Going for a swim?" she asked.

He shook his head. "Sorry, I'm working."

"You hear me when I come in last night?" She grinned. "Up on cloud seven, wasn't I?"

"You were feeling no pain."

"Maybe no, but that crazy Lu sure was. Still is. Well," she said, "I'll be on the beach, happen you change your mind."

"I won't."

She giggled. "That wife of yours sure got you hog-tied, ain't she?"

"Now, you look here—!"

"Never mind. I dig it, Davy. You know where to find me later on."

She undulated down the steps. Dave closed the door with unnecessary violence and wondered, as he did so, whether the violence was directed entirely at Thelma or partly at himself. He was honest enough to admit that he did feel a little flattered by the interest of a young and pretty girl, but he was also realistic.

He wanted nothing more to do with her. It was lucky that his painting only needed a few finishing touches, or, in his confused state, he might have botched the job. As it was, he completed it within two hours, and then did something he refrained from doing as a rule. He mixed a cocktail before lunch.

It was a self-congratulatory gesture of celebration, and he carried the martini to the living room. He was holding it when there came a second rapping on the door. This time it was Lu Warren.

Warren was a thin man who dressed habitually in khaki shirts and trousers. He was a care-ridden fifty with an accent that was the male equivalent of Thelma's. He had a nervous, fretful manner, and Dave had noticed the same manner in Amy Warren. He had wondered what common calamity had formed the worry-lines in their lean faces, and since last night he had suspected that it was each other. That might partly explain Thelma's presence in the house while Amy was away.

"Hello, Lu," Dave said. "What's on your mind?"

"Want to ask you something, Mr. Russell. You're friendly with my cousin?" There was a significant pause before he spoke the final word.

"Friendly?"

"Well, you drew this picture, didn't you?" The sketch Dave had made the day before was thrust into his hand. "Just one thing I want to know," Lu said. "Was it you that took her out last night?"

The creaking of the gate at the head of the stairs attracted Dave's attention. He looked up. Helen was standing there. She had come home unexpectedly and, by her expression, she had heard what Lu had said.

Lu had also seen her. He nodded curtly. "Hi, Miz Russell." He scowled at Dave. "Talk to you about it later." He turned away.

"You'll talk about it now. The answer's no. I heard her come home last night, and I heard you. I heard everything you both said. Like me to repeat the conversation?"

Lu took a backward step, alarmed. "Needn't take that attitude, Mr. Russell. I was just asking."

"You've been answered." Dave ignored him, holding his left hand out to Helen. "Glad you came home early, darling."

Helen said nothing. The cocktail glass in Dave's right hand assumed the proportions of a gallon jug as she came slowly down the steps.

The prowl car cruised north on the stretch between the breakwater and Martinez Canyon. Tommy Riggs was driving. Earl Bingham sat beside him, a placid mass. Earl did not notice the beautiful blonde girl, but Tommy did. She was standing at the gate beside which he had picked her up the previous night. He almost drove past before deciding to give the kid another break.

"Hi. Thelma. How you feel?" he called.

She shrugged a bare, indifferent shoulder. Earl, leaning forward to get a better look, saw that she had a red dingus on her head and that she was wearing a tight black swimming suit.

"Ain't that the girl was on the beach yesterday?" he asked.

Tommy said off-handedly, "Correct."

"You know her?"

"Spoke to her, didn't I? Name's Thelma."

Earl thought about it for a minute. As Tommy turned in to park beside the bridge, he said, "You didn't know her yesterday."

"Yesterday was twenty-four hours ago."

The car was stopped, as usual, facing the highway. Earl waited until Tommy had set the brakes. "You must of met her last night, then."

"That's right, Earl. That brain of yours is working overtime today."

"Yeah," Earl agreed soberly. "Yeah, it is. How'd you make out with her?" he asked.

An expansive grin lit Tommy's handsome face. "Now you've embarrassed me. As a gentleman, I can't answer that.

But I'll tell you this much—she's no different from any other dame; you know how to handle 'em. I know how." He opened the car door. "You got any more questions, prepare to ask 'em. I'm going over to see Mildred."

The furrows in Earl's narrow forehead grew deeper. "I got one more question, Tommy. Yesterday you was talking about the guy that kissed her on the beach. You said seeing an older man making a play for a kid like that—you said it made you sick."

"Did I say that?"

Earl nodded. "Then you go and make a play for her yourself. How come?"

"Well, I'll tell you," Tommy said. "With me, the circumstances are entirely different."

"What circumstances?"

"It's simple. That artist and I are two entirely different people. He's him. I'm me. What's right for me is wrong for him and maybe vice versa, maybe not. It all depends." He jumped out of the car. "You think that over for a while."

Earl watched him swagger across the road. He thought it over. If it had come from anyone but Tommy, he would have said it didn't make good sense. And Tommy or not, he was getting tired of having his questions answered in a sort of fancy double-talk. Just because a fellow thinks slow doesn't mean he doesn't think good, when he thinks.

There was a breeze from the east. Smog settled over the beach like a dirty cotton blanket. The brilliant, energetic day turned glum. Swimmers bundled up their gear, drove home. Dave and Helen went about their individual tasks, treating each other with self-conscious courtesy. Dave got together the materials necessary for wrapping his picture for the mail. Helen compiled a grocery list and crossed the beach road to the supermarket. Walking, she had a tendency to come down hard on her heels.

It was only too clear now that, during the daylight hours while she'd been working, Dave had spent his time lounging on the beach. Playing around with a vicious little juvenile delinquent, drawing pictures of her, arousing Lu Warren's protective jealousy. He could rationalize his behavior all he pleased; the fact remained that he had deliberately concealed the truth about the girl. He hadn't even mentioned that he'd met her. And, since he had concealed their acquaintanceship, it was perfectly obvious that what existed between them was a good deal more than that. It was much more likely—

Helen got that far in her angry reasoning, and no further. She suddenly realized to what end her suspicions must inevitably lead her, if they turned out to be true. A lonely, bitter end. A vacuum, because life without Dave would be no more than that.

She had already paid for her groceries. They boy was putting them in a heavy paper bag. She caught up the bag and almost ran out of the store. A truck slammed on its brakes, just missing her as she crossed the road. She ran through the gate and down the steps. The front door was standing open. She went in.

She came to an unbelieving halt. Dave was leaning out of the window, talking to someone below him on the beach. She knew who it was even before she heard the hateful, whining voice.

"Lu's gone to Palisades City. And your wife ain't here, so why not Davy? I'm lonesome. Come on down."

Helen was not conscious of having made a sound, but she must have done so. Dave whirled around. She studied his guilty face for a long moment, then turned and crossed the living room to the bedroom stairs. Silently, with natural dignity. The door at the head of the stairs always stood open. She locked it as Dave started up the steps.

He banged on the door. She lay face down on the bed, hands over her ears. She could still faintly hear his muffled voice, sense from its changing tone that he was growing angry. But she was too hurt even to attempt a reply.

The noise stopped after a while but she still lay motionless. An hour passed before she got up, washed her face. She went down to the living room prepared to suffer through an explanation and, perhaps an abject apology, but it was too late by that time.

Dave had gone.

There were only a few customers in the cafe and Hazel was taking care of them. Mildred sat beside the kitchen window, fingering a letter. The letter had arrived only that morning, but already she knew it by heart. Unlike Ralph's other letters, this one said something. It said too much.

"Dear Mom.

I'm sending this out by a guy they're turning loose, a friend of mine, so the screws won't get a chance to read it. When I wrote you before that everything was fine and they were treating me okay, I was lying, Mom. Maybe I would deserve to be treated this way if I was guilty, but I'm not guilty. Tom Riggs framed me. He was jealous because he knew you loved me, and he picked up Hank's switchblade after he run us off the road and Hank got killed, and he planted the switchblade on me and swore I pulled it on him. I never did, and I would have told the judge what happened but I thought you was sold on Riggs, so I thought what the hell.

Mom, I'm breaking out of here. This friend of mine they're turning loose is going to get a car and come back and pick me up. There's a place in the wire I can get through, and what I want you to do is pack a suitcase and have it ready when I phone. I'll phone you Monday night. Please don't worry. Everything's all set.

Your loving son…"

Mildred put the creased letter in the pocket of her apron. She tried to decide what she should do and was incapable of reaching a decision. She didn't want Ralph to try to escape. Even if he were successful, the act of escaping would place him in defiance of the law. And no boy, no man, can defy the law without warping something in his character. Something deep inside Ralph that had been straight would be forever twisted out of shape.

On the other hand, she could not bring herself to notify the school's authorities. That would have been treachery. Her lips moved, forming silent words.

Mildred was praying, not knowing that she prayed.

Palisades City is a boardwalk beach town. Until a half-hour after midnight its boardwalk, which is really a broad cement sidewalk lined on both sides with tawdry shops, is a rowdy, garishly illuminated pedestrian thoroughfare. At half-past twelve the colored neons are turned off as though someone had pulled a master switch. After that, only the street lamps are left. They shed a cold synthetic moonlight over shuttered stores and empty benches, all waiting for the returning crowd to bring them back to life.

Dave came out of the Palisades Theatre at ten minutes before twelve. He had sat through the feature picture twice, and had no idea of how he could further pass the time until Helen might reasonably be presumed to have gone to bed. He did not want to go home until that happened.

The center of the boardwalk was occupied by a long line of benches. He went to one of them and sat down. The Rambler had been left in a parking lot two blocks away; in another hour he would reclaim it and drive home. All he had to do was sit still for another sixty minutes. But sitting still was more difficult than he had thought.

His mind was in rebellion, and his eyes were as restless as his mind. Fleetingly they noted individual faces in the crowd, a shooting gallery directly ahead and, to its right, an open counter piled high with salt-water taffy. On his left a sign, above a crimson door read. *The Beach Bar—Cocktails,* and beyond that another sign called attention to the offices of *Dexter.* Somewhere Dave had seen or heard that name before. He got up and crossed to the twenty-foot storefront.

There were no windows, only an open double door across which a black star-spangled curtain had been drawn. A tripod beside the door held a large black placard. In the center of the placard was a photograph of a bearded man who wore a turban. This was presumably Dexter, and grouped around his photograph were a number of glossy prints of moving picture celebrities. All of these were autographed, and curiously all the autographs were in the same scrawled handwriting. Five-pointed tinsel stars were scattered among the glossy prints and, at the bottom of the placard, silver letters read, *The Man Who Guides the Stars.*

The phrase stirred Dave's memory. He recalled the circumstances in which he had heard the name before. Thelma had mumbled it when she had come home drunk the previous night.

Everything revolved around that damned girl. She was omni-present, he thought bitterly, and he was aghast that only that afternoon he had been a little flattered because she had displayed an interest in him. One of her favorite words came back to him: Crazy. It would aptly have described his addled state of mind. He went back to the bench, looked at his watch. Only twenty minutes had passed. The time was ten minutes before twelve.

The world had shrunk for Thelma. She lay on the beach and vaguely wondered why she had ever let herself get steamed up about the things she didn't have. Everything she wanted was right here within reaching distance. Her back itched. She rubbed it against a small convenient boulder that had become embedded between her shoulder blades. A couple of feet away, beside a shallow pool left by the tide, there was a bottle. The moon was so bright that she could see how full the bottle was. The moon was peeking at her over the top of Point of Rocks. It was close. Her right forefinger stirred the shallow pool. If she felt like it, she could have lifted her finger and poked the old moon in the eye.

A man lay on the sand beside her. His arms were around her so tight it hurt her ribs. She tried to remember what his name was. He'd told it to her a day, an hour, a week before, but she'd forgotten it. Ask her right now what he looked like, and she couldn't even tell you that. It didn't make much difference. He was a man.

She wriggled out of his arms and rolled away, for no better reason than to see what he would do. She giggled when he did what she'd expected. He reached out and grabbed, just missing her, and the shadows mixed with moonlight painted funny pictures on his face. His hair was mussed up, so that it looked as though he had two horns sprouting from his forehead. Like a billy goat, or like a bull. She took a drink from the bottle, screwed the top back on again. It was so comical she laughed out loud. She took the red babushka off her head and dangled it in front of her, the way she'd seen a bullfighter in the movies do. She remembered an old song she had learned when she was just a kid. She sang it to him, giggling, waving her babushka in the moonlight.

" 'Toreador-a, don't spit on the floor-a.
Use the cuspidor-a, that's what it's for-a…' "

She was only doing it for kicks, but it turned out that he wasn't fooling. All of a sudden he made a big jump and landed right on top of her, and started getting fresh. Real fresh. That, wouldn't have been too bad if only he'd been nice about it, but he wasn't a bit nice. He was rough, and Thelma wasn't the kind of girl that was going to stand for being treated rough. She told him so and tried to shove him off, but he didn't pay the least bit of attention. He was pressing all the wind out of her and it was getting hard to breathe, so she lifted up her forefinger and poked him in the eye. The left eye. And before he could do anything about it, she poked him in the other.

It was funny how he acted then. He didn't make a sound. He got up on his knees and, for a minute, she thought she'd taught him a good lesson and that he would treat her nicer after that. He couldn't have been seeing good, but he still kept hold of her with one strong hand. The other hand fumbled around beside him on the beach. He picked up something, and Thelma saw it was the boulder she had used to scratch her back. She tried to roll away, but he had her pinned down tight. He lifted the boulder and slammed it hard against her head.

That was another funny thing; it didn't really hurt much. It dazed her, though, and scared hell out of her. And maybe it knocked her out—but only for a second. She knew what was happening when she felt his hand start yanking at her hair. But it was as though it was happening to somebody else, not her. There'd been a mistake somewhere. She'd never hurt anybody. She was just Thelma, out for kicks, an hour late and a dollar short, and she tried to explain this, but he rolled her over and pushed her face down in the pool. She yelled then, yelled loud, but the only sound that got out was a sort of roaring bubble.

Water choked the rest.

CHAPTER FIVE

Dave did not notice the sudden semi-darkness when, within minutes of each other, all the neons were clicked off. He looked up after a while and found himself alone on a deserted boardwalk. It was time to start for home.

He got up wearily and returned to the parking lot. On the beach road going north, he had to slow down because of a gang of men in hard ship workers' helmets who were staring apprehensively at the overhanging palisades. Since the spring rains there had been trouble with landslides, and Dave recognized the men as a work crew bent on preventing traffic tie-ups before they happened. As he was waiting for the signal to resume normal speed, he heard a shout and felt a sharp jolt against the car. He stopped, knowing what had happened: a boulder had rolled down the palisades and hit his right front wheel. There was no damage.

That did not prevent the foreman from taking down his name and license number. When he was permitted to go ahead, it was with the understanding that he might be called upon to testify to the foreman's competence and to the accidental nature of what had happened. That was all right. He did not expect ever to be called. There was no other incident on his way home. He reached there at twenty minutes after one.

The window of the bedroom was dark, and now glow came up the exterior stairway from the Warrens' place. Dave had to feel his way past the porch and down to his front door. He unlocked the door and let himself into pitch-blackness, made his way uncertainly to the couch. He took off his jacket, shoes and trousers, and lay down in his shirt and shorts.

He lay down but did not immediately go to sleep. Seconds later he heard the soft shutting of the bedroom door. Helen had been awake; she had waited in the darkness until he came home. Dave smiled grimly in the direction of the unseen ceiling. He closed his eyes.

They opened again at twenty minutes before two. He verified the time by looking at the radium dial of his watch. It was less easy to be certain of what had awakened him but, listening, he heard footsteps passing the front door. There was no other sound except that of the sea.

The footsteps went heavily, slowly down the stairs. Dave thought of them as heavy because the steps creaked under their weight. A picture formed in his mind of a grotesquely fat man tiptoeing down to the beach.

He fell asleep and dreamed of the fat man standing knee-deep in surf, washing away layer after layer of adipose tissue. When the man returned to the house, he was no longer fat. His footsteps, as they climbed the stairs, were stealthy but brisk and light.

Dave was suddenly wide-awake. The sounds were real; they were not part of his dream. Footsteps were again passing the door, this time going up. It was ten minutes before two. He got up, exasperated, went to the kitchen, and looked out of the window.

It was too dark on the beach road to see much. Another car had pulled in behind the Rambler. Someone had opened the door, was climbing behind the wheel. It was a man; Dave could tell that much, no more. The car was only a black hulk. He could not even be certain of its make.

He turned away—and was stopped by an odd tinkling sound. At almost two in the morning, an ice cream truck should be in its garage, but Dave distinctly heard familiar notes. They formed the refrain, *Oh Where, Oh Where Has My Little Dog Gone?* that he had heard the afternoon before.

He went back to the window but by that time the truck had passed beyond his range of hearing. The car that had been parked behind his own was just starting to drive off. Dave did not wait to see it disappear. He returned to the couch, fell instantly asleep, and did not wake up again until six-thirty in the morning.

He was still tired. Normally he would have slept for another couple of hours. Some unaccustomed deviation from routine must have pulled him back to consciousness. There was an appreciable lapse of time before he became aware of what the deviation was. Helen's most prized luxury was having her breakfast coffee in bed. But this morning the familiar odor was already perceptible in the living room.

It was a bad sign. It probably indicated an unwillingness on her part to accept any favors from him, even so slight a favor as making morning coffee. Dave pulled on his shoes and trousers. If the cold war was going to continue, he might as well get dressed. He approached the kitchen warily.

Coffee was bubbling in the percolator and Helen was busy at the kitchen table. A wicker hamper was on the table and she was making sandwiches. She looked up as he came in.

"Picnic today," she announced. Her voice was gentle and subdued. "We need a change of scene. I'd like to go up in the hills to our old place. Maybe when we come back we'll be more like we used to be." She smiled uncertainly. "Okay?"

"Okay."

215

"Sometimes you provoke me beyond the limits of my patience. But I love you," she said, after they had kissed.

The canyon wound inland for thirteen miles, climbing between rocky hills that were high enough to be small mountains. The last few miles were up a steep grade until, just below the crest, they reached what Helen had referred to as their "old place," They had come here often during the first years of their marriage, a shady spot fifty yards off the road, from which the surrounding country unfolded far beneath them like a lumpy green and yellow bedspread. There were no rusty cans or other evidences of previous picnickers; apparently few people wandered this far from the road. They ate their lunch in privacy and an atmosphere of renewed serenity, and Dave gave her a detailed account of how he'd spent the previous evening. He told her about the footsteps and the ice cream wagon, too.

"And don't say I was dreaming. I actually heard them. I was as wide awake as I am now,"

"Wider, by the way you're yawning."

He nodded. "That reminds me. It's time for my siesta now."

There was a beach mat in the car. He spread it on the grass and lay down on it. He slept with his head on Helen's lap.

The sun sets early in the mountains. At six, when they went back to the car, it was already getting dark. They ran into sunlight again, however, as topping the crest they came for a moment in sight of the sea. They drove inland five more miles, then doubled back southwest, and they had dinner at a restaurant overlooking the ocean. It was a good dinner. Afterwards, they started for home by what they thought was the shortest route, along the beach.

But the road was blocked; the expected landslide had taken place. They were forced to detour inland and return through Martinez Canyon. Lights were burning in both sections of the house when they finally reached home. A sheriff's car and a police cruiser were parked beside the gate.

Helen touched Dave's hand. Her voice was puzzled. "Why the police? You suppose Lu's in trouble?"

"Lord knows." He indicated two deputies standing at the gate. "They'll tell us."

Dave stopped behind the sheriff's car. Before he could slide from under the wheel a deputy was at his side.

"Russell?" He was a flashily handsome man, his features aquiline as an Indian's.

Dave nodded.

"This your wife?"

"This is Mrs. Russell."

The deputy opened the car door.

"Bingham," he called, "take this woman down to the lieutenant." His hand closed forcefully around Dave's wrist.

A second, massive deputy showed up on the right side of the car. He said, "This way, ma'am," Helen silently climbed out.

Dave controlled his anger. He waited until she had been escorted through the gate. "Am I under arrest? If so, for what?" he asked.

"Ask the lieutenant. He's waiting to talk to you."

"Unless I am under arrest, take your hands off me," Dave said.

The first deputy grinned. He twisted Dave's wrist and gave it a vicious jerk. As Dave came out of the car, his left arm was doubled painfully behind his back.

"Damn kid-killer." The deputy ran him forward and around the car; he was pushed through the gate. "Get down there," the man said, and shoved him down the steps.

There was a dazed period wherein things happened, he was pushed and pulled, and voices spoke to each other, but it was like watching the screen of a drive-in movie from far away. He saw moving figures but could not distinguish one from another. He heard blurred sound but could not make out words.

Then abruptly there was silence and the scene swam into focus. He stood in the middle of the living room. Deputies stood beside him, one on either side. In front of him was a lean man with graying temples. At first glance he appeared to be intelligent, but Dave was in no mood to take people at face value. He reserved judgment, concentrating on the fact that the man, although obviously a policeman, wore well-cut civilian clothes. That might, or might not, be an indication that he was less brutal and moronic than the others. Helen leaned against the wall. Her eyes were anguished; her face was pale and drawn.

"It's the truth, Lieutenant!" she was saying. "My husband was at home last night!"

"Not all night, Mrs. Russell," the lean man said gently." "We have a witness who saw him about one o'clock." He turned to Dave. "I'm Lieutenant Morgan, temporarily attached to the sheriff's sub-station. I'll need your statement."

"I'd give it to you, if someone would tell me what the statement is supposed to be about."

The lieutenant frowned. "Don't you read the papers? Thelma Grant was found this morning—murdered."

The name meant nothing. "This is ridiculous," Dave said. "I don't know anyone—" Then a message Helen had been trying to flash to him suddenly grew clear. He took a quick step forward. "You mean Lu Warren's cousin?"

Lieutenant Morgan nodded. The breath went out of Dave. He felt as though he had been kicked in the solar plexus. "So help me," he said slowly. "I hardly knew her. This is the first time I ever heard her full name." He took another step. The handsome deputy stopped him by grabbing at his arm. "You say she's murdered?"

"That's what we're trying to establish," the policeman said. "Mind coming along?"

Dave frowned at the hand clasped around his arm. "Do I have any choice?"

"We just want a few people to see you, and to ask some questions. I'd appreciate it if you came willingly. It would make things easier."

"By all means, let's make things easier," Dave said.

Morgan nodded to the deputies. "Mr. Russell will ride with you. I'll follow. I want to talk to Mrs. Russell for a minute."

The deputy jerked Dave's arm. "Let's go." Dave said nothing. He allowed himself to be led out.

He was hit the instant the front door shut behind them, hit hard back of the ear. He fell forward, landing on the steps.

"Take it easy, can't you?" The voice of the deputy named Bingham seemed to come from a great distance. "You don't know he's guilty. Nobody knows that."

"As far as I'm concerned, he's guilty," Tommy said.

Helen waited for Dave to call but the hours passed and the telephone was silent. A clock ticked, waves tumbled on the beach, the tide ran out, and still there was no message. At two o'clock she lifted the telephone but, after holding it for half a minute, slowly replaced it in its cradle. She went back to the couch, picked up the evening paper. She shuddered as again she saw the glaring headline, GIRL'S BODY FOUND ON BEACH. The paper came out while she and Dave were in the mountains.

She sat on the couch and for the sixth time read the story. It was a sensational story. The body, dressed in green panties and brassiere, had been discovered about breakfast time that morning. It was lying, hidden from the house where the girl had been visiting, at the foot of a small embankment near the sea. Thelma's other clothes were neatly piled some distance away. A preliminary medical examination had disclosed the presence of water in her lungs, and police had first supposed her death to be suicide or accidental drowning.

Helen raised her hand to the Venetian blind. If she had lifted the blind she could have seen the embankment at the foot of which Thelma's body had been found. She did not lift it. She went back to the story.

Two hours after the discovery of the body, a red babushka identified as Thelma's had been picked up miles to the north at Point of Rocks; and a more thorough examination, conducted about the same time, had shown a swollen bruise on the girl's head. The babushka was torn, and other signs of a struggle had been found in the area. Thelma, it now appeared, had been knocked unconscious shortly after midnight and her head held under water in one of the pools left by the tide at Point of Rocks.

Lucius Warren, brought in for questioning, had admitted that the girl was not a relative. He had met her in Palisades City where she had been employed as a salesgirl. He was being held tentatively on a charge of contributing to the delinquency of a minor. Police, acting on information furnished them by Warren, were looking for David Russell, an artist who occupied the upper part of the Warren house and who was said to have been on familiar terms with Thelma Grant.

Familiar! The hateful word stirred Helen into action. She dropped the paper, went to the phone, and told the operator to ring the substation.

She gave her name to the man who answered, and told him she was calling about her husband. "He hasn't come home. I don't know what to do."

"Hold the line, please." There was a pause while the man asked muffled questions. Then he spoke into the phone again, "They took him to the city, Mrs. Russell. They haven't booked him yet, if that's what you mean."

"Of course they haven't booked him!" Helen sounded more indignant than she felt; actually she was relieved. "He didn't take his car. I just wanted to know what time I can pick him up."

"Couldn't tell you, ma'am," the man said.

Helen hung up and walked to the ship's clock hung decoratively on the wall beside the bedroom stairs. She checked the time, then she straightened magazines on a table at the far end of the room. She moved like a somnambulist, and when she suddenly climbed to the kitchen, her action was compulsive, governed by no motive known consciously to herself.

In the kitchen she opened the refrigerator. It contained, among other items, a plate of cold sliced meat left over from the picnic. She was not hungry but she crammed two slices of tongue and one of turkey in her mouth, and was only stopped from eating more by the creaking of the gate out by the porch. Someone was coming down the steps.

She almost fell in her hurry to get to the door. She pushed it open and ran out.

"Dave!"

The man on the steps continued downward. She knew instantly that it was not Dave, but he had come within six feet before she recognized Lu Warren.

"Mr. Warren, have you seen my husband?"

"I seen him," Warren's voice was bitter. "Told the cops about him, too." He passed her and kept on going down the steps. "Hope they put him in the gas chamber. It's what he deserves."

Helen's hand groped blindly for the banister. She watched the landlord until he had reached the sandy patio and passed from sight. Then she returned to the living room and lay down on the couch, forearm covering her eyes. Her eyes ached with the pressure of accumulated tears, but she did not cry. There would be time for crying later. Lots of time.

It was dawn when Dave finally came home. Helen heard him on the stairs, but this time she did not go running to the door. She sat up and waited. He saw her as soon as he came in.

He smiled faintly. "Tough night? I know how you feel."

She said, "Sit down. Tell me what happened."

"Isn't there any coffee?"

"I'll make some. You sit down and rest."

When she returned with the coffee, he was asleep sitting in his chair. Her instinctive pity put up only a token struggle before anxiety completely routed it. She set the coffee down and shook his shoulder.

"Wake up, dear."

He woke as a hunted animal wakes—standing, poised to run. "What's the matter?"

"That's what I want to know," she said.

He sat down again, sipped coffee, lit a cigarette. She noted the dark circles under his eyes, and gave him all the time he needed. When he seemed more relaxed, she said, "Tell me about it. Start from the beginning."

He gave her a lopsided grin. "They questioned me. Know what a police questioning consists of? The same old questions asked over and over again for hours and hours. It seemed to disappoint them that I kept on giving the same answers. Finally they let me go—drove me home, as a matter of fact. That's all for tonight. My present status is a polite form of house arrest. I'm supposed to be here when they want me."

"Why?"

"Look, darling, they have to have a suspect. The public expects it of them. It's a rule. Lou Warren's out. At the time she was murdered he was looking all over the place for her, and people saw him. Ken Hurley, among other people. They may still get him on that contributing charge, but not for murder. He's clear on that."

"You're not?"

He shook his head. "Lu spent a lot of time upon the road last night. I wasn't home at the time the murder was committed, and he knows it. Then there's the foreman of a gang of road workers. He talked to me at one."

"But how about the ice cream wagon? How about those footsteps you heard?"

"I told all that to Morgan. Told him about Dexter, too." Dave shrugged. "He said he'd look into it…"

His voice trailed off. She had to prompt him. "Well?"

"I don't think he believed me. He didn't seem impressed." Dave got up. "I'm going to have to go to bed."

"When does Morgan want to see you again? What about?"

"Ask him. He'll be here at eleven. Please, Helen," he begged. "I've got things to do. Before I do them I have to get some sleep."

She let him go. By that time it was half-past five, and she'd had no sleep herself. She lay down on the couch but could not keep her eyes closed. At eight she got up. She could no longer be inactive, waiting submissively for terrible things to happen. What Dave had described as a polite form of house arrest did not apply to her.

Dave seemed to be sleeping. She hurried from the house and down the road to the cottage occupied by the young man who drove the ice cream truck. She'd known Ken Hurley, as Dave had, when he'd worked at the service station. Her heart beat rapidly as she knocked on the cottage door.

No one came to open it. She called, "Mr. Hurley—!" but there was no evidence of life beyond the door. She didn't give up. It had been a good try, and she could come back later.

Helen went back to the house. She called the shop and left word for Mr. Victor that she would not be able to work that day. Hanging up, she heard Dave coming from the kitchen. She turned toward the steps.

She started to explain, "Just calling—" and broke off in surprise. "You're going out?"

He nodded. "All dressed up to have my fortune told. Morgan didn't believe me about Dexter. I'll have to see the guy myself."

"You're not supposed to leave the house. Morgan will be here at eleven."

"So will I. Fresh coffee will be ready in a minute. If Morgan expected me to stay in one place," Dave said, "he should have kept me in his jail."

CHAPTER SIX

There are some people a guy just naturally hates on sight. They affect you like an overdose of raw corn liquor. Tangle with one of them, and you wake up next morning with all the symptoms of a hangover. Tommy Riggs woke up Monday morning with a dry mouth and a headache. If it hadn't been for Dave Russell, he would have got to bed earlier and slept better. He would have wakened feeling fine, ready to go to work.

But work, today, wouldn't have been a good idea anyway. Some of the people at the sub-station—Corporal Gonzalez in particular—were gunning for him. Tommy had to keep a jump ahead of them. Right now he had to get himself in a position where he could just sort of casually mention what he had been doing Friday and Saturday nights. Block any thought of a connection between Thelma and himself before it could get started. There was no telling what might happen if word that they had known each other got around.

It would be easy enough. Mildred and Earl could be counted on to give him alibis. Mildred was nuts about him, and Earl would do anything that Tommy said. Nobody had actually seen him with Thelma, so he didn't have to worry about that. Tommy dressed, and drove his yellow convertible down the beach to Mildred's place.

He turned the motor off, staring moodily across the road at the window of Russell's bedroom. What a racket! Russell was probably still asleep while he, Tommy, had been forced to haul his backside out of bed at dawn to make a third-rate living. Around noon, Russell would get up, slap a little paint on canvas, and sell the canvas for a couple of thousand bucks. It wasn't fair.

But the hell with thinking about Russell. What he had to concentrate on right now was being nice to Mildred. And what she'd always liked best was a little sweet talk about the future. She needed something to build on, hope for. He got out of the convertible, opened the door of the cafe.

"Hey, Mildred!" he called.

It was Hazel's day off. Mildred sat in the kitchen by herself. She turned as he came in, and Tommy saw that something must have happened. There were new lines in her face, and she looked old. He gave her a winning smile.

"Honey, I got a proposition to make. You interested?"

She shook her head. "No proposition of yours would interest me."

Tommy's voice dropped in pitch, became utterly sincere. "You just listen for a minute. I do a lot of horsing around, but actually I'm a very serious type," he said. "A family man, you know? I don't like the way things are with you and me. I live all by myself up in this room, and all I do is sleep and look at television and go to work. And I don't like the kind of work I'm doing now. It's got no future in it, understand?"

Mildred said quietly, "You're a little late worrying about your future. That was all decided long ago."

"You may be right. I always felt I was intended to do something big." He smiled ingratiatingly. "Well, what I got to say boils down to this. How's about you and me getting together again? I could come down here and run this restaurant. Maybe I could handle a few cars—clean ones, strictly high-class—on the side. When Ralph gets out, and if he's learned his lesson. I might be able to throw a job his way. All we need is a little capital; we'd have it made. So how's it strike you, Milly—pretty good?"

There was a silence. Then Mildred got slowly to her feet. "Get out. Get out, you son of a bitch," she said.

Tommy was so shocked that he started to obey. He had turned toward the front door before he thoroughly realized that she had meant what she had called him, and he got mad.

"Hey!" He turned back quickly. "Nobody, least of all a damned woman, can call me that!"

Her hand was in the pocket of her apron. "Tom, I haven't even begun to tell you what I think of you. You don't want to hear it; you'd better get out fast." She took a slow, determined step in his direction. "You framed Ralph."

"That's a lie!"

"It's the truth. I know that now; I know a lot about you, and every bit of it is bad. How about that little blonde girl that got murdered—Thelma Grant?"

Tommy shivered. It was as though someone had poured a bucket of ice-cold water down his spine. "Well, what about her? I didn't even know the girl," he said.

"Is that what you'll tell the district attorney? I don't think he'll believe you. I saw you with her Friday. Suppose I tell him so?"

"This is a sample of what you'll get," he said, and clipped her on the jaw.

She crumpled to the floor. Tommy looked at her a moment, then suddenly he got frightened. He hadn't meant to hit her. He didn't like to hit women as a rule. He'd have a hell of a job now, talking her into doing what he wanted. It might be better to wait a while before he tried. He went out to his car.

But he was nervous. His mind was working frantically, much faster than it usually did. He'd thought he was safe but if Mildred had seen him with Thelma, it followed that other people might have seen him, too.

Abruptly, he remembered Dexter. He hesitated a moment. The fortuneteller didn't know his name. There was a possibility that Dexter wouldn't remember him at all. Just the same, he had to make sure. There was no use trying to do anything with Mildred until he had made sure. He started his convertible, turned south into the beach road.

Just before he reached the Warren house, a Rambler nudged into the traffic ahead of him. Dave Russell was driving it. Tommy scowled, wondering where Russell was headed for. Then, as the blocks passed and the Rambler anticipated every turn that would take both it and the convertible to Palisades City, that icy feeling began playing up and down Tommy's spine again. Even before the Rambler turned into the parking lot near Dexter's place, Tommy knew it was a good thing he hadn't gone to work. He had to get to the fortuneteller before Russell did.

The telephone booth was in front of a drug store on the east side of the boardwalk. From it, Tommy could see the entrance to Dexter's place. That damned attendant in the parking lot had held him up. Russell had beat him by a whole half-block.

Tommy was dialing the telephone as he watched. He heard it ring; heard the gruff voice of Corporal Gonzalez at the sub-station up the coast.

"This is Riggs," he said. "Corporal, I don't feel so good. Doctor says I shouldn't work today."

"I feel for you, Riggs, but I can't quite reach you. Bingham got less sleep than you did, but he's on the job."

"Swear to God, that's exactly what I told the doctor. Said it'd look funny as hell, my partner working and me not. You want to talk to the doctor, Corporal? He's right here."

"No. I don't want to talk to any doctor. But there is a matter I'd like to discuss with you. A personal matter. At your convenience, of course."

The connection was broken but Tommy still held the receiver to his ear. As long as he looked like he was talking, nobody would pay any attention to him in the booth. He was sweating, although the day's heat had not yet begun. That damned Gonzalez had the knife in him all right!

He was still at the telephone when Russell came out of Dexter's. Russell headed back toward the parking lot. Tommy darted from the booth as soon as he was out of sight.

He ran across the boardwalk, did an about-face, and walked right back into the booth again. He'd nearly run into a guy he knew, Dick Swope, a plainclothes man attached to the city force. A disturbing possibility occurred to him. Swope might be standing as a plant outside of Dexter's place.

But why? How could first Russell and then Swope have known that he'd brought Thelma here to have her fortune told? It was all very confusing, but Tommy dismissed the idea of personal danger after a moment's thought. For one thing, Swope was paying no attention to Dexter. His interest was centered on a cute little redhead he'd just run into on the boardwalk. Tommy watched the detective sit down beside her on a bench. Swope's back was turned. Once more Tommy left the booth.

And once more he was forced to return to it. A couple of yokels—they looked like honeymooners—stood giggling in front of the black placard until the old fortune teller, complete with beard and turban, came out and roped them in.

Swope was still on the bench when those two came out again. But he was making good time with the redhead; Tommy knew from experience that a man in Swope's position couldn't think of two things at once. He didn't bother to take precautions. He hurried over to Dexter's, brushed the yokels aside, and went in the door.

Dexter met him in the tiny, curtained reception room. He bowed, touching his forehead, lips and heart. "Good morning," he said, his accent as thick as it was fake. "You are deeply disturbed, sair. I 'ave known that you were coming. I 'ave seen it in the stars."

He was a slight old man. Tommy rushed him through a second door into the rear, private room. He shut the door, turned the key, and popped a chair beneath the knob.

"I'll get to you in a minute," he said, as the old man mouthed silent, frightened words. He crossed to the window, opened it, and looked out. A stationary ladder descended from the window to the beach. Dexter had provided himself with an emergency exit. He'd been smart, but not smart enough.

Tommy shut the window. He returned to the trembling fortuneteller. "Remember me?" he asked.

"You...you... No! I never seen you in my life!" Dexter's accent was forgotten. He was so agitated he could hardly speak.

"That's the right answer, but you took too long to say it. Now we got to make sure, next time somebody asks you, you come up with the right answer and come up fast."

Tommy took a blackjack from his pocket and went scientifically to work.

It was only a little after ten when Dave got home, but a police car had parked beside the gate and a uniformed policeman waited at the wheel. Dave wasn't worried. If Morgan wanted to get tough, he had material now with which to soften him. He got out of the Rambler, went down the steps and entered the living room. Lieutenant Morgan was with Helen.

As far as he could tell, Helen was perfectly at ease. She was sitting on the couch, drinking coffee and talking to the lieutenant. Morgan rose as Dave came in. The policeman's face remained expressionless but, as Dave approached, he saw that Helen's calm had been assumed. The sight of him had brought relief into her eyes.

"Lieutenant Morgan's been waiting to talk to you," she said.

Morgan nodded. "Mr. Russell, I understand you went to call on Dexter. I thought I asked you to stay at home."

"What did you expect?" Dave shrugged. "Somebody had to talk to him."

"Dexter's place has been staked out since six this morning. He was the next man on my list. Now—" Morgan sighed, went over to the phone. "Mind if I make a call?"

He dialed a number. "Lieutenant Morgan. Have Swope bring Dexter in immediately." He read the number from the telephone. "Call me back."

He hung up, and thoughtfully recrossed the room. "Well, Mr. Russell, what did you find out?"

"Two things," Dave said. "Thelma was there Friday evening with a man."

"Description?"

"No luck. That rear room of his is heavily curtained and he keeps the lighting dim. The man stood over in the corner. Dexter couldn't see his face."

"Curious. Even a shadow in a corner has dimensions," Morgan said. "If it talks, it has a certain kind of voice. You said you found out two things, Mr. Russell. That's only one."

Dave said quietly, "The man with Thelma was a policeman. He wasn't wearing his uniform, but Thelma had been drinking. She let it slip."

There was an intense but only momentary silence. Dave looked at Helen, and she looked back at him. Morgan had been smoking. He crossed to an ashtray, snubbed out his cigarette.

"May I have more coffee, Mrs. Russell, please?" he asked.

Grudgingly, Dave admitted to a sneaking admiration for the lieutenant. Morgan had poise. He gave no indication that he had just lost his Number One suspect and, as a substitute, been handed one of his own men. He stirred his coffee, sipped it black.

"We'll wait a minute. Maybe Dexter will be able to tell us a little more," he said.

The telephone rang as he was putting down his empty cup. "That's probably for me." He crossed the room to answer it.

"Yes? ...Speaking." Dave, watching, saw quick anger form in the policeman's eyes. He saw the effort with which Morgan fought it down. "Well, you know what to do. Tell Swope—" he said, and checked himself. "Never mind. I'll talk to Swope myself."

He hung up and turned to Dave. "Dexter's not talking to anybody. He's on his way to the hospital with a fractured skull."

"An accident?" Dave got his answer from the expression on Lieutenant Morgan's face. "Hey, wait a minute—you're not accusing me! Somebody must have done it after I left. Somebody—"

"That's right, Mr. Russell. Somebody. I'll have to go now. Will you stay put this time, or must I lock you up?"

Dave had been pushed around too long. "On what charge? You can't lock me up without a reason. Do you have one?"

Morgan ticked off several. "Material witness, suspicion of murder, assault with a deadly weapon. How about—?"

"Never mind. You win," Dave told him. "I'll stay put."

CHAPTER SEVEN

There were people on the beach but Tommy saw them only as mobile obstacles between which he must make his way. He went north, plodding through soft sand toward questionable refuge. Fear prodded him so sharply that once he lost his head and broke into a run.

But he got hold of himself almost immediately, and slowed to an inconspicuous walk. What the hell was the matter with him, anyway? He was a cop; he knew that a cop's attention is always attracted by a running man. Particularly when the man doesn't seem to be running anywhere. The cop instinctively looks to see who's chasing him.

There wasn't anybody chasing him that he knew of. He had a good head start. He'd got out of the window and down the ladder a split-second after the first knock on the door. He had gone so fast that he'd been halfway down when he'd heard the shouted, "Open up—police!" He had not heard Dexter's answering shout.

Why hadn't he heard it? He hadn't hit the old man often or very hard. He'd pulled his punches, or meant to pull them, because he didn't really give a damn about Dexter one way or the other. All he'd wanted was to throw a scare into the guy. Scare him enough so he wouldn't blab the little that he knew.

But when you came right down to it, what did Dexter know that was worth blabbing? He might be able to say that Tommy was tall and dark, and had been wearing a sports shirt, but they could walk along the beach and drag in a thousand guys that looked like that. Fingerprints? Prints must be so thick in Dexter's greasy shack, the chances were a hundred to one against them finding a single positive.

So he was safe, or reasonably so, and all he had to do was get out of the neighborhood, act natural and fix up those two alibis. Just the same, he wished Dexter had sung out when that knock came on the door. The old guy had either been too scared to answer, or—

Tommy refused to consider the alternative. His head was still splitting and Palisades City was a half mile behind him now. He wanted a drink. But all they sold at the makeshift stands along the beach was beer. The bars were on the far side of the boardwalk, and he didn't want to go up on the boardwalk yet. He stopped at a stand and bought a can of beer.

It tasted like carbonated quinine water, but he got it down. He came to the crowded pier at last, and had a double shot of bourbon at a bar. The whiskey warmed him, cleared his thinking. He knew exactly what he had to do.

There was a liquor store across from the end of the pier. He bought a pint of bourbon, put it in his pocket, went to the corner, and caught a southbound bus. The bus line paralleled the boardwalk. He got off a block east of Dexter's place, walked to the parking lot and got his car. Then he drove inland, approaching Martinez Canyon by a roundabout route. He parked behind Mildred's cafe, drank from his bottle, and got out of the car. He opened the kitchen door of the cafe, but did not enter.

"Mildred—" He kept his voice low as he called.

She was in the kitchen, as he'd figured she would be; it wasn't time for the lunch crowd yet. She looked at him with sullen resentment from the far side of the stove.

"Come back to hit me again. Tom? Didn't you do it hard enough last time?"

"Honest to God, Mildred, I wouldn't hurt you for the world. Wouldn't have touched you if you hadn't gone haywire on me. What you said—about me and Ralph, remember—it just wasn't true,"

"Why did you come back?"

"There's a little something you can do for me. No trouble, honey, or I wouldn't ask you. Just give Earl a message."

"Earl?"

"Earl Bingham. He's probably parked across the road. Will you do that for me?"

"Why don't you do it for yourself?"

"There's a reason, a good reason. Just get Earl off by himself and tell him I want to see him. I'll be in Manny's joint next door."

"Suppose he isn't there?"

"Tell him when he comes. I'll wait. And Mildred, anybody asks you, I been in and out all morning. I want to talk to you, too, as soon as I've seen Earl. See you later," he said, forcing a hard quality into his voice. "Let me give you some advice—don't cross me up."

Mildred said quietly, "The way you're acting, something tells me you're crossed up already. Can't say it breaks my heart."

"I could break your heart, if that was what I wanted. I hope you won't make me," Tommy said.

He left her, slipping around the corner of the cafe and into Manny's. He bought a can of beer and carried it to an empty booth. There was a window on his left. A thick curtain was drawn across it. He parted the curtain and looked out.

It took a moment for his eyes to adjust to bright sunlight after the gloomy interior of the bar. When they did, he saw Earl in the prowl car across the road. Earl was alone. Mildred stood beside the road waiting for a break in the traffic that would enable her to cross. The break came, but the prowl car moved away before it did. It merged with southbound traffic, headed toward the breakwater and the pier.

Never mind. Earl would come back, although that landslide might slow him down a little, and if Mildred knew what was good for her she would be waiting for him when he did. Tommy dropped the curtain, and immediately parted it again.

The scene was unchanged, but now he was able to identify a couple of people he had only glanced at casually before. The ice cream wagon was parked in front of Mildred's place. A man was standing beside it talking earnestly to the driver—Dave Russell!

Tommy slapped the curtain back in place. He took the bottle from his hip pocket, helped himself to a slug, and chased it down with beer. He put the bottle back, and for a time did absolutely nothing. He didn't even think.

He knew that something was wrong at least a quarter of a minute before he was able to put his finger on exactly what it was. The knowledge felt, at first, like an emptiness in his stomach. Then, with realization sudden and complete, he stiffened as though he had been given a severe electric shock.

The breath went out of him. He clapped his hand to his right hip pocket. Nothing was in it but the pint of whiskey. The left pocket contained only a handkerchief.

His blackjack was gone.

"But I heard you!" Dave insisted. "Early Sunday morning. You drove past my house."

Ken Hurley answered impatiently, "You couldn't have heard me. I'm always in bed by ten-thirty. That's my rule."

"Then someone was driving your truck. I recognized that little tune it plays."

Hurley shook his head. "Every evening all trucks get turned in to the company garage. The garage is locked. There's a watchman in the place all night."

"But—?"

"Say, tell me something, will you? What's everybody picking on me for, anyway? Lieutenant Morgan gave me the same line. I told him just what I've told you." After a moment, he added coldly, "Sometimes, or so they tell me, people hear things that just aren't there. Particularly when they're under a strain."

"Oh, for heaven's sake!" Dave said, and turned away. Abruptly, he turned back. "Hey...wait a minute. You told Morgan a lot more than that. You alibied Lu Warren, said you saw him on the road. How could you have seen him if you were in bed?"

Hurley's shrug expressed disgusted resignation. "Okay, okay—Morgan knows, so I might as well broadcast it to the world. Saturday night the wife and I had a small difference of opinion. She threw a book at me and ran out of the house. I met Warren when I went out to see which way she was heading. When she came home around two, I saw him again. Asked him what he was doing. He said he was looking for his cousin. Satisfied?"

"If the police are, I suppose I'll have to be. I'm also satisfied," Dave said, "that I heard an ice cream truck, but you've convinced me that it wasn't yours." He went home, not nearly as convinced as he had said he was.

Helen came down from the kitchen. "Find out anything?"

"I drew a blank." He told her Hurley's revised story.

She said thoughtfully, "That's not necessarily a blank. He's a big part of Warren's alibi. If he and Lu turned out to be friends, or if—"

"Please, darling," he begged, "we can't go around suspecting everybody. Let it rest."

She sighed. "I really botched things, didn't I?"

"Botched things—you?"

"This whole thing started because of my darned jealousy. If I hadn't nagged you so, you would have stayed home Saturday. You would never have been dragged into this. It's all my fault."

Dave was astonished. "Careful, girl—humility's rich food."

"I can swallow it. It's taken something like this horrible murder to make me see the truth. Darling, you know those long strings of colored electric lights they hang on Christmas trees? I'm like they are."

"You're prettier."

"No. I'm trying to be serious," she said. "The tree's all lit up, everything is lovely. Then one tiny light flickers—and the connection's broken. The whole string goes out. That's me. We're getting along fine. Then some small thing happens, and it may not even be your fault. But suddenly there's no more light and you're the world's worst heel. How can two people who love each other, as we do, act like that?"

"I don't know," he said, "but I do know one thing. We're not going to do it anymore." He put his hand out, and she took it solemnly. "Agreed?"

"It's a deal," she said.

They had a light lunch. Afterwards, Helen refused to let him help her with the dishes. The telephone rang as she started carrying them to the kitchen. She put the dishes down to answer it.

"Yes? Oh, hello, Mr. Victor. No, I was standing right here by the phone." She was silent for what seemed to Dave a long time. Occasionally she frowned, "I understand," she said at last. "You'd better wire them.   Hammerschlag & Vincent; my address book's on the desk." Her frown was deeper this time, really troubled. "Oh, Lord! Will you hold the line a minute, please?"

She cupped her right hand over the instrument.   "I've goofed," she whispered. "Darling, would you mind terribly if I ran into the shop just for an hour or two?"

"Go right ahead." He waved permission with a lightness that he did not feel.

Helen spoke into the phone again. She told Victor to hold everything, that he could expect her at the shop within an hour. But as she talked, her eyes were fixed questioningly on Dave. He turned away, looked out the window. He was no longer listening but he knew when she hung up. He knew what she was going to say before she spoke.

"Dave, the way you looked just now—are you *sure* that you don't mind?"

He turned back after a moment, smiling. "Mind? Of course I mind. You're not the only one whose wiring is a little faulty. But run along, darling. My lights may have flickered for a second, but now they're screwed in tight."

"Okay," She was responding slowly to his smile. "I'll leave as soon as I've done the dishes."

"You'll leave now. I'll do the dishes, and have a good time doing them," he said.

Tommy heard someone speak his name. He opened his eyes. Mildred was standing beside the table. He shook his head in an effort to clear it, and felt for his bottle. It was empty. Someone had stolen his liquor while he slept.

"You take my liquor?" he asked Mildred.

"No. And after you've heard what I've got to tell you, you better layoff the bottle. I talked to Earl Bingham."

Earl. The necessity of seeing him, and all the pressing reasons that made it a necessity, swept over Tommy in a nauseating wave. "Where is he?"

"He can't come here. Not until much later, after work. He says they found your blackjack. There's an all-points out to pick you up."

"Oh, my God!" Tommy struggled to rise, but couldn't make it. He fell back heavily against the booth. "Why would they do a thing like that to me? I'm a cop, just like they are. They're my friends!"

"You don't have friends. Tom, unless maybe Earl is one. Outside of him, all you've got is a lot of people that you've used."

Mildred left him. She went back to the cafe, and did not permit herself to think of him again. That wasn't hard; she was utterly preoccupied by something more important. This was Monday. In a few more hours, with the coming of darkness, her son planned to escape. If it took all night, she would wait beside the telephone to hear from Ralph.

At half-past six Dave crossed the road to the supermarket and bought a can of roast beef hash for dinner. He bought canned stuff because it would be easier to prepare, and he chose the smaller size because Helen had just telephoned that she and Victor were still trying to straighten things out at the shop. Something about an order from Hammerschlag & Vincent that had been shipped to the wrong address. She would have dinner in town and come home afterwards as soon as she could get away.

Dave had accepted it serenely. Only a few hours before, he realized, the message would have left him wallowing in resentment. Now he could take it, not only without wincing, but without feeling that his masculine pride demanded at least a token wince. He left the market with a small bag of groceries, shouldering the glass doors open wide.

"'Evening, Mr. Russell," a man said.

The man was getting out of a parked car. Dave recognized him as one of the deputies he had ridden with last night. The fairly decent deputy, as opposed to the one who had clouted him behind the ear. A huge man in uniform, he seemed even bigger in civilian trousers and white shirt.

"Hello, Bingham. Thanks for holding your partner back last night."

The deputy looked sheepish. "Tommy wouldn't have really hurt you. He's a nice fellow, just sort of...excitable."

"He's that, all right. You know why I haven't filed a complaint against him? I hope to be clear of this mess soon," Dave said. "Then I'm going to find him off duty and out of uniform. I'm going to take him apart. You tell him that."

"I'll tell him, Mr. Russell, but he ain't going to like it," Bingham said.

Trying to pound something into Earl's thick muttonhead was like slapping water with a stick. He just sat there on the other side of the table, meaning well, but nothing you said to him left much impression. Tommy sighed, went over it again.

"Look, Earl, maybe you better write this down and study it. Friday night I was with Mildred. I haven't talked to her yet, but I know she'll back me up. Saturday night—well, where was I then?"

A frown formed slowly on Earl's narrow forehead. "I know what you want me to say. You want me to say you was with me."

"That's it! I knew you'd get it, given time. We bought a six-pack of beer and drank it on the beach. That's where I lost my blackjack. Then we drove up to Santa Barbara just for the ride. At 3:00 am you drove me back to my place and spent the night. Got it?"

Earl nodded, and Tommy gave him a relieved smile. He killed the rest of a can of beer. "Wish I had a decent drink."

Earl pulled two full pints of bourbon from his pockets. He pushed them across the table. "Mildred told me you was drinking. Figured you'd be needing a pickup about now."

"If you wasn't so ugly, Earl, I'd kiss you," Tommy stowed away one pint, opened the other, and tilted it against his lips. "Well, now we got everything settled, haven't we?" He drew the back of his hand across his mouth.

Earl shook his head. "It won't work. Morgan's already asked me about both nights. Told him I went to a picture show Friday, and then went home. Did the same thing Saturday; it was a real good show. Asked me if I'd seen you. I told him no."

Tommy didn't move. Only his sick eyes betrayed the way he felt. All his plans, and all the hopes founded on those plans, had suddenly been smashed. Mildred might have alibied him for one night, but not for both. Hazel would have known that she was lying. She wouldn't have let Mildred get away with it. She hated Tommy for some reason he had never been able to understand.

Earl was still talking, but his voice was only a semi-intelligible rumble in Tommy's ears. "I'd do anything to help you, if I could. If I'd known what you wanted me to tell Morgan, I'd of told him exactly what you said. I'm sure sorry."

"You're sorry."

Earl nodded. "You're my friend. Everybody knows that. Why, Morgan put a tail on me hoping I'd lead him to you. It's okay," he raised a reassuring hand. "I shook him. But I'm taking a chance just being seen with you. That's all right, too. Us cops got to stick together. I want to help you all I can."

"How?"

"You better hole in somewheres. This'll all blow over," Earl paused, and after a moment added, "It'll blow over, that is, if you didn't really kill that girl."

"Hey!" Tommy sat up straight. "What is this? You know damn well I didn't kill her!"

Earl soothed him down. "Sure, Tommy, sure. I know you didn't, and I got a pretty good idea who did."

"So have I. Russell."

"Well, maybe—maybe not. Maybe it's another fellow doesn't live so far from here. People don't know, but he's been having trouble with his wife. Had his eye on Thelma. Anyway," Earl said, "you better keep away from Russell. Next time he sees you, he says he's going to take you apart."

Tommy leaned forward, his elbows heavy on the table. "Did he actually say that?"

"Sure did. Not ten minutes ago, out here in front. Hold on, Tommy." Earl rose, gently restrained his friend. "You can't tangle with him now. Where's your car?"

"Back of Mildred's. Why?"

"You better stretch out in it and get a little sleep. Then find yourself a place to hide."

"Just like that, huh? Where?"

Earl said thoughtfully, "You got a private entrance to your room. They already went there to look for you. If you was to leave your car somewhere, your own place might be the safest place there is."

There was a short silence. "I'll think about it," Tommy said.

"You do that." Earl asked one more question just before he left, "Say, Tommy—tell me the truth. Where was you Saturday night?"

Tommy stared at him furiously. "It's sapping Dexter they want me for. That's all. I had nothing to do with that blonde girl. I didn't even know her, understand? You remember that, and keep your nose out of places where it don't belong."

"Sure. Tommy—anything you say." The big deputy left the table, walked out of the beer joint. Tommy was alone. He thought about the girl he'd had a date with Saturday night. There was a fat chance of getting Maria Gonzalez to give him an alibi. If Corporal Gonzalez knew the truth, he'd beat hell out of his wife. And if he didn't do the same to Tommy, he'd certainly have Tommy's job. It was a terrible thing to be suspected of something that you haven't done, and not be able to prove you haven't done it because what you had done was, from certain prejudiced points of view, almost as bad.

Tommy pushed Maria from his mind and concentrated on the guy who'd really killed poor Thelma. He was going to have to have a showdown with Dave Russell, beat the truth out of him if it was necessary. But Earl had been right about one thing. Before he tackled Russell, before he did anything, he was going to have to get a little sleep.

At ten minutes past seven the pay telephone in the front part of the cafe rang shrilly. There was only one customer at the counter. Mildred went over to the phone. Her movements were unhurried. She had been waiting hours for this moment, and she had schooled herself not to betray excitement. Her hand was steady as she lifted the receiver and held it to her ear.

"Hello," she said, expecting to hear Ralph's voice.

A woman answered. "This is Western Union. I have a telegram for Mrs. Mildred Riggs."

"This is Mrs. Riggs. Read it to me," Mildred said.

There was a pause. Then the woman said slowly and with terrible distinctness, "Message follows. 'Regret to inform you Ralph accidentally killed while attempting escape. Please wire as to disposition of body.' " A shorter pause. "The telegram is signed—"

"Never mind," Mildred said. "I know who signed it."

"Would you like us to mail you a copy?"

"I don't care. It makes no difference."

She hung up. The customer was drinking coffee. "Leave your money on the counter," she told him. "Shut the door when you go out." She went into the kitchen and sat down beside the window, her accustomed place.

She was sitting there when Tom Riggs came out of the beer joint. She saw him stand unsteadily for a moment, staring at the house across the road. Then he lurched around to the rear of the cafe. Presently she heard him climb into his car. He slammed the door but did not drive away.

An indeterminable period of time went by. It could have been three minutes or three hours, Mildred didn't know. She was waiting for something—something significant to happen. She did not know what it would be, but she knew that it would happen, and that she would recognize it and be guided by it when it did.

Then Tom Riggs snored, and apparently was awakened by his snoring. The car door creaked as he opened it and got out.

CHAPTER EIGHT

Dave went up to the bedroom and changed to pajamas and a dressing gown. It was a gesture supposed to show that he wasn't a bit worried. But he was worried. It was ten o'clock and Helen had not yet come home.

The doorbell rang. He was running down the stairs before he realized that it could not be Helen who had rung it; she would have used her key. That only increased his anxiety. She might have been in an accident. This might be someone bringing him the news. His hand was damp, turning the knob.

The door was violently pushed open. The deputy named Riggs stood there. He was no longer handsome. His face was lined and puffy, his half-closed eyes were red. He looked as though he had been drunk, and shortly might be drunk again, but right now he was sober. Fairly sober. He took two lumbering steps into the room.

"Smart boy, Russell. Murder Thelma, then make 'em think I did it!" He swung a powerful but misdirected fist.

Dave hit him twice. The first blow caught him in the belly and won a spray of vomited bourbon. The second, as Riggs doubled up, came from below to connect with the point of the deputy's chin. He went down but, falling, he wrapped his arms around Dave's legs.

They were strong arms. Dave tried to smash his knee into Rigg's face, but the dragging weight threw him off balance. He fell, but managed to free himself. Once more he slammed his fist against the sagging chin. He sat on top of Riggs and banged his head against the floor. Suddenly all resistance stopped. The man's head lolled to one side. He had passed out cold.

Dave slapped him, first on one cheek then the other. There was no response. He got up, went to the kitchen for a glass of water. Returning, he poured it on the upturned face. Riggs gasped. His eyes came into bleary focus. He stared at Dave.

Dave nudged him with his foot. "So now they think you did it, do they? Well, that figures. A cop was at Dexter's Friday night with Thelma. You're a cop. Suppose you tell me all about it, friend."

Comprehension came back slowly to the staring eyes. "Gimme a drink."

Dave grinned. "What would you like? Water, whiskey, gin?"

"Whiskey."

"There's a whole fifth in the liquor cabinet. But you'll have to earn it. Want to talk?"

"Got nothing to lose. Gimme a drink," Riggs said. "I'll talk."

Dave crossed to the cabinet. He filled a shot glass, and brought back both the glass and bottle. Riggs gulped the whiskey. He got groggily to his feet, held out the empty glass. Dave refilled it. Riggs threw the second glass of whiskey in Dave's face.

Alcohol seared his eyes. Through a burning haze, he saw the deputy stagger toward the door. Half-blind, he plunged after him. He almost caught him on the outside stairs, but Riggs kicked backward. His heel hit Dave in the chest. Dave saved himself by grabbing at the banister, but the delay had given Riggs too big a start. He had already crossed the road when Dave got up to the gate. Riggs was running in the general direction of Mildred's cafe, and Dave started after him. He stopped when he heard his name called softly.

"Mr. Russell?"

It was man's voice. Dave thought he recognized it. It came from the shadows on the far side of the gate. "Let him go, Mr. Russell. They'll pick him up now. Poor fellow hasn't got a chance."

"Bingham?"

"Yes, sir. Hope Tommy didn't hurt you. I tried to get here sooner. Had trouble with my car."

Dave's eyes had adjusted to the night, and they no longer burned. He could see Bingham quite distinctly now. The deputy stood beside an old sedan. It was a black Buick with a damaged right rear fender. There was something about its presence here, and about Bingham's presence, that didn't fit in logically with the time and place.

"Why didn't you warn me Riggs was coming? You didn't have to drive; you could have phoned."

"Didn't have anything for sure to tell you. I didn't know what Tommy was going to do. He was in bad enough trouble. Didn't want to make it worse."

"He's in trouble, all right," Dave said. "And so are you. You're a deputy sheriff. Riggs is wanted for murder. Why didn't you grab him? You practically had him in your hands."

The huge deputy was silent. He produced a pack of cigarettes, methodically opened it. He offered a cigarette to Dave.

Dave shook his head impatiently. "Well?"

"Just couldn't do it, Mr. Russell," Bingham told him. "Deep down inside me, I still can't believe that Tommy killed that girl. Sure, I *know* he did it, but knowing ain't believing. Anyway, I can't arrest him. He's my friend."

There was another silence, longer than the one that had preceded it. Then Dave said, "He's no friend of mine. I'll have to telephone Lieutenant Morgan. Bingham, I'm going to do it now."

Bingham shrugged. "I see what you mean. It all depends on how you look at it. I won't try to stop you. Guess it's the only thing you can do."

Dave turned away, feeling no sense of vindication or of triumph. Feeling, on the contrary, unsatisfied. Something was lacking, but what it was he didn't know. He would do what he had to do. From then on it would be up to the police. He started toward the little gate.

Then he stopped, becoming suddenly and absolutely rigid. From close at hand—from very close at hand—there came a tinkling little tune. Dave had an instant of total recall. It was two o'clock in the morning and he was standing in the kitchen, in the dark. Outside, beyond the kitchen window, a man had just climbed into a car. Its motor started and Dave distinctly heard familiar notes. They formed the refrain he had always associated with the ice cream wagon. *Oh Where, Oh Where Has My Little Dog Gone?*

Dave turned back slowly. He looked at the deputy, at the cigarette lighter in Bingham's hand. That's where the tune was coming from, the lighter. It was one of those Swiss gadgets that played when its top was open. In the excitement of discovery, Dave stared at it too long.

He looked up to see that Bingham was watching him, and he saw that Bingham knew he'd been found out. Neither man spoke. After a moment, Dave turned away again.

This time he hurried. When he heard footsteps close behind him, he broke into a run. He ran down the steps and slammed the front door as he went in. He crossed to the telephone. He had just picked it up when the door shuddered under the impact of Bingham's heavy shoulder. He dialed rapidly.

The door burst open. There was a gun in Bingham's hand as he came in. The gun was pointed at Dave's stomach.

"Put the phone down, Mr. Russell," Bingham said.

Dave dropped it in its cradle. When Bingham told him to turn around, that's what he did. Something heavy crashed down on his head. He heard a groan, and vaguely recognized the sound of his own voice. Then the room tilted up on end and slid away.

Helen turned into the beach road from the canyon at twenty-eight past ten. There was a light still burning in Mildred's cafe as she passed. That was unusual, but Helen was so angry that she didn't even notice. She was furious with Victor for keeping her so late. Goodness only knew what Dave would say when she got home.

A car was parked just beyond the little gate, and she slowed down to stop behind it. Her headlights illuminated the crumpled fender of a black Buick sedan. The Buick moved out as her car crept up on it; it made a fast U-turn and headed north. The Rambler slid into the place where it had been. Helen climbed out and started down the steps, coming to an abrupt stop as she neared the door.

The door stood open, and something was the matter with it. Light streamed through the doorway from the living room. She went down the rest of the way and saw that the door was hanging awry on its hinges. She walked past it, looked up the stairs toward the kitchen. No sound came from the kitchen; it was dark.

"Dave—?" She ran up the stairs.

The bed was unrumpled. His shirt and slacks were lying in a chair. She looked in the closet. His pajamas and dressing gown were gone. Where, dressed only in a dressing gown and pajamas, could Dave have gone at this hour of the night? And who had broken in the door?

She remembered the black Buick with the crumpled fender. Panic clogged her throat.

She ran down to the telephone. She told the operator to connect her with the sheriff's sub-station, that it was an emergency.

A red-hot spike had been driven through Dave's skull. He was burning up, but his forehead, curiously, was cold. And wet. There was a rumbling nearby crash of heavy surf. He opened his eyes and, by the gritty feel of it, knew that he was lying face downward on damp sand. His hands were locked behind his back. He moved them, but only for a couple of inches. They stopped then; the metal was tight around his wrists.

He rolled over on his back, willing the pain to go away. It didn't go, but presently it became supportable. A man stood near him, thick legs spread apart. It was Earl Bingham.

The deputy must have heard him move, but he paid no attention. He was staring northward, up the coast. Dave knew where he was now, on the beach near Point of Rocks, beside one of the pools left by the receding tide. One of the pools in which Bingham had drowned Thelma. By turning his head and craning back his neck, he was able to see what the deputy was staring at. There were red flares on the road ahead.

"What is it, Bingham?" he asked. "Your first glimpse of hell?"

The deputy looked down at him. "Trouble of some kind. Don't know what. Sorry you woke up, Russell. Hoped I could get this over with before you did."

"Must you get it over with?"

Bingham's voice, when he answered, was puzzled and surprised. "Well, sure. What else can I do?"

"I don't know what you hope to gain. They're sure to catch you. I don't know why you killed Thelma. Tell me, Bingham—why?"

"I am not as slow-thinking as everybody says I am. Fellow gets tired of always being pushed aside, seeing other fellows get the gravy, the good-looking girls. There was something special about Thelma. She was beauty-full. Tommy didn't see that; all he saw was another dame, and he treated her like one. He didn't have no trouble. So I tried, but she just laughed at me. Made me pretty mad. Guess I sort of lost my head."

"What makes you think she didn't laugh at Tommy, too?"

"Because he told me. He told me she was easy. Tommy wouldn't lie to me. He's my friend."

Dave looked past the deputy at the zebra-shadows on the beach. He had thought he'd seen one move, but now it was quite still. He kept on talking, and tried to keep Bingham talking. Kill time. Hope that something, anything, would happen. It was the only thing left.

"Riggs is your friend, but you went out of your way to make him look bad. You wanted him to be suspected. Why?"

Bingham chuckled. The muscular spasm accompanying the chuckle was like a small earthquake. "Sure played that one smart. Yes, sir—Tommy might of pulled that trick hisself."

"How smart can you get? Would you have let him go to the gas chamber in your place?"

The earthquake chuckle gradually subsided. "Why not?" Bingham said. "I don't want to die, and it's what Tommy would of done to me. He's told me so a hundred times. He always said a guy's got to look out for hisself."

He reached down then to put his hands beneath Dave's arms, to drag him over to the pool. For an instant he was in a vulnerable position. Dave drove his right foot up with all his strength.

Bingham's breath *whoosed* out of him. His hands went to his crotch; he doubled over. Dave tried to get his legs out of the way. Too late. The deputy landed on them as he fell.

His huge arms encircled them and held on tight. Presently, when his breathing had grown normal, he got back on his feet. This time when he approached, it was cautiously, from Dave's head. The shallow pool was less than a yard away. One heave pulled Dave up beside it. A big hand grabbed his head and pushed it down. Dave tried to shout, and gagged on brackish water. He breathed, and water rushed into his lungs. He had not known there could be red flares beneath the surface of the water... But they were there, lots of them, when they should have been up on the road. He watched them, growing strangely incurious as time passed.

One by one the red flares all went out.

The mindless night was alive, groping and sentient. It seeped through the kitchen window, dimming the single electric bulb suspended from the ceiling. Mildred knew that when the light was gone, when the darkness was complete, she would go, too. Not bravely, not with a gallant gesture. The night would simply take her over. She would cease to be.

Someone opened the front door of the cafe. "Anybody here?" a man's voice called. She got up slowly, went to, the service panel remembering that she had not locked the door.

"Sorry. Closed for the night," She looked through the service panel at the man who had come in.

He was dressed in working clothes: high laced boots and a yellow metal helmet. The helmet was shaped like those worn in the First World War. He turned in the direction of her voice.

"Have to use your phone." He had already started toward it, feeling in his pocket for a coin.

Mildred pulled her head back from the panel, heard him dial, heard the bell ring as he dropped his dime. "Put Mike Collins on. Emergency," he said.

Five seconds passed while his fingers impatiently tapped the coin box. Then he spoke urgently. "This is Art. Mike, you know that fault a half-mile north of Point of Rocks? It gave way twenty minutes ago." A pause. "The biggest yet. Knocked out the whole road—nothing left but a sheer drop to the rocks. Better get the gang here on the double."

He listened, nodded briskly. "Yeah, set up a road block— route traffic through Martinez Canyon. Will do. I already got flares going. Hurry up."

He hung up, started for the door. Mildred came into the front part of the cafe.

"What happened?"

"Landslide," the man said. He hurried out.

Mildred returned to the kitchen. She took a switchblade from the pocket of her apron, and dropped it on a table. The knife was part of her defiant, bitter past; she wouldn't need it anymore. She took her apron off and hung it on a nail. She picked up a bright scarf from the table and tied the scarf around her head. There was something almost coquettish about the manner in which she adjusted it and tied the knot. She smiled at her reflection in a mirror. She might have been a young girl going to a dance.

She didn't bother to shut the kitchen door as she went out. She walked around the parked car, opened the door, got in behind the wheel. Tommy was huddled in the corner of the front seat, head drooping on his chest. He didn't awaken until she had started the car, backed up and turned into the beach road.

He stirred then. His head came up, but it was at least a minute before he spoke. "Well, what do you know! Old Mildred," he said thickly. "You taking me for a ride?"

"That's right."

"Cops looking for me, Milly. Where we going?"

"We're going home," she said. A man shouted at them as the car sped north. He wore a yellow helmet, and Mildred swerved to avoid hitting him. A few yards south of Point of Rocks three cars were clustered together off the road. Two of them bore the official insignia of California, but Mildred didn't notice that. She was staring eagerly through the windshield at red brilliance on the curving road ahead. The brilliance came from flares. Black moving dots were silhouetted against them. The moving dots grew larger, became distinguishable as men. One of the men threw up his arms in an arresting gesture. He shouted; there was a whole chorus of warning shouts. Mildred ignored them. Her eyes were fixed on a wide gap in the road ahead.

Beyond the gap was nothingness. The flares were on both side of the brink. Their redness had a stimulating effect on Tommy. He started bragging about his twenty-one inch color television as the car shot into space.

It was a hot day. The window by Dave's bed was open.

A young man stood by the window studying a chart. He wore a stethoscope around his neck. When he saw Dave looking at him questioningly, he smiled.

"Awake, Mr. Russell?"

"What hospital is this?"

"St. Mark's. It's eight o'clock in the morning. Your temperature is normal, and if you don't let yourself get excited you'll probably be discharged this afternoon."

"How did I get here?"

"The usual way, an ambulance. Don't talk too much, Mr. Russell; I'll tell you anything you want to know. You can thank your wife for being here. She telephoned Lieutenant Morgan, described Bingham's car. They'd been looking for it already. Morgan showed up at Point of Rocks in time to pull your head out of the water; the ambulance crew got the water out of your lungs. Bingham's in jail. He's a celebrity. His picture's in all the papers, and he's making the most of it. That's all, I think," the doctor said. "Or is there something more?"

Through the window came familiar notes, a tinkling little tune. It passed. Dave listened until it had faded in the distance. It was a hot day, but it wasn't ice cream that he wanted.

"Where's my wife?"

THE END

If you've enjoyed this book, you will not want to miss these terrific titles…

ARMCHAIR SCI-FI & MYSTERY CLASSICS, $12.95 each

If you've enjoyed this book, you will not want to miss these terrific titles…

ARMCHAIR SCI-FI & HORROR DOUBLE NOVELS, $12.95 each

D-121 **THE GENIUS BEASTS** by Frederik Pohl
THIS WORLD IS TABOO by Murray Leinster

D-122 **THE COSMIC LOOTERS** by Edmond Hamilton
WANDL THE INVADER by Ray Cummings

D-123 **ROBOT MEN OF BUBBLE CITY** by Rog Phillips
DRAGON ARMY by William Morrison

D-124 **LAND BEYOND THE LENS** by S. J. Byrne
DIPLOMAT-AT-ARMS by Keith Laumer

D-125 **VOYAGE OF THE ASTEROID, THE** by Laurence Manning
REVOLT OF THE OUTWORLDS by Milton Lesser

D-126 **OUTLAW IN THE SKY** by Chester S. Geier
LEGACY FROM MARS by Raymond Z. Gallun

D-127 **THE GREAT FLYING SAUCER INVASION** by Geoff St. Reynard
THE BIG TIME by Fritz Leiber

D-128 **MIRAGE FOR PLANET X** by Stanley Mullen
POLICE YOUR PLANET by Lester del Rey

D-129 **THE BRAIN SINNER** by Alan E. Nourse
DEATH FROM THE SKIES by A. Hyatt Verrill

D-130 **CRY CHAOS** by Dwight V. Swain
THE DOOR THROUGH SPACE By Marion Zimmer Bradley

ARMCHAIR SCIENCE FICTION CLASSICS, $12.95 each

C-55 **UNDER THE TRIPLE SUNS**
by Stanton A. Coblentz

C-56 **STONE FROM THE GREEN STAR**
by Jack Williamson,

C-57 **ALIEN MINDS**
by E. Everett Evans

ARMCHAIR SCI-FI & HORROR GEMS SERIES, $12.95 each

G-13 **SCIENCE FICTION GEMS, Vol. Seven**
Jack Vance and others

G-14 **HORROR GEMS, Vol. Seven**
Robert Bloch and others

If you've enjoyed this book, you will not want to miss these terrific titles...

If you've enjoyed this book, you will not want to miss these terrific titles...

ARMCHAIR SCI-FI & HORROR DOUBLE NOVELS, $12.95 each

D-141 **ALL HEROES ARE HATED** by Milton Lesser
AND THE STARS REMAIN by Bryan Berry

D-142 **LAST CALL FOR DOOMSDAY** by Edmond Hamilton
HUNTRESS OF AKKAN by Robert Moore Williams

D-143 **THE MOON PIRATES** by Neil R. Jones
CALLISTO AT WAR by Harl Vincent

D-144 **THUNDER IN THE DAWN** by Henry Kuttner
THE UNCANNY EXPERIMENTS OF DR. VARSAG by David V. Reed

D-145 **A PATTERN FOR MONSTERS** by Randall Garrett
STAR SURGEON by Alan E Nourse

D-146 **THE ATOM CURTAIN** by Nick Boddie Williams
WARLOCK OF SHARRADOR by Gardner F. Fox

D-148 **SECRET OF THE LOST PLANET** by David Wright O'Brien
TELEVISION HILL by George McLociard

D-147 **INTO THE GREEN PRISM** by A Hyatt Verrill
WANDERERS OF THE WOLF-MOON by Nelson S. Bond

D-149 **MINIONS OF THE TIGER** by Chester S. Geier
FOUNDING FATHER by J. F. Bone

D-150 **THE INVISIBLE MAN** by H. G. Wells
THE ISLAND OF DR. MOREAU by H. G. Wells

ARMCHAIR SCIENCE FICTION CLASSICS, $12.95 each

C-61 **THE SHAVER MYSTERY, Book Six**
by Richard S. Shaver

C-62 **CADUCEUS WILD**
by Ward Moore & Robert Bradford

B-5 **ATLANTIDA** (Lost World-Lost Race Classics #1)
by Pierre Benoit

ARMCHAIR MYSTERY-CRIME DOUBLE NOVELS, $12.95 each

B-1 **THE DEADLY PICK-UP** by Milton Ozaki
KILLER TAKE ALL by James O. Causey

B-2 **THE VIOLENT ONES** by E. Howard Hunt
HIGH HEEL HOMICIDE by Frederick C. Davis

B-3 **FURY ON SUNDAY** by Richard Matheson
THE AGONY COLUMN by Earl Derr Biggers

If you've enjoyed this book, you will not want to miss these terrific titles...

ARMCHAIR SCI-FI & HORROR DOUBLE NOVELS, $12.95 each

D-151   **MAGNANTHROPUS** by Manly Banister
       BEYOND THE FEARFUL FOREST by Geoff St. Reynard

D-152   **IN CAVERNS BELOW** by Stanton A. Coblentz
       DYNASTY OF THE LOST by George O. Smith

D-153   **NO MORE STARS** by Lester del Rey & Frederick Pohl
       THE MAN WHO LIVED FOREVER R. De Witt Miller & Anna Hunger

D-154   **THE CORIANIS DISASTER** by Murray Leinster
       DEATHWORLD by Harry Harrison

D-155   **HE FELL AMONG THIEVES** by Milton Lesser
       PRINCESS OF ARELLI, THE by Aladra Septama

D-156   **THE SECRET KINGDOM** by Otis Adelbert Kline & Allen S. Kilne
       SCRATCH ONE ASTEROID by Willard Hawkins

D-157   **ENSLAVED BRAINS** by Eando Binder
       CONCEPTION: ZERO by E. K. Jarvis

D-158   **VICTIMS OF THE VORTEX** by Rog Phillips
       THE COSMIC COMPUTER by H. Beam Piper

D-159   **THE GOLDEN GODS** by S. J. Byrne
       RETURN OF MICHAEL FLANIGAN by S. J. Byrne

D-160   **BATTLE OUT OF TIME** by Dwight V. Swain
       THE PEOPLE THAT TIME FORGOT by Edgar Rice Burroughs

ARMCHAIR SCIENCE FICTION CLASSICS, $12.95 each

C-63   **THE OMEGA POINT TRILOGY**
      by George Zebrowski

C-64   **THE UNIVERSE WRECKERS**
      by Edmond Hamilton

C-65   **KING OF THE DINOSAURS**
      by Raymond A. Palmer

ARMCHAIR SCI-FI & HORROR GEMS SERIES, $12.95 each

G-17   **SCIENCE FICTION GEMS, Vol. Nine**
      Ben Bova and others

G-18   **HORROR GEMS, Vol. Nine**
      Emil Petaja and others

Made in the USA
Lexington, KY
31 May 2017